About the Author

Oliver Friggieri, born in Malta in 1947, is a renowned novelist, poet and scholar whose works have been translated into numerous languages and published throughout the world. He is Professor of Literature at the University of Malta and the winner of various international prizes. His long list of books includes about sixty which have been launched outside his native country. His novels *Children Come By Ship* and *Let Fair Weather Bring Me Home* were launched by Austin Macauley Publishers Ltd (London) in 2013 and 2015.

To Eileen
Sara and Ivan
Elise and Luca
with all my love

Oliver Friggieri

SAFE AT ANCHOR IN MID-HARBOUR

Translated from Maltese by Rose Marie Caruana

AUSTIN MACAULEY
PUBLISHERS LTD.

A CIP catalogue record for this title is available from the British Library.

ISBN 9781785547362 (Paperback)
ISBN 9781785547379 (Hardback)
ISBN 9781785547386 (E-Book)

www.austinmacauley.com

First Published (2016)
Austin Macauley Publishers Ltd.
25 Canada Square
Canary Wharf
London
E14 5LQ

Chapter 1

It was that time of day when the sun was sinking in the sky. A deep silence was settling down everywhere. Now that those last minute noises from the village and the surrounding countryside were dying down, it was becoming clear that the day's stress and fatigue was beginning to ease. The last straggling flocks were being shepherded towards their covered pens or some other shelter, some cave already hollowed out by nature In the solid rock face, where the animals could snuggle up against each other to pass the night, waiting for the light of a new day. Each little flock moving across the stony ground of the garigue looked like a carpet, coloured dirty-white, with many delightful heads nodding to a single rhythm, ears pricked up, stepping daintily on, making a beeline for their destination. A flock consisting of many siblings and many friends. The thin ringing of the little bell strung across the neck of each sheep and goat was a continuous song of innocence. The farmers who had stayed on last had already shouldered their hoe and were walking back home. There they would find their wife waiting quietly for them so that together they would recite their evening prayers, eat their supper and go to bed.

In a little while, the entire village would look deserted, with empty streets and locked-up houses, where not a single glimmer of light would be seen from outside, with no sign of life except for Baskal's wine tavern that would stay open till late. There would only be some streak of light stabbing the darkness from the tavern's little door to illuminate the street, and the sound of some men talking, but otherwise, nothing.

Katarina gave the footrest of her rocking chair another tap with her foot to set it in motion, in the way she enjoyed most. At regular intervals, without a break in-between, she would give it a tap to keep up the steady rhythm, rocking backwards and forwards, with her head tilted to one side resting against the chair's back. It was that time of evening, more than any other time of day, when her thoughts flew back to range over her own past. The evening's deepening silence made her feel more uneasy than a long night's solitude.

In contrast, she felt that she had been able to better endure those long-ago moments of misunderstandings and disagreements between her and her husband. Once, she had expressed a wish to have a hand in managing the household, holding it by right. She had raised her voice to Saverju and told him that her say was just as important as his.

"Your say doesn't have the least importance," her husband had roundly declared in a loud voice.

"I'm your wife, Saverju, don't forget," she had answered him softly.

"That's why your say is supremely unimportant. Because you're my wife. You're nothing more than that."

"I will always be your wife, at least till Susanna grows up and settles down in her own household. I'm ready to wait till that day dawns, even though I know I'll have to endure some hard times. I'm ready to go through everything for Susanna's sake."

"You'll do whatever I say for Susanna's sake, nothing more."

"What do you mean?"

"You'll soon find out."

"Very well," she muttered beneath her breath. In her heart of hearts she swiftly decided she would spite him, but quietly and secretly.

One day she met a woman at the market, a few streets away from the village square fronting the parish church. The woman drew her aside and whispered in her ear, "I need to tell you something, Katarin."

"Oh? And what's that? Go on, tell me," Katarina replied.

"No, no, not here. Somewhere where we won't be overheard," the other woman answered her.

The two women were both of the opinion that the matter would be best discussed in church. Thereupon they retraced their steps, going back inside the church, nearly empty now that mass was over. They sat down on two chairs at the side of the nave and began the conversation in earnest.

"I don't really want to interfere. It's not really any of my business," the other woman began apologetically. "But your Susanna is meeting a young man. They've been seen together going down into the Valley, holding hands, and there..."

"Really?" Katarina had cut in shortly.

"I didn't want to tell you but I had to," the woman floundered on.

"And whom is she meeting? Do you know him? Do you know his family?"

"I don't know. All I know is that he's not from these parts. The person who told me, the man who wanted me to have a word with you, doesn't recall seeing him around here. It looks like he's the kind of roving young man who's always on the lookout to have things falling in his favour."

Katarina thanked her, saying, "Every word you told me counts as pure gold and I wish to repay you."

"Pay me nothing. The only thing I ask is that you don't tell your husband that I'm the one who told you all this," the woman spoke to her anxiously. "I know you, only you personally."

Katarina remembered how she had kept all of this secret from her husband. Deep in her heart she was uncertain whether to be glad or sorry that her daughter had found somebody to love her. The uncertainty she had felt long ago

3

kept flitting through her mind as she was rocking to and fro, in solitude.

The silence blanketing the entire village was almost complete.

"How many years have gone by! How many changes there have been! And as for Saverju, how far away he seems to be, God forgive him!" she mumbled the phrases, alone.

Earlier that same day, only a few hours before, Susanna had spent some time over at her house. She had come bringing some of her mother's clothes, freshly laundered and ironed, and had also brought bread and pastries she had baked herself.

"When you come over, there's no need to bring anything with you. Remember, all you have belongs only to you and to your husband and to Wistin. I have nothing to do with it. I'm your mother, that's all." Katarina paused for breath and then hesitantly asked her daughter, in a whisper and almost against her will, "Is Wistin still behaving in the same way?"

Susanna approached her mother and slowly, slowly pushed the rocking chair as if to draw her mother's attention to her and make her reply without any need for words, words she was unwilling to utter.

Her mother gazed steadfastly back at Susanna, waiting. "You don't want to tell me, it seems, my dear daughter. Is that it? I don't want to poke my nose into your affairs. Wistin has grown up now and he seems to have become an angel butterfly."

"An angel butterfly? What on earth is that, Mother?"

"A butterfly that's always on the wing, almost all the year round, and it flutters around mostly down in the valleys."

Susanna kept rocking the rocking chair, as if she was rocking a cradle with a babe on the brink of sleep. She did not say another word.

"I know, all the same, my dear daughter. People told me. Where is Wistin drifting to? Is he going down to the Valley, by chance? Him too?"

4

"You mean him too, just like his mum did, don't you Mother? Isn't that how the story goes? Once upon a time there was a young woman called Susanna, and one fine day..."

"No, no, daughter, that's not what I'm saying at all. When things turned out the way they did, I was behind you, ready to help you out in any way I could. And your father, God grant him eternal rest, was right there behind you too, steadfast. Both of us were there for you."

"Well then Wistin has nobody."

"Wistin has both of you, but..."

"But, but... you mean to say both of us have no say over him. Arturu in one way and me in another."

At that moment someone rapped on the door and Susanna opened the window, peered out and closed it again. "There's a lad with a sheaf of papers in his hand. I think he's the boy who comes round with the story sheets," she reported to her mother, uninterested.

"Yes, yes, that's him. Who else could it be? Open the door, go on. Take the latest instalment and pay him. Look, there's the money on the cupboard, it's ready. I've been expecting him to turn up one of these days."

Susanna opened the door and took the proffered story sheet and paid the boy.

"When you come round next time, read me some more of the story. Somewhere there in the drawer, on top, there are the previous story sheets. So far the story–"

"I'll read it to you next time I come round. And tell the neighbours to come and hear the story, too."

"Yes, yes, stories keep us alive. They're too beautiful for words! But when you read them out as they're written, God bless you! Not me, no of course, because I can't read. Ooh, stories are wonderful but not when they happen for real! Wistin, huh, Wistin! I'd never have supposed...!"

As Katarina kept up her rocking, steadily tapping her foot, Susanna informed her that she was going to take another

5

bundle of clothes to be washed, and would be bringing them back to her ready laundered and ironed, as usual.

"Oh no, no," Katarina exclaimed. "You're too good to your mother. Children aren't like that anymore!"

"Don't say that, Mother! I'm still hoping and praying that Wistin will start loving me back again."

"Love is a heavy burden, my dear daughter. That's what my own dear mother used to say."

"A heavy burden? What do you mean, Mother?"

"Ooh heavy! Love's a heavy burden because it falls down easily with no trouble at all, just as when you let something fall and it drops right down to the ground instantly. Isn't that what happens when you drop something?"

"Yes, of course, Mother, everyone knows that."

"Wait, wait a bit, let me explain. But then, when love tries to rise, well up from below, you understand, well then, that's a different story and love struggles. It can only do so with great difficulty. A mother loves her son with no difficulty whatsoever. But for a son to love his mother, ooh, that's not easy at all."

"He doesn't love me anymore?" Susanna drew closer once more and with both hands gave the rocking chair another light push. She bent her head and kissed her mother on her forehead.

Katarina heard Susanna's ragged breath and realized that she was on the brink of tears. "You should go back home, now, Susanna. It's time. Arturu will be waiting for you. Maybe he won't like being left on his own with Wistin in the house; maybe he'd rather not. And I don't want him to think that I keep you far too long here."

"Wistin isn't often at home, Mother. Bless me. I'm leaving now."

"Bless you, my dear," Katarina gave Susanna her blessing and rising from the rocking chair accompanied her daughter to the door. She then closed it behind her, also raising the bar across to make it secure. She returned to her rocking chair to continue reciting the prayers from where she had left off when Susanna had arrived. "Where was I? Which decade in the Rosary had I reached?" she asked herself. She kept clasping the rosary beads but disturbing thoughts continued to intrude, taking her hither and thither along with them.

***

Arturu entered the room and softly approached Susanna on tiptoes, not wanting to startle her. She saw him from the corner of her eye before he reached her, and she smiled back at him turning her head to face him. He kissed her lightly on her forehead and told her, "I'm going out into the garden for a while. I intend to do some weeding and gather a few flowers and fruit. As soon as the meal is ready, call me."

Susanna raised her face to his and flung herself in his arms, as if she had been waiting for him.

The time they had spent separated from each other had served to remind them of each other's good points; and it also brought home to them the realization that the spark between them, which had brought them together in the first place, had not died. They could not have come to know all this if it were not for the divide that had yawned between them, making them take stock of their own situation, far from each other, with both of them coming to the same conclusion that at the end of the day they did not want to lose all that they had found in each other. It was all very clear to them now.

During that difficult time, locked up all alone in a large house overflowing with riches, Arturu had learnt that he could not live a full life in spite of all his wealth. He knew he had made the right decision and thought that if his mother and father had still been alive, they would have urged him to open up his house once more to the woman he had married, even though at that point she was living far away from him. He knew all too well that they had held strong beliefs and had upheld traditions, ones that instructed him which step to take. Both of them were children of their own time, a time of decisiveness and certainty. But then, since he had taken that first fatal step, the same strong principles that had nurtured them would have made them unhappy to see him destroy the relationship he had built up. In that house, an ancient abode full of dark portraits of people far more serious looking than him, adorned with the accumulated riches of entire generations, everything reminded him that his father wanted him to set up his own household, get married and guarantee the future of his family line.

Arturu had never forgotten all the occasions when the three of them would meet around the dinner table: simple affairs but taking a long time, so long drawn-out that it felt as if they would never end, when he, and Lady, and his father, each with a plate heaped with warm food in front of them, would glance surreptitiously at each other weighing up every movement of a spoon or fork, politely trying not to make the least sound with their mouth, and using their napkin frequently, and talking, and talking, non-stop. Good meals, all according to tried and tested recipes and serious conversations and discussions, all following ancient rules and regulations that had been laid down. He was the one who spoke up least of all, because that was the way he had been brought up in that adult world. At the time, Arturu was still learning by listening to his elders, and his father always spoke decisively, for a long time, gesticulating with his hands as if he was a preacher, and with a clear strong voice. Dinner was the time when the three of them would discuss everything.

On the other hand, Susanna, always with her mother at her side, had long felt that even this good and decent woman, an illiterate one but blessed with a remarkable memory, was waiting for her to return to her husband's house. Susanna was certain that even her father would not have been pleased with her situation, separated from her husband. She could just imagine his fury at such a state of affairs! The days passed tranquilly enough, in the peace and quiet of that neighbourhood and immediate surroundings, but she still felt that this was simply not enough. Her mother constantly urged her to take the first step to resolve the situation, even though

8

she was not to blame. There was someone on whom she could call for help, and Susanna was quite sure that in this, at least, she was most fortunate. The path was not always an easy one to follow, but she was not alone. Katarina frequently reminded her of all this.

The moment Wistin had been found, Susanna's life was turned upside down, and so was Katarina's. The latter began to feel that finally, after Saverju had passed away almost without a word, she had taken up the reins in her hands and was able to achieve something she could never have managed before.

Susanna's memories remained sharp in spite of her endeavours to forget, or at least to stop feeling that the past was still so very important.

***

Her father held all the power. Her mother had to obey his every command.

"When I'm dead, well then, you can do what you like. The reins will be in your hands. Ask your conscience, ponder everything, don't be in too much of a hurry to take decisions and then decide what you will. But for now, all you have to do is wait," Saverju had enjoined Katarina a short while before he passed away.

"That's what I'll do. Just that," Katarina had promptly replied. "But you need to tell me where I have to go," she went on in terror. "And you need to tell me whom I have to look for. I hardly ever set foot outside this village. Really and truly I have hardly ever been far away from here. I'm so afraid of getting lost if I wander away, oh dearie me! But for my daughter's sake, and for the sake of her baby, I'm ready to journey to the end of the world if needs be."

"Then you can stay right where you are, wife. You ninny, don't you know that the end of the world is here, this village?" he snapped at her.

"Very well, I'll go wherever needs be. I'll hire a *karozzin* and leave. I'll pay and it will take me to my destination. When I won't know the way I'll ask and I'll get there in the end. Just you wait and see."

"Wait and see nothing! When you get there I'll be long gone. I want nothing to do with this business!"

"Tell me whom I have to search for, and where."

"I've taken care of everything, absolutely everything. As long as," he warned her, pausing to give weight to his words, "as long as you wait." Saverju had got up from his place, gone into another room to open a drawer, and after rummaging around in it, he took out a scrap of paper. He went to the lamp standing alight in the centre of the table, raised the paper to his eyes to check that he had got hold of the right piece he was looking for, slowly drew his finger along the writing as if reading it, and recognized the pattern it made. "This is it, this is it, it's the one," he muttered to himself. There were few other papers, only those pieces he had no other choice but to keep. He closed the drawer once more and walked back to where Katarina was still standing, telling her, "This is the paper. Everything is written down here for you. You won't be able to do anything without it. Only with this. There's nothing to confuse you, wife."

Susanna had come to know of this a long time before; her mother had told her all about what had happened. During those long hours they spent together in the fields while Wistin played some distance away with a toy or with his kite, Katarina would embark on some story, dredging up some memory or other, to make sure that Susanna would learn everything there was to know about what had happened. The baby was to be found after so many years had elapsed because Saverju had laid his plans in order for that scrap of paper to bind one time to another.

"As long as this doesn't happen whilst I'm still alive!" Saverju had insisted with Katarina.

"At least, well then," she had replied, mollified, "at least one day the time will come when it will happen."

"The day will come? What, you're wishing I was dead already?" he had thundered at her.

"No, no, Saverju, don't misunderstand me. I don't want you to die. I would like you to live for a very long time, for ever..."

"Forever? Remain here forever? What can you be thinking of? Some future you're wishing on me! What on earth would I do here, day after day? Right in front of your eyes! Don't you still believe that we're not meant for this world? Hey there! Make up your mind!"

"There you are! I just don't know what to say to please you. If I say one thing I make you angry and if I say the exact opposite you still get angry with me!"

"Look, there's the paper, and when the time is right all you have to do is to take it with you and hand it over to the person you've judged is the right one. From your hand to his... And in the meantime say a prayer for the repose of my soul."

"Say a prayer for you, of course. Why, let me say one right now."

"No, no and no! Not now!" Saverju had bitten her head off.

"But to whom shall I give the paper?" she implored him, thoroughly confused.

"To whom? Don't you know? To that tame priest of yours!"

"You mean, Fr. Grejbel?"

"And then let him guide you. He knows whom to ask. He knows people because he's always mingling with them."

"Have you spoken to him, in the meantime?"

"Yes, I have. Against my better judgement, but I went through with it. Since it had to be done I did it. He knows all about it now." Saverju took a long look at that fateful scrap of paper once more and very carefully tucked it back inside the drawer at the bottom. He had not wished to reveal its

11

whereabouts to his wife but realized that there was no help for it, he could not do otherwise.

. Katarina had remained standing on the spot, alone in the room, more confused than ever before.

"Look, look here, here's the paper. Look for it at the bottom of the drawer."

"But since I can't read what am I going to do?" she wailed, trailing his footsteps, seeing him putting it back in its place, almost furtively.

"That can't be helped! There's no need to try and start learning to read. Why should you want to, at your age and considering what you are? What is this folly? Haven't we lived our entire life, you and me, without letters? If they ask you to sign anything just draw a cross. You know how to draw a cross. Look here," he paused to show her. "Look, draw a line across, as if it's lying down, just like this, see?"

Katarina drew near to see better, taken completely by surprise.

"And then you draw another line to cross it, straight down. It has to go straight down through the first line. See, there's nothing to it! That's all the writing you need to know. Do you think you're still young enough to learn how to write? You're not all that much younger than I am. And even I don't know how to read, either. Haven't I lived as fully as any other person?"

"Well then, all I have to do is to take the paper and give it to Fr. Grejbel."

"That's it. That's all you need to understand. He knows how to read," Saverju closed the conversation with a disparaging tone of voice.

***

Susanna could see all this before her eyes, even now. Katarina knew how to tell stories but Susanna also knew how

12

to listen and remember. After all this time, now, lying beside her husband, she wanted to fit all the pieces of the puzzle together, to make all the parts of her story make sense, and to look back on it with satisfaction.

Arturu was worried about her. This was a new time they were going through, full of renewed hope for them both. "I don't want to see you cry. This is no time to feel sad, or to wish for things that your nearest and dearest can't give you. A wish is always a wish, just like a vow. Isn't that what our ancestors always believed, dear heart?" he told her tenderly. She nodded her head in assent.

"Are you wishing for something right now? If you are, I'll run and get you whatever it is, I can't deny you anything. What are you wishing for? Tell me!" he exclaimed, wanting to cheer her up.

"Don't you know what I wish for? My entire life was one whole wish, right from the start. A wish, a wish. I want you. You can be sure of that, Arturu. Now that I have you once more I'm very happy and content." She replied, her answer muffled by sobs.

"But don't forget, Susanna, a baby has every right to feel happy and content from the very beginning. And you can do much to bring about its happiness, if you want. Don't wish for anything, or if you do, tell me and I'll give you whatever your heart desires." Arturu knew very well what was in her thoughts but he waited for her to broach the subject.

"If it depended on you, Arturu, I know you'd do your utmost to satisfy my every desire. You've given me so many things that were in your power to give. But you can't give me this thing, gratify this great wish I have. It's a wish that has no hope of being granted."

"Up to now. Don't lose hope. Keep on hoping but don't let this burning desire overwhelm you. Remember."

Susanna kissed him again, withdrew from his embrace and returned to the kitchen to continue cooking. The kitchen table was covered with vegetables and their fresh scent was strong. The fragrance of fields. She had learnt much from her mother. And there was no traditional recipe she did not know, and sometimes she tried her hand at one.

"What do you fancy eating today, Arturu?" she called out, seeing him leave the room.

"My wishes aren't important now. Your wishes are the ones that count at this time."

"Never fear. You can express a wish for things too."

"I'd like to see you perfectly content, even today, in spite of everything."

"Oh very well. But tell me, what would you prefer to eat? Green beans *à la siciliana*? A spinach omelette? Potatoes *à l'anglaise*? Artichokes stuffed with ricotta cheese?" She was about to go on with a list of dishes she could cook that day but she stopped. "Don't you have any wishes, Arturu?"

"I wish for the very same thing you're wishing for. Count on it."

Arturu left the room, went down to the garden, put on his gardening overalls and began hoeing the ground and watering some trees. He spent some time pruning shrubs and then flung himself onto a bench under an old tree, waiting. A few birds swooped down near the fish pond in the centre of the garden, looking around and pecking at the breadcrumbs left out there for them, and then they flew back up to the branches. Arturu had kept up the custom he had learnt in childhood. He would scatter breadcrumbs on the path and around the fish pond for the birds. Only a few minutes would elapse before all the crumbs would disappear. It was a custom Lady never neglected and Arturu learnt to read her kind heart in her actions.

"Arturu!" Susanna called him some time later.

Arturu rose from the bench, removed his soiled overalls and went to the dining room. A long time before, when Lady ran the household, she would call them in for meals by ringing a small bell. As soon as Arturu remembered this, he smiled ruefully. Those days had gone forever.

"*In the name of the Father, and of the Son, and of the Holy Spirit,*" Susanna began saying grace.

Arturu took up the recitation of prayer. And they began to eat.

"Enjoy your meal, Arturu," she told him, gazing at the heaped plate in front of her.

"Enjoy your meal, dearest, but it all depends on you how good this meal will be. I'm not happy at all to see you so sad. We had been separated for so many years and now that's all behind us. We're together. And now you're expecting a baby. What else is there to make you happier than you've ever been?"

"This isn't a calm pregnancy for me, Arturu. Before Wistin changes his behaviour towards..."

"Before he changes his behaviour towards me. Me, you mean, don't you?"

Susanna slowly raised her gaze from her plate and nodded assent, giving him a long look, waiting for him to confirm her previous words.

"Towards me, towards me. Wistin knows there's no special bond between us. We share nothing. He feels nothing for me," he voiced his thoughts, unwillingly. "In his eyes I've always been, and will always remain, an outsider. An outsider who's infiltrated his life. This doesn't surprise me in the least because I know it. And I accept it."

"I know you accepted him. And from the very beginning."

"So why are you cut up about it now? Life is what it is and we have to accept it. You're his mother but I'm not his father. A fact of life. What's so wrong with that? Something that Mother Nature produces. Our mother, Mother Nature. Isn't that what we were taught? And isn't it so? You'll always be his mother but I'll never be his father. That's all. No one can erase what has been written by..."

"Mother Nature," Susanna interjected promptly. She would have liked to smile more, and even laugh, but she could not.

15

"Very good! Well done!" Arturu exclaimed happily. "That's what I was going to say." He put down the cutlery, made as if to applaud her and rose from his seat to come round the table to her, taking away the cutlery from her hands and clasping her to him in a strong embrace. "Well done!" he reiterated.

Susanna burst into tears. She had been holding back her tears before the meal had started but she could not hold them back any longer. She wept, collapsing into his arms.

Arturu gently disengaged himself and returning to his seat continued to eat. By finishing his meal he wanted to show her how good her cooking was.

"He didn't come home last night, again. He slept somewhere else once more," she continued voicing her fears. "I tiptoed to his room late at night and his door was ajar so I went in. I didn't touch anything. I don't want him to realize I've gone inside his room. God forbid he catches me going into his room! His bed was still made up, just as it had been all day."

"I didn't want to tell you but I knew it somehow. I felt that he was not in the house. I know that even when he's home he hardly makes a noise, perhaps because of my presence. For some time now it's been as if he doesn't want to be under the same roof. But I usually still hear him make some noise or other. But last night... nothing. There was perfect silence."

"You're right, Arturu. He didn't sleep here last night. Where could he be staying? I can imagine where, but that's all. I just don't know."

"Did you tell your mother?"

"No, I didn't say a word to her. I don't want her to worry if possible."

"But your mother isn't gullible. And she isn't a little girl, either."

"I know, I know. Mother thinks he'll probably leave one day and we'll never set eyes on him again."

"And why does she think that?"

"All that my mother has learnt, she learnt from the fields, and from the fastness of the village. And she's never been far out of her reckoning. The land has taught her many things. It taught her not to expect too much, not to wish for the moon and not to be surprised with whatever befalls. As she worked the land and looked at the soil, she always thought she was discovering something new. And my father was the same. No one could make him change his mind, no one. He was absolutely certain that all he'd been taught was right and proper. Nothing more. And perhaps he was right."

"And Wistin? Where is he now? He's his father's son."

"But where is his father? Up to a little while ago my son thought his father lived here."

"No, he never believed that, Susanna. He's no fool. I too am no fool. I married you because I loved you, only you. Do you remember? It feels like yesterday."

"It feels like yesterday. That's how it will remain, forever. Yesterday."

In that long ago, the two of them were there in Lady's house. And they were attracted to each other. She was pregnant with Wistin, but Arturu was irresistibly drawn to her. He wanted her to give birth soon so that afterwards he could love her in the way he wanted, free of any ties. She was the first love of his life, the only maiden, and she was more than enough for him. Lady had immediately suspected that love could be kindled between them and she had warned Arturu off in no uncertain terms as soon as she became aware of it.

"Come outside, Susanna. First finish eating and then come outside. It's a lovely day today with not a single cloud in the sky. It won't rain. The countryside will make you forget your worries," Arturu coaxed her.

Susanna rose from the table, put away the plates and cutlery and went to change. She was soon ready.

"Lovely as ever, I see. You're beautiful," Arturu told her admiringly, trying to change her mood.

17

The two of them left the house and strolled along the country lanes. It was calm and peaceful. Birds sang uninterruptedly and white wispy clouds peeped from the sky. They walked hand-in-hand, without haste, and glanced around to see where they could stop and rest. Occasionally, a church bell could be heard ringing nearby. Soft peals, simple peals filling the air all around. The loud burdensome noise of the wider world was far away from that place. The peaceful tranquillity of that hour enhanced the beauty of that wide expanse of green, thickly interspersed with flowers.

"This is an old carob tree. I wonder how old it really is." Arturu idly wondered aloud to Susanna as they approached a tree, intending to lie down beneath its spreading branches. "A carob tree can live for hundreds of years, you know."

"I wonder, where can Wistin be at this hour?" she answered him with her own thoughts.

"Wistin is where he wants to be. That's all there is to it. Ever since he found out I'm not his real father he felt at liberty to wander off wherever the fancy took him. I don't want to hurt you, Susanna, but I think that for some time now he's been feeling a new man, free of all ties. It's as if he's been born again, a baby with several years already behind him. That's what he's like."

"And he's left me, his mother, all alone."

"He left you with me, Susanna."

"Yes, I know, he left me with you. But where is he?"

"Ask the wind, Susanna! From now on, if you want to know that, you're going to have to go far and wide and start searching for him again."

"Just like I did right after he was born till he was a little boy. That's what you're telling me, aren't you?"

"Yes, that's what I'm saying. But talk to me about something else now, please!"

"Do you want me to tell you that long ago we used to come to this area and we used to spend hours here together? We would bring a picnic with lots of savoury bread and we

18

would lie down on the grass and talk and talk. We were happy in each other's company, owning nothing. These wide open spaces were ours to enjoy. No one ever forced us to leave. We felt at peace here and wished for nothing more."

"He used to like flying a kite, you told me once."

"Once I took him to a shop which has since closed down when the owner died, and I bought him a kite. And we used to fly the kite together; he and I, and he loved that immensely, seeing his kite rise in the sky and fly higher and higher. And I would embark on some storytelling and we would be like two children together, fooling around, happy with each other, full of imagination. And that's how we were able to bear all that happened to us." Susanna paused, lost in thought and then spoke again in a different tone of voice. "And I used to think about you, too. My mother wouldn't let me forget you, don't worry!"

Arturu hugged her warmly and the two of them fell back on the grass, hard. A little way off, some boys were flying a kite and their mothers were nearby. Some of the women were singing, others were reciting the Rosary and yet a few others were chattering endlessly.

"Wistin himself would choose to come here, enjoying himself listening to my stories even though he'd be eager to go back to flying his kite. He was my pride and joy. I'd never have imagined that in a few years he would change so much. I can hardly recognize him nowadays."

"And he'll be changing even more, Susanna. Do you remember when we first came to know each other, you and I? Weren't we very different then from what we are now?"

Susanna could recall all that had happened and could hardly believe that so many years had gone by. "If you don't mind, Arturu, I'd like to go back home now. It's time and I'm not feeling too well."

They picked themselves up and began walking slowly back home. The green countryside seemed like an enormous carpet spread before them. Field upon field full of crops and flowers, farmhouses and dwellings, and narrow winding paths separating fields. Beyond lay a huddle of houses that formed the village core, and the parish church could be seen with its central dome and steeples, above the rooftops.

"Oh, oh!" Susanna suddenly cried out in terror as they were walking. "Arturu, hold me, hold me!"

Arturu was startled and held her as firmly as he could to allow her to regain what little strength remained in her legs, but she was heavier and bulkier than his two hands could grip and soon slid to the ground in a heap, like a heavy sack. "Oh my God! What's happened?" he cried in alarm.

"All of a sudden I felt dizzy, somehow... I don't really know... oh, it's nothing, it's nothing, Arturu. Don't worry about me."

He left her lying on the grass to recover and then helped her up. She held on to him and slowly put her weight down to stand on her feet, taking a tentative step. He helped her along resting against him and together they made slow progress.

A few minutes later, Wistin appeared across the boundary of the field. Walking with a light step, aimlessly, he seemed to be coming in their direction.

"Wistin's coming," Arturu told her.

"I know, I know. I saw him from afar. He must have guessed we'd be here and came to meet us. That means he won't be sleeping somewhere else tonight, then. Maybe he didn't find a shelter for tonight. Who knows what he intends to do?"

"Susanna, don't be angry with him. It's better to deal calmly with him and act sweetly, otherwise goodness knows what he'll do next!"

"What more can he do that he hasn't done already? He knows very well I can't keep up with him. He defies me and disregards whatever I say to him. It's as if I mean nothing to him. Sometimes he even answers back. He's already brought me nothing but trouble. What else can he do?"

Wistin continued walking towards them but as soon as he saw them draw near, he halted in his tracks, put both his hands in his pockets and ducked his head, as if he did not know what to do. He glanced at Arturu and Susanna walking hand-in-hand and turned his face to avoid their gaze. They did not speak to him and he fell into step behind them. When they arrived back home, the three of them keeping up a perfect silence, Wistin went straight up to his room, took off his shoes and outer clothes, pushed the door closed and flung himself on the bed to lie full stretch on it. The door did not close properly and he got up again and slammed it shut.

"There, did you hear him? He must have gone to bed, then," Susanna told her husband. The two of them were in the dining room around the table. The loud noise, coming from his room which was quite close to them, startled Susanna and she cringed.

"That came as a shock to you, Susanna. Are you alright?"

"Don't worry, Arturu. I need to get used to this state of affairs. I know that my son is like this now, not the way he used to be at first. What I can't understand is how this can be the same Wistin he used to be such a short while ago. I don't know what sort of company he's keeping."

"Go and talk to him, say something to him. Maybe if you were to speak gently to him you might succeed in changing his attitude a bit. A sweet word can never come amiss."

"I've tried that already but it was no use. I don't feel I should do that again. He's being quite beastly to me. And he's doing it on purpose. Not by mistake or beside himself with anger, but in a calculating manner. That hurts me so very much."

"Not just you, Susanna."

"Yes, you too. More so, actually. Out of the three of us, you're innocent. A victim. I know, I know. This is your house and it's as if you're the outsider in it."

"It's your house too, and his, if he wants. What more can I offer to do?"

"He doesn't want anything to do with us. I know that all too well. It's as if he feels nothing here that binds him to us, to home, this house."

"Go and have a word with him, listen to me," Arturu urged her once more.

Susanna rose slowly from the table and began climbing up the stairs. After having mounted a few, she was suddenly gripped with a stabbing pain and froze, crying out and sliding down, but she managed to keep herself from falling by clinging to the banister. She was frightened and took shallow breaths till the pain eased.

"Susanna!" Arturu shouted in alarm.

"I'm alright, I'm alright," she soothed him and continued going up.

In that grand old house all that could be heard was her laboured tread, going up the stairs. "Oh, oh!" she still whimpered softly, in a whisper, determined not to be heard.

"What do you want? What is it?" Wistin spoke brusquely to her as soon as she tapped on his door.

"You haven't gone to sleep yet, my dear son?" she asked him tenderly.

"I'm not sleepy."

"Aren't you going to eat anything this evening? Have you eaten already? Aren't you hungry?"

Wistin did not reply.

"Would you like me to go downstairs and fetch you something to eat? Your dinner is in the kitchen. I cooked for us three. I always cook for the three of us and so yours is still there."

"No, don't bring me anything."

"Or maybe you'd prefer coming down to eat? Nobody's in the kitchen. Come, Come down. Shall we go down together?"

"No, I don't want to, no."

"Are you going to sleep without any dinner?"

Wistin did not answer her, again.

"Well then, tell me what's happened to you," she asked him wistfully, trying the doorknob gently to enter the room.

He pushed at the door to keep it closed. "Don't come in! Don't come in!" he ordered her. "You can't come in unless I tell you to. This is my room."

Susanna withdrew her hand from the doorknob and moved back a step.

The door cracked open slowly and he appeared in the narrow gap. "Come in," he told her, looking down at the floor to avoid looking directly into her face.

"I'm coming in, but before that I want you to tell me what's happened to you this evening. You're not the same."

"How do you know?"

"My heart tells me."

"Your heart tells you? Well then, at least there's something that speaks to you. And what does it tell you?"

"My heart speaks to me of Wistin. Tell me, what's happened?"

"Nothing's happened." He paused and in a changed tone of voice asked harshly, "Where were you this evening, you and that other one?"

"We went to the field."

"Did you go to fly a kite or to tell stories? Or maybe you had other things to do?"

"There were a few boys flying their kite, and I think a few mothers were telling stories to their children too. That's what I think. And you can remember this well."

"I do remember it and I'd like to forget it if I could."

"You'd like to forget it? But why?"

"Why?" he repeated in a harsh tone. Then he fell silent.

"You still haven't told me what happened to you this evening."

"My girlfriend is leaving me. And she's leaving me because of you."

Susanna burst into tears, went up to Wistin and flung out her arms, bending to hug him but he drew back and did not allow her near him and she straightened up and slowly left the room.

Only the sound of her weeping could be heard echoing hollowly in that large domain, and her dragging footsteps going down the stairs. She held on tightly to the banister, all the way down, afraid of falling again.

At the foot of the staircase Arturu was waiting for her. As soon as she approached, he mounted a few steps and clasping her around her forearms, drew her towards the bedroom.

Wistin slammed his door shut and the loud bang echoed around the house, a startling noise, like a bolt out of the blue. And then perfect silence reigned once more.

Chapter 2

A light breeze, fresh on one's face, came drifting across the worked fields of the neighbourhood and wafted through the entire room, like a butterfly familiar with its surroundings. The curtain behind the window billowed out afresh, as if it was greeting nature and welcoming the peace bestowed by that hour. As usual, a deep tranquillity had settled over the place. The last random birds sought their nightly resting place, swooping back and forth nervously, flying in circles silhouetted across the darkening sky as if they had forgotten their house address, seemingly momentarily forgetful of those majestic densely-leaved ancient trees where they had grown up. In a little while, all the birds would have settled in their place and gone to roost. Then, even their shrill chirruping abated and died down completely and the silence remained unbroken. Their evening prayer was finished and done with and night time could proceed. Another full day of labour had been laid to rest. This ancient rule had never been broken in the village, a rule stipulating a long day's work from dawn to dusk; otherwise life could not go on. The villagers also knew that hunger was the main driving force behind the greatest rule of them all. They followed it to the letter, living their life in an unchanging routine and rhythm, generation after generation.

A tiny village, an ancient one, situated at the end of the world as the villagers liked to say, would not have been the way it was were it not for this bond between life in the open air and life indoors. A natural rhythm had succeeded, working in full order for countless years holding sway over an entire village. A village that, withal, was a world in itself, from the cradle to the grave. A village where its inhabitants would quickly gather in their own separate household. With the exception of the same handful of men who habitually gathered at Baskal's wine tavern, none of the villagers tried to lengthen their day.

Katarina, comfortably ensconced in her rocking chair, was craning her neck to peer out of her window. Sometimes she stared, sometimes she fixed her gaze somewhere in the distance, or nodded her head as if she was holding a conversation with herself or with someone who could not be seen at the window. Though her husband had been laid to rest many years before, she could always picture him in front of her eyes, staring back at her with a fixed gaze. His memory was part of the pride she held onto, the fact that she had been a married woman once.

"Why doesn't Mum want to tell me any more stories?" Wistin asked her. "That's how she brought me up, with storytelling. She was always making them up, both whenever I asked her to and whenever she felt like it herself. I know they weren't real, but maybe that's why I liked them so much. Though not all of them. To get up from bed in the morning, to go to sleep at night, and to do whatever she wanted me to do, and to eat. Always with some story or other."

"Did you know they weren't real?" Nanna Katarina asked him, rather taken aback, straightening up in her rocking chair. "I suppose you did know really, didn't you?"

"Of course I knew. Nobody could fool me completely. Even your stories, Gran; I knew you just made them up. But lately, I don't know what's with Mum. She doesn't know how to imagine and make up stories anymore."

"Can't you guess why? Because now you're growing up into a young man, Wistin. You're no longer that little boy you were a while ago, always imagining and dreaming up things, enjoying yourself playing around, and wanting a bedtime story every night to set you off to sleep! And at your age, now, what sort of story would interest you? Why are you finding this so hard to understand? Everything happens in its own time and place. Don't you see how the crops grow in their own season in our fields? If you look around you at God's creatures you can learn. It's like clockwork, a law which no one can break. No one, except mankind, poor deluded mankind. I've told you all this already, please, believe me! Your gran doesn't lie. She's never lied to you. Isn't that true or not? Tell me, yes or no?" Katarina insisted in a firm voice. "I haven't lied to you. Answer me!"

Wistin remained dumbstruck.

"I'm asking you a question, so you must speak up. Aren't you going to answer me?" she asked again in an even more decided tone of voice, wanting to know how he would answer her.

"I don't know what to tell you, Gran. I don't mean to let you down. I know how much you've done for me. Have I ever let you down in all this time? You brought me up and I always found you by my side whenever I needed you. But... I don't know... I've never failed you before but then neither..."

"No, no, my dear, you've never let me down. You've never hurt me, up to now. Ooh," Katarina replied pensively, taking a deep breath and falling silent as if she was about to start talking to herself. "Up to now, never, never. I can only say up to now because everything changes and people, huh, people change from one day to the next. A person's heart is like a leaf resting on wind, fluttering wherever it wills. Winter can mingle with summer if they want. It's the seasons that command. But let me stop right there otherwise you'll think I'm the one embarking on another story now. What do you say, Wistin?"

Wistin did not answer her.

"The time for stories has gone. Isn't that so?" Again he did not answer her and she lowered her head and closed her eyes.

The village church bell was ringing out, signalling the time for the *Ave Maria* prayer. One stroke after another, with just a short pause in between, reminding people to stop working and to say a prayer. The men folk would remove their caps and together, men and women, would clasp their hands across their chest in reverence. It was that time of day when daytime would stop for a while and let evening beckon.

"All I know is that Mum behaved very differently with me until a short time ago. Now, all of a sudden, she seems to be another woman, one whom I don't know. Don't I have the right to know what's happened?"

"Your mother loves you very much, and I know this because she's my daughter, and she loves you more than anyone else, Wistin."

"That's not the real reason, Gran."

"Well then, the real reason must be something else and I'm going to tell you what it is, now. You're no longer a boy. Since you're growing up you need to pass through a great change. We all went though it at your age, and it's your turn now. If we overprotected you, forgive us, we didn't know any better. We did the best we could. Nobody taught us how to live our life. We had to learn with the passing of time. But if we made mistakes, we made them out of love."

"Is that your opinion, Gran?" Wistin said scornfully, putting his hands in his pocket.

The silence outside was suddenly broken. "Wistin, Wistin," a couple of youths called out, standing a few steps away from the window.

Wistin went up to his grandmother and told her, "I'm going out, Gran."

"You're going out now? Where are you going? Is this a decent time to be going out?"

Wistin went to the window and called out to his friends that he would be joining them in a few minutes. "Wait for me, wait for me, I'm coming, I'm coming!"

"Ohh" Katarina moaned with resignation, the loser in the battle of wills. She set herself in motion again, a regular, steady rhythm in her rocking chair. She used to spend hours in it, sometimes dozing off or even falling asleep, and sometimes praying or staring vacantly, lost in thought or preoccupied with troubling reflections. Many thoughts would pass through her mind and she would worry, or cry solitary tears, or smile, or talk to herself and then say a prayer, enthusiastically like a little girl. She got up from the rocking chair and went to the window, peeking out. She hid behind the curtain to prevent anyone seeing her and by pushing the curtain slightly aside, she could make out Wistin and his mates disappearing down the street and reaching the far corner.

The young men looked to be Wistin's age.

"Don't stay out too late, dear," she called out. "Don't forget it's getting dark."

Wistin kept pace with his mates without giving her an answer, and she was wounded to the quick. But she was unwilling to admit it even to herself and often took herself to task about it. His mates had taken up a more important role in his life now. The three of them went out together and idled around in the village square or on the outskirts of the village, making plans for their future when they would be young men looking for work and courting a maiden. They were in the habit of observing the young women of their village as they would be entering and leaving church, admiring their beauty. These maidens were all somewhat different from each other though their clothes looked more or less the same. The lads would stare at them from beneath their brow and sometimes would pluck up courage to approach them and whisper some word of praise and admiration in their ear. Occasionally one of the youths would be cheeky enough to blow them a wolf whistle. The young women would walk on, blushing with embarrassment, bending their head and whispering among themselves, and smile. Their heart would have been broached. The young men would know this straightaway.

"If I start courting a girl, I don't want to find her from this village," one of them said.

"Why ever not?" the other one asked him.

"I'd like a different girl," the first one replied.

29

"The main thing is that she's pretty," his mate answered him again.

The noise of their chatter followed them, but as soon as they were out of earshot, peace and tranquillity settled down once more in the street. Katarina drew back from the window and pulled the curtain back into place.

Wistin said nothing and the three continued walking aimlessly on. Wistin had set his sights on a young woman some time before, seeing her enter church, and he waited for her on the church parvis on the lookout to see her emerge, plucking up his courage when she came out to approach her and tell her how pleasing in his eyes she was. They spent some time meeting on the outskirts of the village, and they also liked to go down into the Valley sometimes, lying down full stretch under an ancient carob tree watching birds and butterflies flutter around or stepping into little puddles of water just for the fun of it. They had spent quite some time courting till someone saw them and reported him to his mother straightaway. Susanna had brushed it off, telling the man who had come telling tales that her son was grown up and adult enough to see to his own affairs.

However, it did not end there and that same man went up to Fr. Grejbel telling him, "You should know about this. Wistin, Susanna's boy, is courting a young woman in the Valley. These aren't the sort of things we tolerate here. Don't let such new habits take root here. Do something about it. That's what you're supposed to be here for, to oversee what happens in the village."

"That's not what I'm here for," Fr. Grejbel had answered him sternly.

"Then go back where you came from," the man had replied, mortified and angry.

The two young people went on courting till one fine day, Wistin's girlfriend told him she was fed up and they quarrelled furiously till she got up and ran away. He ran after her, calling out to her telling her he still loved her. "Antonja, Antonja! I'll give you everything! The little I have is yours, all

30

yours! I'll tell you sweet stories, make them up especially for you, just as they used to do for me when I was a little boy. I'll give you everything they gave me. My grandpa left me many things, a large linen shirt, a lambswool cloak, a waistcoat with silver buttons, and a sash of carded cotton worked on the loom, and his knapsack. I have everything I need to set up my own household, Antonja. Just wait and see! And I'll work hard for you and in time build you a beautiful house, and you'll see that out of all the women in the village I love only you. I promise you: I'll never leave you!"

"I don't want to know, I'm fed up!" Antonja shouted back.

"But why? Is it my fault?"

"I don't know why. Don't ask me anymore! This is it!" she insisted putting more distance between them and sprinting away. Sometimes she glanced back fearfully to make sure she was keeping up the distance between them, holding back her long hair with one hand to prevent it impeding her vision and with her other hand raising her skirt slightly in order not to trip over it in her haste. Finally she made the village square, but in her eagerness to escape she stumbled and fell at the feet of an old man who was standing there chatting to another villager, both of them having just left the church as soon as mass ended.

"Oh, excuse me please! I'm so sorry I cannoned into you!" Antonja exclaimed in total confusion.

"Never mind. What's happened to you?" the old man asked her full of concern.

"Look there, he..." she began but could not bring herself to name Wistin who had arrived on the scene, out of breath and feeling slightly fearful and embarrassed.

"Who's he?" the old man queried.

Antonja did not reply and patting her hair and dress neatly into place made to go on her way but was rooted to the spot, undecided.

"That's Wistin, Susanna's boy, Katarina's Susanna," the old man muttered to himself, quite certain.

Wistin continued approaching slowly, as if he was walking on tiptoes, appearing confident and ready to face all the villagers and make them aware that he was a personable young man, handsome, courageous, proud. A knot of people had gathered round by this time and they all stared, full of curiosity and pleased that something out of the ordinary was finally happening in that sleepy village. They all waited to see what would happen next. They exchanged questions and traded gossip, who was that young woman and who was that young man, until Wistin and the old man came face-to-face.

"Of all the young men in the village, did it have to be you? You, of all people?" the old man rebuked Wistin in front of everybody.

Wistin dropped his gaze to the ground, balling his hands into two fists but held his tongue, as if controlling himself from uttering a single word from all the words rushing angrily to his mind. He raised his eyes and turned his face around taking all of them in, and said, "Yes, that's who I am."

"Susanna's boy," the people whispered to each other in barely audible tones.

Wistin still did not speak and he looked around to see a way of escaping the crowd and go back home. He searched for some way out of the throng but could not move for people massed around him. Staring faces with watchful expressions gazed back at him, some of them from little children held up in arms, all staring at him and whispering among themselves. He did not want to show any fear but he did not have the audacity and aplomb to part the crowd and make his way back home. His mates were somewhere in that crowd and he was certain they were feeling the same as he was.

"Here, here he is, it's Wistin," someone shouted.

Among the many people that had gathered round, Antonja spied her father Tumas and her mother Ester and she quickly went to them.

One of the women there silently left through the crowd and went to look for Susanna at home. "Come, come quickly," she told her.

"Oh dear Lord, what's happened? What's happened to Wistin?" Susanna moaned.

"Oh nothing very much, just the usual trouble with young people," the woman tried to soften the blow with this answer.

Susanna ran as fast as her legs could take her. She parted the crowd and went right up to Wistin who was standing in the middle. She was hoping against hope that all the anger that had been roused would quickly evaporate. She had immediately realized what must have occurred. She had been through far worse but this was a new kind of trouble and she was still unsure how to tackle it. All she knew so far was that she had to keep calm, wait and pray. That's what she had learnt to do in the face of trouble and it had always stood her in good stead.

"Don't ever let him set his sights on my daughter! Don't you dare let him even look at her again! Do you hear?" Ester shouted angrily at Susanna. "My daughter will court only whom I decide upon. I will choose her bridegroom how I please. I didn't choose your son. Let your son go somewhere else looking for a woman. Let him go to the Port! Don't you know how many people there are over there? It's full of seafarers, and townies. Send him there to search for a woman."

Tumas kept his gaze on Antonja and held his peace without making any move to interfere, trying to hold his wife from continuing with her loud abuse. "That's enough, now that's enough, wife," he coaxed his wife, holding her back from her shoulders to prevent her squaring up to Susanna.

"Are you lily-livered, husband?" Ester rounded on him in plain view of all. "What sort of man are you? Huh, some husband you've turned out to be! You're not worth the trousers you wear! Do you want your daughter to wed into a family you haven't chosen? Yes or no? Is your daughter really your daughter or not?"

"Very well, you're right, but that's enough now. You've said all you had to say to her," he countered.

"Don't tell me you're taking her side, by any chance?"

"Her side? What do you mean?"

"Don't play the fool with me! As if you weren't old enough to know better. But this isn't the time to give you a good talking-to as you deserve. We'll see all about that when we get back home. At the moment, my duty is to defend my daughter to the best of my ability, and she's your daughter too! Tell everyone that she's your daughter and we've never done anything to be ashamed of. Be a man, husband, and tell everyone that you don't want your daughter to keep company with just anyone who comes along."

"Very well, very well. I declare that I too do not wish my daughter to keep company with anyone without our approval," he quickly said what his wife wished to hear, hoping to calm her down and prevent her voicing all that came to her with as shrill and penetrating a voice as she could produce.

Antonja hugged her mother, burrowing into her bulk and trying to avoid the taunting gaze of all those people thronging around her.

"The town, the town! Send him to town! To the Port!" Ester took up the shout once more. "That's where he can find a young woman good enough for him. A young woman who knows how to dance and waggle her hips, to paint her face all colours of the rainbow and know how to dress and show her cleavage, and other things too! We know nothing about these things. We only know how to till the soil, plant and harvest crops and live along the dry-stone walls and farmhouses and *giren* stone-huts. Don't you know all this, you? But in the Port, huh, in the Port it's like another world. What do you say to that Susanna? See how different we are!"

Wistin quickly looked at his mother, mortified to have been the cause of this angry scene. Susanna gave him a hug and then disengaged herself and approached Ester, hoping to soften the harshness etched on her face.

"Do you have the cheek to approach me? Do you think your noble marriage has made everything alright? We're not wealthy like you, riches didn't rain from the sky and conveniently fall in our lap, but we're village women just like you. Just see to it that from now on your son takes up a different path and that will be the end of the story! Understand?"

Susanna nodded her head twice in assent but drew nearer, still wanting to talk to Ester. But Ester held firm, drew back in scorn and pushed her husband along as well. Tumas looked at Susanna, silently admiring her beauty, from the top of her head to the tips of her toes. He too thought in the same way as his wife because that was the way he was brought up to think, but he could not altogether feel things the same way she did.

Antonja raised her head and left her mother's protective arms. Giving Wistin a long stare she gave him a little smile, conveying the knowledge that she still loved him.

"Antonja!" Wistin exclaimed silently, mouthing the word with his lips so that she, in turn, would get the silent message of love.

Ester, Tumas and Antonja made for home straightaway. The three of them succeeded in keeping silent till they arrived home and went inside. Antonja bent her head and immediately went up to her room, bursting into tears the minute she entered it. Her mother made to follow her.

Tumas grabbed his wife from her shoulders and pulling her back, brought her headlong rush to a standstill. "Now, don't take on so, Ester," he advised her. "Mind you don't antagonize her!"

"Let go of me! You! Today you've shown me again your true colours as to what sort of father you are!" Ester glared at him, slapping away his restraining hands off her shoulders. "I'll talk to you later. Now I have to talk to her!"

"To her! You mean me! Go on, tell me what you have to say to me, Mum, before I start on what I have to say to you!" Antonja said, appearing at the head of the stairs and starting to come down slowly.

"Are you talking to me, in that manner?"

"Yes, to you, Mum."

Ester was totally taken aback because Antonja had never behaved in that manner to her. She stared back at her daughter in shock, stupefied, waiting for her daughter to speak, her hands raised to her face in alarm.

Antonja came down all the steps and faced her mother. "From today onwards, you're not going to poke your nose into my affairs. I will choose my boyfriend myself. And he only has to please me. In time, then, you too must be pleased with him."

Ester felt overwhelmed and drew closer to Antonja trying to embrace her.

"Mum, Mum, out of my way! Let me pass!"

"How can I leave you on your own, my dear daughter? I don't know how! And my heart wouldn't let me if I did."

"Well you'll just have to learn now, Mum."

"What's happened to make you change so much? In such a short time! How long have you been meeting that young man, then?"

Antonja pulled her veil across her head with both hands, turned and walked out of the door. "Ask me where I'm going! Go on, just ask me!" she taunted her mother as she left the house.

Ester was lost for words, unable to pluck up her courage. "But how can this be happening?" She turned to her husband and asked him, "What's happening, Tumas? How can Antonja talk to me this way? She's never done such a thing before. I'm afraid to quarrel with her, now." She paused and then threw herself in his arms, "Maybe she doesn't love us anymore? Is she going to abandon all she grew up with? All that we went through for her sake counts for nothing? She didn't appreciate it?"

"She's fallen in love. That's all! It doesn't mean she doesn't love us anymore, wife. The heart can accommodate many people."

"But, then, have you changed as well? Don't I know you the same way as before? Since when have you thought in this way? You left me to stand alone facing her. Antonja has already won and I have lost. Do you want her to go courting with Wistin?"

"I want to see her happy and content, that's all."

"If you and I never agreed on anything, I thought that on this at least we were agreed and shared the same opinion. But even about this, Tumas..."

"Ester, Ester, only time will tell. Do you remember those days when you would pick a flower and tear off the petals one by one, chanting 'He loves me, he loves me not'?" He paused and repeated the words in a changed tone, "Do you love me?"

"I love you, Tumas. I love you in the way I know how. And that's why I'm so worried about Antonja. I don't know how else to bring her up if not in the way of our people, keeping to our traditions. I didn't bring her up this way."

***

That evening, in Baskal's wine tavern, the evening did not turn out as it usually did. It was still the same place, a quiet place where people could argue to their heart's content, cut off from the rest of the world and it was a place where a drop of wine could fill up any void. Every evening, the talk would turn to the doings of that same day, something out of the ordinary that would set a few men discussing it. The scene with Antonja and Wistin in front of a crowd of people a few hours before was far more interesting than the usual tales those few men kept recounting to each other time and time again. The wine tavern was the place where they bared their soul to each other. It was quite impossible for them not to comment on what had just occurred.

"What happened long ago is dead and gone. But for goodness' sake, we can't allow some youth to think he can get away with breaking all the rules of behaviour we've grown up with. If he's village bred and born, he should stick to our village rules," Ġamri fumed, raising his glass of red wine to his lips.

Ġwakkin agreed with him. "If the village elders won't speak up to prevent such happenings, our village will slowly crumble to pieces. Both our village as well as the neighbouring ones. Let only a few other youths like this young man loose and there we are, lumped with new customs copied from goodness knows where and we might as well be dead and gone! Either they stick to our rules or else they can jolly well leave this place!"

Kieli had not interjected so far but then he spoke up, "The youths of today won't be like us, my friends. They mingle freely with people from other villages, much more than we ever did. We've spent all our life here, closed in within these walls, within our fields, and we never even realized that there was a whole new world out there, only a short distance away. Times change."

"No, no, times don't change, we won't let them, Kieli. This is how we were brought up and lived our life, and now, that's how we want to get old and die. From the cradle to the church square and from the church square to the grave. That's how it used to be and that's how it should remain, forever! Maybe you're thinking our ancestors were at fault?" Ġwakkin raised his voice getting hot under the collar. "We've got children in our midst who seem to mingle freely with people from other places, far away from these streets of ours. We're no longer alone, my friends!"

A perfect silence fell all of a sudden in Baskal's wine tavern, as if they had all lost the power of speech.

"Don't you have anything to say? None of you have the courage to say something? Do you want our village ruined, yes or no?" Ġwakkin hotly insisted, raising his voice.

"Come on, if a young man goes down to the Valley to kiss a young woman, is that going to ruin our village and all that our ancestors built up? I don't think so. Here, Baskal, refill my glass will you, maybe I'll get some inspiration and tell these two others my bright idea," Kieli scoffed in derision.

"Are you referring to us, by any chance?" Ġamri and Ġwakkin burst in with one voice.

"No, of course not, God forbid," Kieli replied sarcastically. "No such thought crossed my mind. You're old friends, just like this, look at this, mates," he shrugged off the hostility, raising his brimming glass of red wine, giving it a kiss and downing it in one gulp.

"Huh, that's why you're talking nonsense, Kieli," Ġamri admonished him.

"The wine's gone to your head and no one can bring you back to your senses, willy-nilly. You've gone a long way down that road," Ġwakkin added. "Calm down a bit, think properly and you'll see we're in the right of it. No one will change our village under our noses, least of all a slip of a lad like that one."

"A young man familiar with the Port," Ġamri interjected, with the air of someone revealing something nobody would have guessed at.

"Familiar with the Port?" Baskal asked with his mouth agape. "I didn't know that, mates."

"Don't you know whose son he is? Blood will tell, Baskal." Ġamri replied.

"That's right, Ġamri's giving it to you straight," Ġwakkin told Baskal.

"A son of the Port? How can that be? The Port is very far away from here. We've been brought up in the middle of fields, not the sea," Baskal went on, amazed, seemingly speaking to himself.

"We know all about the hoe, nothing about oars," Ġwakkin took up the complaint. "The hoe digs deep into the soil but the oar turns in the emptiness of water without any direction."

39

"Now I can really see the difference between them," Baskal reflected. "The hoe searches for something sound and solid, but oars..."

"Search for nothing. They have nothing to search for. Everything moves below them; there's nothing but water, waves that come and go. Nothing you can hold on to. That's the difference between us. Don't you understand, Baskal?" Ġwakkin asked.

"You mean, we're very different from them, don't you?" Baskal asked.

"That's right. Maybe at last you're beginning to understand, Baskal," Ġwakkin shouted at him in exasperation.

"Don't shout at me, Ġwakkin! I was born here just like you were, and I was brought up here too, and I know where the Valley is and what happens down there, even though I myself have never been down that road. If by that it means I have no knowledge of the Port, it simply means that I've remained a villager, from the top of my head to the tips of my toes. There, do you understand now?" Baskal replied roughly.

"I did go to the Port, true enough Baskal. But I only went there out of necessity. And I saw it from afar, without touching it at all. It's not for me. Life is very different from ours over there," Ġwakkin went on more calmly. "Over there they live right up against the water, near ships, and they constantly see the doorway of the Port open in front of their eyes, day and night, always ready to allow them to pass and go beyond. We are stuck fast here, far away, at the end of the world. We lack nothing!"

"That lad is trying to bring in the way of life he knows amongst us. My friends, do you know what his father does? He works as a trader on a bumboat." Ġamri spoke in an even tone.

"A trader on a bumboat?" Baskal asked in astonishment and some envy. "Then he has far more custom than I do in this tiny hole of a wine tavern. And I wonder how many more people he meets by dint of his boat than I do! How many clients he must have!"

"Aren't you glad of our company every evening, Baskal?" Ġwakkin asked, affronted. "Aren't we good patrons?"

"Of course, of course! I'm always very pleased to welcome you," Baskal answered hastily, afraid that a careless word from him would put customers off. "I open this tavern every evening for your sake. Now mind that you keep coming, my friends, or I'll be forced to close shop and seek other employment."

"Why don't you try your hand at being a trader on a bumboat, Baskal?" Ġwakkin asked sardonically, getting his own back. "Furnish a boat, fill it up with goods and go row it around in the Port. You might even manage to sell everything."

Baskal looked as if he had taken umbrage but he controlled himself and did not let a word of censure escape him. "Shall I refill your glass, Ġwakkin?" he replied in a subdued manner in as few words as he could manage.

"Yes, fill it up again for me, because I once heard tell that truth only lies in wine," Ġwakkin answered, dropping his head to the table and falling silent. "I don't know why I'm speaking this way, my friends, I really don't. It's not the wine but something stronger."

"Something older than this wine, Ġwakkin. All of us are older than we look," Baskal felt fit to explain.

"It was Wistin who brought all this trouble about, Baskal," Ġwakkin went on.

"Wistin is a nobody, only Susanna's boy," Ġamri interposed.

"A youth of the new age, mates. That's what he is! We're old, or nearly so. It's true that we're the ones who built up this village but it seems the moment has come for us to step aside," Kieli interjected.

"Step aside, step aside! That's all very well but we'll do so only on the condition that nothing that we've built up gets broken," Ġamri declared.

Baskal waited for everyone to fall silent and then he told them, "If our village isn't to get broken up and ruined, my friends, we must learn to read and write. Otherwise everything is going to die with us."

"Read and write? Now, after all this time? How can we?" the other three exclaimed with one voice.

"Yes, that's what we have to do," Baskal insisted.

"Very well, if it's necessary," they acquiesced. "Who's going to teach us?"

"Can't you guess? As soon as he finishes his duties in church, after giving the Blessing and hearing Confession, and after closing up the church, he'll come here," Baskal informed them.

"Really? Who told you?" they wanted to know.

"He himself told me. I believe him because he's always been a man of his word. You'll see!"

***

Not a single sound invaded the street and one could hear a pin drop. The church clock marked the passage of time every quarter of an hour, precisely, with many strokes, a system that hardly anybody understood. That time of evening was not a time to stay out on the streets.

Katarina spent all that time pacing the room, looking at the framed picture of Our Lady in front of which she kept a tiny lamp, constantly lit, and praying and gripping the Rosary beads tightly with all her fingers.

"Holy Mary, let him come back home soon. We only have him. We struggled so hard not to let him die before he was born, and to see him coming into this world, and to find him at last and bring him up. Will he be the one who'll break our heart now? What wrong did we do to him that makes him bring more bitterness upon us? Haven't we been hurt enough? Didn't we do our duty entirely? Haven't we waited many

42

years? Why is he doing this? Maybe it's not entirely his fault? He doesn't seem to care too much about his mother. He almost seems to be repelled by her. He doesn't obey me. He hardly goes to church anymore. He isn't even paying attention to days of fasting and hardly ever makes the Sign of the Cross before eating. He no longer wears a holy medal around his neck and nor does he keep a holy picture on his person somewhere, in a pocket, nothing! What more is he going to do?" Katarina continued talking to herself as she went to the kitchenette and poured some water into the kettle to make herself a cup of tea. She took a lemon, cut it in half and squeezed it into the cup. Some sugar, a quick stir with the teaspoon and her drink was ready. But her appetite was wanting, even though taking tea with lemon was an old tradition going back to when she was a little girl.

Suddenly, the front door opened and a few light steps broke the silence of the hour.

"He's come home, he's come home!" she said to herself in a whisper.

"Gran, I'm home!"

"Wistin, Wistin! Where were you at this late hour? I couldn't sleep before you came back. Where were you? Why are you so late?"

Wistin stood there before her with his head hanging down, utterly silent.

Katarina opened her arms to hug him but he drew back. "What's happened? Oh dear Lord!" she exclaimed, startled and apprehensive.

"Nothing, Gran, nothing's happened. You taught me there's nothing new under the sun. Everything has a long tradition in our village, isn't that what you like telling me?"

"Yes, that's what I said to you. That's what I was taught, after all, by my ancestors and what I learnt all by myself as the years went by and that's what I still think. This is all very well but what's it got to do with anything, now? Tell me, go on."

Wistin tried to pat his hair down because he suddenly realized it was in a mess. It had got all tangled when he was down in the Valley and was running after his sweetheart, bumping into branches and feeling gusts of wind pluck at his hair. He knew there was no taming that rogue lock of hair now but indeed all his hair was quite tangled and mussed up.

"Where were you, dear?"

He also had his shirt coming out of his trousers and as soon as he noticed, he tried to tuck it back in.

"What's happened? Don't you want to tell me? Is it none of my business? I won't poke my nose into your affairs. After all, you're growing up now and I'm not your mother. And talking of your mother, she must have her mind at rest thinking you're here! Your mother, oh dearie me, your mother! That's another problem."

"In this village there are only problems it seems, aren't there, Gran? A problem to find work, a problem to love somebody, a problem to have your mum agree with you, a problem to find out what lies beyond the fields surrounding the village, problems upon problems! Isn't that what you want to say?"

"No, no, that's not what I want to say, my dear Wistin. I love the village, I like it. I mean, the village is home to us all, and we are all brothers and sisters. And we have the occasional spat, as all brothers and sisters do. We quarrel, are disagreeable, hate each other and sometimes succeed in loving each other too."

"You succeed in loving each other too?" he asked her with a taunt but still betraying his hurt feelings.

"Yes, yes, we often managed to love each other. We learnt to love each other, me and your grandfather, God forgive him! Yes, yes, God will forgive him because God forgives and forgets all sins. God forgets and makes people forget, too. Praise be to God! Mind you never forget what I'm telling you, ever, ever. Not even if you're dying of hunger and no longer have the strength to use the plough. Never, understand, never! If I don't tell you this, I'd be tricking you, selling you to nothing! And when I'm no longer here, you might end up without support. God is always there for us, my dear, always, and mostly in stormy times. But on fine days too, of course, of course."

Wistin let her finish, and then, plucking up his courage said, "Gran, Gran..." and then he burst into tears, sobbing his heart out.

Katarina went up to him and hugged him to her. Life had taught her not to be surprised by anything and not to feel overwhelmed whenever some new trouble was brewing. She did not want to ask him what had happened because she preferred to let him tell her in his own words. She did not want to pester him, especially now that he was confiding in her and seemed to trust her more than he did his mother. He had been seeing his mother in an ugly light for some time now, for one reason or another, too high-handed and overpowering in her dealings with him, and almost mocking him when trying to interfere and lead him in the way she wanted. It seemed he did not appreciate the way she showed her love for him and indeed he had begun to doubt that she even loved him! And what was even worse, he had begun to lose all interest in all of it.

"I had a girlfriend, Gran, but everything's finished between us now."

"Did you love her, Wistin?" she asked him gently.

"Yes, Gran, I loved her."

"And how did you love her, Wistin?"

"The way I know how, I loved her in the way I felt I should. I used to smile at her, tell her stories, try to make her laugh, remind her how beautiful she was, how attracted I was to her, and I used to promise her that by and by I would get a job and be able to keep her in comfort, happy and content. I told her that I would start working in the fields, planting and pruning, ploughing, cultivating crops and selling them and that I was so very happy with her, as if she was everything to me," Wistin told her in a rush.

"You told your girlfriend many wonderful things. And how did you know about all those things? Who taught you?"

"Don't you know that we were told many wonderful stories when we were little? And they were all love stories. I'm grown up now but I still think in the same way. But I don't think the village is like that. Those decent and kind women who used to tell us those stories about the world around us didn't know enough about it! They were lovely stories but..."

"And so you loved your girlfriend. Where did you use to meet her?"

Wistin paused to gather his thoughts, between embarrassment and worry, but he knew his grandmother would understand him straightaway. And she would never go so far as to be angry with him or condemn him. She was patience itself, listening without getting tired or fed up, and she always took his side, even though she might order him to do something in a loud and firm voice. Sometimes he used to wish his grandmother was his mother.

"Where did you use to meet her? Come now, Wistin, you must tell me," she asked him once more.

"In the Valley, Gran."

"In the Valley? Just like an angel butterfly then. Do you know what the Valley signifies, dear? It signifies life. Life is born there."

"What do you mean, Gran? Can life be born in the Valley?"

"One day I'll tell you, the day will come when you should know. But it's too soon. And then?"

"And then we began to love each other, but she came today and told me that she couldn't love me anymore. That was to be the end of it because she couldn't love me any longer."

"Another rule, just like the rest, my dear. Life is full of rules and regulations, some sweet and some bitter. Go on, go on."

"She told me that her parents didn't want her to fall in love with me."

"With you? And why not?"

"She told me: 'You're Susanna's Wistin'. She used to love me before, but not any longer. I am Susanna's son. Which means the village doesn't want me."

"Never mind, Wistin. There are many other young women, and you might find one to love from amongst them. And then you'll promise her too that you'll work in the fields, and plough and plant, and harvest and everything else. There are many others, just you wait and see."

"But maybe, Gran, I'll also be Susanna's son to them all."

"Is that what you think?"

"Yes, that's what I think. And do you know why? Because they all seem to be the same."

"How well you can think and speak! You've started reading books it seems. I can just imagine."

Wistin left her arms and patted his hair into some semblance of order. His thoughts were all on his girlfriend and he felt convinced that she, in turn, was locked up in her parents' house thinking of him. He got up and left the room.

Katarina remained there, thinking about all that she had said to him. She felt no need to remind him that there were plenty of other fish in the sea. After turning it over in her mind she asked him, loudly, "Wistin, does your girlfriend know how to sew and embroider?"

Wistin was silent at first, unsure of his answer. "I think so," his reply came from the room next door.

"And does she know how to cook?"

"Yes, yes of course, Gran. She knows how to cook, though not everything."

"Does she go to church regularly?"

"Yes, of course she does."

"Did she often tell you she loved you?"

"Many times, Gran. And sometimes I'd get fed up hearing it, she said it so often. She'd start on it and wouldn't stop! And I would beg her to stop..."

"If she tells you once, gently and seriously, that's enough," Katarina declared solemnly. "And if she'd never said she loved you, would you still be certain that she did, Wistin?"

"Yes, I'd still be sure, Gran."

"But how do you know?"

"Because my heart tells me so, Gran."

"Well then, Antonja is the one for you."

"How do you know, Gran?" he asked her eagerly.

"Because my heart tells me so, my dear."

***

Katarina went to lie in her rocking chair, and closed her eyes. She could not stop thinking and worrying, dreaming of all that she thought could ever befall Wistin and fearing it was happening. She had never resolved the dilemma, whether she should give Susanna some word of warning or not, but had always ended up never uttering a word so as not to add any more worries to her daughter, in spite of not being able to dislodge those thoughts from her own mind. She kept every thought locked up within but there were moments when these thoughts spilled out of her mind and marched in front of her eyes; she could feel and touch everything as she was imagining it. She wanted to rise and fling such thoughts aside, to think of other things, but her imagination ran riot, continuing to accompany her rocking. And this is what Katarina imagined...

As people would have it, beyond the village there was a different world, completely different in all respects. Wistin's village appeared in the distance, very far away, and Wistin himself too seemed to be very far away. He had become familiar with the Port, having left the village in exasperation, hoping to find a future somewhere far away from it. He worked at any job that came to hand and frequently slept outdoors, waiting for the new day to bring him some opportunity for work. In the beginning he was a beggar, running after soldiers and sailors and asking for a penny with both hands cupped in front of their faces. After that he was lucky to find a café owner who gave him work. He had to take cups of tea or coffee to people in the vicinity and this earned him a few extra coins. In time, he became used to living in the Port's environs and changed jobs to help a boatman in rowing his ferryboat. Wistin gladly set himself to the oars, rowing without getting tired or bored. He often sat at the quayside and invited passers-by to take a ride on the boat with him and the boatman. And then Wistin became familiar with the bars that opened in the evenings. He would plunge his hands in his pocket and out of the few coins he would have earned in an entire day, he would bring up a few precious ones and buy a bottle of beer. He would feel a certain pride as he delved in his large and deep pockets of his long, wide trousers. He would drink and stand around others in the hope of making friends and maybe finding some means to continue living in those parts. He had no wish to return to the village for the Port offered him more and far better opportunities than those offered by his upbringing. He offered to run errands for the bar owners, perhaps by carrying boxes of bottles or by cleaning the tables. It was not long before one of the bar owners recognized Wistin for the decent boy he was and took him under his wing. And so Wistin became a waiter. He began to wear a smart outfit with a white shirt, a black pair of trousers, a black bow-tie, and a long white apron wrapped around his waist. With a polite word, a natural smile, and quick and precise hand movements, Wistin was able to serve everybody and become friendly with many people and he managed to draw the sympathy of everyone who entered the bar into the bargain. He quickly served all comers and did not loiter around in idle talk but the owner always urged him to "stop and chat with clients as long as necessary. Be polite, friendly, kind, and take your time. People come to this bar because we treat them well." Wistin understood everything and took it to heart.

The bar used to fill up with people who lived in those parts and who wanted to spend their evenings chatting with others and having a drink. The deep sea of the Port meant that many people lived there and it ensured a considerable amount of trade. Enormous ships would bring many people from overseas, all of them looking forward to a few hours of rest and evening entertainment. There was nothing better to look forward to than meeting friends over a drink and many people went to a bar in spite of the fug from cigarette smoke and people's loud chatter.

Beautiful women used to frequent these bars. Some of the women had grown up in the neighbourhood and preferred to earn a living by keeping company with the men who went there, but others hailed from distant parts. Wistin was struck by their comeliness but did not allow these beauties to hinder his work.

One of them caught his eye and he could not get her out of his mind. She used to enter the bar with two women friends and always had some extra words to say whenever he approached their table. She used to smile at him and order a gin and tonic. Always the same drink.

"Would you like something else?" Wistin plucked up his courage to ask her once, in his strong country accent.

"No, dearie, nothing else."

"Nothing else? Are you sure?" he replied.

"No, nothing else, really!"

Wistin smiled back at her, went to have the order made up and came back with brimming glasses, smiling conspiratorially at the woman to show her that he appreciated her compliment.

It was not long before they began courting. They used to meet in the same area of the Port and she often remarked how taken she was with the place, and with him, but she was thinking of returning to her own country. She could come and go as she pleased.

"But do you want me to leave everything I have behind?" Wistin asked her.

"Do you really love me?" she replied with her own question, firmly.

"I love you, darling, truly," he answered in as decisive a tone as hers, "but..."

"But, you have me. Never mind the village. Do you need it? Do you still want to be with your relatives? You have me now! Just wait and see the new world I can show you. Shall we go?"

Wistin was quite confused but knew nonetheless that the Port was part of his life now. He had discovered a new way of life in the Port and there was nothing to draw him back to his old village.

The two of them went abroad and lived together for a while. But in a short space of time Wistin realized that the way of life there was not to his liking. There was nothing rustic about it, true, but then there was nothing in comparison with the things he enjoyed in his own country either.

"Now that we've come here, we'll stay here," the woman insisted. "I was brought up here and I'm not going back there again."

"Then why did you come to my country? How did you come to be down South? Couldn't you have stayed here?"

"No, I couldn't. I had to accompany my husband. "

"You're married, then?"

"Of course I'm married! Don't tell me you've only just realized now! We left each other a long time ago. It's all in the past and behind me now."

"How could I know that you're a married woman?"

"Can't you tell the difference between a married and a single woman? Not even that a woman has already borne children?"

"What are you saying? Are you telling me that...?"

"Of course."

"And how many children do you have?"

"Two. A boy and a girl."

"And where are they?"

The woman fell silent, lowered her head and burst into tears.

"Where are they?"

"I don't know."

"Don't you wish to see them? Don't you miss them?"

"I don't know."

"Meaning too much time has passed for you to remember?"

"No. I mean not enough time has passed by for me to forget. I know that there was a woman who wanted to raise them as her own and they're with her. I never intended to search for them. What's past, is past. Maybe in time I'll feel like looking for them, but it's too soon and anyway, I'm not even sure I want to take that step. I thought I could forget and start over with a new life in your distant country, but I was wrong."

Wistin made it clear that he was none too happy with the situation and had decided to return to his own country. He went on board a ship and came back, returning to his mother. She told him roundly that she had not brought him up in such a manner. She was very angry with him.

"Well then, I'll go and live with Gran," Wistin told her.

"No, son, I'll take you back, all the same," Susanna told him.

"No, Mum, I'll go to Gran's. And if she doesn't welcome me back with open arms I'll go back to the Port. The Port always welcomes me."

Katarina went on imagining and making up an entire story as she gently rocked to and fro in her rocking chair. She used

52

to spend many hours of the day in that rocking chair, which lulled her to sleep whenever she felt like taking a nap and it also helped her to think, each little jerk seeming to jog her memory whenever she felt like looking back in the past. This time round she closed her eyes and imagined Wistin and what could befall him in a few years' time when he would be a fully grown man.

She was afraid for him and burst into tears, putting her feet down to the ground to still the rocking motion of the chair, and taking hold of the rosary beads she began to pray earnestly, "Holy Mary, please deliver us from all this... *Let us contemplate and think of...* Don't let Wistin distance himself from here."

She was ever so pleased when she came fully awake to find that it was her thoughts that had run away with her.

"Wistin, Wistin! Where are you?" she cried out loudly, in alarm.

"I'm here, Gran, I'm here," Wistin answered her from the room next door. "What is it? Do you want something?"

"No, dear. No, nothing. Just for a moment I thought you weren't here. I imagined the worst but it was a passing thought. I wanted to hear your voice. That's all."

Chapter 3

For Susanna this was a special time. Ever since she had returned to Arturu's side, she had wished he would become a father and not simply her husband. "Do you think that day will come again?" she used to ask him eagerly.

"The day will come. Wait and see," he had encouraged her.

She had always wished him well, since the day she had entered Lady's house as a servant many years earlier, when she was a young woman who was expecting a child, hoping that the entire world would not come crashing down on her and that she would find work to earn a living. She had never forgotten that it was Fr. Grejbel who had intervened with her mother and father on her behalf and then made it possible for her to earn a decent living without having to turn to other ways to keep herself, ways which were distasteful to her. In Arturu's large and luxurious house she had found much more than she had expected. Indeed, she had never even imagined that such a beautiful life could exist behind those walls in the humble streets of the village, a very different life lived by a couple of people who lived quietly and hardly ever set foot outside, except when necessary.

Arturu soon fell in love with her and she was wise enough to return his love at an opportune moment, when the time was right. She had never learnt the ins and outs of love games and so knew instinctively, by nature's gift to her. A short while later, when she had become used to the way of life in there, Lady passed away precisely at the moment when Susanna's life was to turn upside down. She could still remember every detail. In spite of all the twists and turns life had dealt out to her, and to Arturu as well, and in spite of their separation and the hurtful words they inflicted on each other which caused their rift, there they were, together again. Wistin was with them and her heart was full of hope as she waited upon events. Both Susanna and Arturu had gone out of their way to mend the past, and to close each other's wounds.

In the silence of her house, quite alone, Katarina kept tapping her foot against the footrest of her rocking chair. She opened her eyes and closed them again, and from one moment to the next, kept seeing everything pass before her eyes, as if it was all happening right there and then. As time went by, when she met Saverju and had Susanna and discovered all the bad with the good, her memory served her well. Now in her old age, her memory was still as keen as when she was a maiden, happy with every wonderful thing she was discovering about herself and her surroundings. In time, especially after her daughter got married, she learnt that not being able to read nor write made her memory sharper.

Wistin arrived just then at his Gran's, out of breath. He knocked on the door, once, twice, and waited with his hand resting against the wall. Susanna had sent him with a message to his grandmother, urgently telling him, "Wistin, go, go quickly to your grandma and tell her, 'Mum tells you,' say this exactly, 'come, come quickly, right now. Mum is waiting for you!' Go now, quickly!" Wistin obeyed her promptly and ran out of the house.

"What's happened? Dear Lord! What's come up now? What else can happen?" Katarina moaned loudly as soon as she saw Wistin before her unexpectedly, exhausted and out of breath. She asked him in, ready to close the front door behind him.

"No, no. Don't close the door. There's no time to lose, Gran. Come immediately, Mum said."

"But what's happened? Aren't you going to tell me? Tell me, tell me! The baby! Has something happened to Susanna?

Her pregnancy? You're not a child any longer and anyway you grew up in the fields and know all about childbirth. Ohh! Nature teaches us all about what's right and proper. What's happened? What has happened to her?"

"Nothing's happened to Mum, Gran. Set your mind at rest."

"At least! I'm going by your words, mind! I'll believe you," she replied hastening to fetch her * għonnella*.

"There's no time to lose, Gran. I've already told you."

"I'm not to appear decently dressed outside. But what could have happened?"

"You'll soon find out, Gran."

"Is it your father? Has something happened to your father? Tell me, tell me."

Wistin stood mute before her, standing up straight as if he was one of those tall trees which abounded in the village. He did not answer her.

"Ahh! I understand you now. Something's happened to Arturu. Dear Lord! He's my daughter's husband. So he's my son too. Arturu, Arturu! What's happened to Arturu?"

"Arturu, Arturu," Wistin repeated in an icy voice.

"Arturu's your father, my dear," Katarina told him without looking at him. She quickly picked up the large iron door key and locked the door on her way out. The two of them walked quickly towards Susanna and Arturu's house.

Wistin held her by her forearms and helped her hurry along as much as he could. She tried to increase her pace but her legs could not keep up. She had always insisted she would never use a walking stick. The youth knew his grandmother was feeling terrified and he heard her ragged, laboured breathing. There was no other sound in the street. The houses were all closed up with bolted doors and only glimmers of light here and there softened and soothed the evening darkness. Nothing broke that deep silence except the howling of some stray dog or the mewling of some cat teetering on the brink of a roof or crouching in a corner. The church clock, with its solemn strokes every quarter of an hour, had not enough presence to lessen that great solitude. The villagers had gone to bed a long time before, ready to rise at an early hour to greet a new day and head for their fields where animals and crops waited for their usual ministrations.

"Don't hurry so, don't hurry so, please, dear. My legs don't have much strength left in them to run anymore," Katarina pleaded. "I'm not young like you any longer!"

Wistin did not reply, again, but he did not slacken his pace. He too was feeling worried.

***

A few months earlier, in Susanna and Arturu's house, the long awaited event had arrived. Both of them had waited and prayed for this moment.

"Don't lose heart. Mother used to tell me that I need to pray, and to keep on praying till I receive whatever grace I'd been praying for. Heaven's wall leads on to somewhere. If you knock on the door, it will open but not after one tap or two, after you continuously knock on it, as much as you can without stopping."

"But that's pestering someone," Arturu had told her jokingly.

"That's having faith, it's faith itself," Susanna had answered. "Whoever loves someone stays at his or her heels."

"And so, whoever is a pest knows how to love?" he had asked her teasingly.

"Of course not! Every fly can fly but not everything that flies is a fly!"

"Are you reading books, Susanna?" he had queried.

"No, I discovered all this before I discovered books."

"You mean from my mother."

"Very well, from your mother."

"I don't remember what I learnt from my mother. Mother was Lady, as you know. Lady was Mother. I don't know who my real mother was. I never saw her. I'd like to see her and I often dream of her, without knowing who she is. I look at my father's face, at his portrait, and tell myself: he certainly doesn't resemble her. But then I go in front of a mirror and stare for a long time at the face that appears, my own, and tell myself: maybe this is the face that resembles most my mother's face, the face I've never seen."

"Arturu, my dear Arturu, do you love me?"

"Don't you know that I love you very much? If I didn't love you I wouldn't have changed my life for you. I'd never have broken with family tradition. Maybe when I took that step I trespassed against my father's wishes, but that's life for you. Everything changes with time and my father left this world too early to see it happen."

"If you love me, I pray you, forget it all now, for my sake."

"I do love you, but how can I forget? My mother will always remain my mother, all and none of the women I see. Only my own face can give me some hint of how hers was. Who knows where she is? In which distant place she lies? All I know is that she came and went away, leaving me here, searching for her forever more, but all in vain! In the meantime, Lady was always there for me and she's my mother, too."

"You'll soon become a father, Arturu," Susanna told him with great certainty.

"Really? Are you really...?"

"Yes, Arturu, this time there will be no grief but great joy. I just know it. I can feel something inside me telling me so."

Arturu took her in a strong embrace, giving her a long deep kiss till he was out of breath. He drew his head back, drew in a few shallow breaths and kissed her again. Susanna was not displeased.

"I'm certain, this time I'm certain. You're going to become a father, Arturu. Your wish is going to be granted and I hope that this time I'll make amends for the grief I caused you that time, long ago."

"Forget that, Susanna. What's done is done. It's all water under the bridge."

"The past does not pass by, my darling. The past is saved up, shelved in one's memory. It's stored in there and we carry it around with us, till the very end."

"Till the very end? Do you really think so? Don't you know that my father ended up forgetting everything, Susanna? He couldn't even remember that I was his very own son. He ended up not recognizing me, or Lady, his wife. It was as if I no longer had a father."

"That's another of nature's laws, Arturu, nothing more."

"Nothing more, except a gaping wound inside me, forever."

"No, not forever, dear."

"Not forever? Till when, then?" he asked her, his tone verging on ironic.

"Only till death!" she exclaimed firmly and proudly, happy to be finding exactly the right words to say. She was feeling very happy and quite content.

"How well you can speak, Susanna!"

"The books you taught me to read, Arturu. It all comes from books," she assured him. "Do you remember the very first book you gave me, wanting me to read it?"

"No, no, it doesn't all come from books," he replied, "and you yourself told me that you'd learnt some things from somewhere else."

"From the fields, Arturu."

"True, from the fields, for fields are also books."

"Fields are books?" Susanna's jaw dropped. "Where did you come up with this?"

Arturu did not reply but caught hold of her and kissed her long and deeply once more, not allowing her to speak.

"And what would you like to name the baby?" she asked him.

"Susanna, if it's a girl."

"And I'll call it Arturu if it's a boy," she responded jokingly.

"I'm not joking. That's what I think is right and proper."

The months of pregnancy began passing by. Katarina related all the pieces of advice she knew from folk knowledge but constantly warned Susanna not to let Wistin know what was happening. Children really did come by ship; she had to stick to that rule which only time would reveal was false. It was too soon to unveil the truth. Susanna obeyed her mother in all things and Arturu was prudent enough to follow suit. He too had grown up in a house where certain things were not discussed openly. In hindsight, Arturu realized that this was an essential part of the beauty and innocence of childhood and early adolescence. He was still able to let his imagination soar, dream and wait. "I wonder, I wonder. How are children born?" he had gone through a period asking himself, and Susanna.

"It all depends on the ship, Arturu! A big ship, a small one? A ship with many sailors on board?"

"When have you ever seen a ship full of sailors, here in our village or in your mother's village, Susanna?"

"Yes I have, a ship full of people in uniform, a smile on their lips, longing to disembark in our land and discover what it holds, by day and by night. They would go drinking till they became boozy and sometimes dead drunk. Holding hands they would jump and dance around, as if they'd become children again, and then start singing love songs. What lovely melodies they sang! They longed for love."

"How do you know all this too, Susanna?"

"Don't I live in this land too, Arturu? The Port is important. That's where ships come and berth, both those that bring children and those that carry off adults."

"Adults you say? Who are these adults?"

"Those who never come, who never arrive. Children may be told lies but then..."

"Yes, I know. You mean that Wistin, at the age he is..."

"Yes, I'm talking about Wistin. I very much fear the day will come when he'll have to know who his father is."

"That's what I think too," Arturu told her against his will, in a subdued voice.

Arturu did not allow Susanna to do anything. He used to take whatever she held in her hands, heavy or not, not wanting to see her carrying anything and straining herself. He even did some housework in the way he knew how and she looked on indulgently at him, even when he made a mess of things. She would smile frequently and then end up laughing at him and he would first feel hurt but then would take it with a good grace.

"It doesn't matter. That's not your work," she would tell him encouragingly.

"It's the thought that counts, isn't that what they say?" he would say in his defence, with a smile, especially when he tried his hand at cooking and nothing came right, and they ended up having to throw everything away, and when he did not wash the laundry properly and the clothes were still all smeared and grimy, and when he hung out the wet load on the washing lines on the roof and the strong wind blew them down.

"True, it's the thought that counts, but it's not everything."

"What do you mean?"

"Ohh!" she smiled ruefully. "Then you haven't read enough books."

"You know which book I haven't read yet? That one in my father's hands, God forgive him, the one he was holding when he died. That day when Lady called up to him and he didn't answer and she kept calling him and finally the two of us went upstairs and found him."

Susanna gently held the fingers of her right hand against his lips to prevent him from uttering the word.

"Dead, he was dead," he still managed to say. "He died and will never come back again."

"But, please try to forget all this, Arturu. Remember that somebody is about to be born. One ship leaves harbour and another one arrives."

Arturu was pleased to see Susanna expecting her baby with pride, all the while continuing with her work as usual. She did not mind going to the market to buy groceries, especially vegetables and fruit, and still stopped for a chat with the few friends she had, all of them women who passed on to her snippets of advice which they too had had from their forebears. She went to church to hear mass every morning, always stopping for a few moments in front of St. Joseph's niche. She did not have the heart to ask for a favour. She felt he had granted more than enough favours for her mother and that it would be too presumptuous of her to continue asking for more. But she still sneaked a glance at him, a sweet and slightly teasing glance to make him understand that she was certain he would stand by her this time too, and everything would go well.

Sometimes Susanna went down to the garden and picked a fruit, but instead of eating it she would put it in one of her large skirt pockets. And sometimes she would pick up the hoe and scrabble around the soil desultorily. She would walk amongst the trees and tear off a leaf, looking at it and smelling it, and then she would throw it away.

Wistin was not often at home. He used to find jobs he could do in those parts and even beyond the village. Sometimes he ran errands for the tavern landlords or went to the market and asked if he could help out the hawkers and traders for a few coins in return. It was not easy for him to find some sort of employment. He soon passed from some light work that did not take long to other heavier work or to none at all. He used to pass the time running around in the fields, hoping that some farmer would ask for his help in return for some money. He did not hold out much hope and in the meantime he could not complain about Arturu since Arturu did not keep him short of money.

Arturu and Susanna used to go down to the garden every evening, when it would be neither hot nor cold, and they would stroll together arm-in-arm, from one side of the garden to the other, trying to imagine how the baby would look.

***

As soon as Wistin and Katarina arrived at Arturu's and Susanna's house, Wistin pushed the door open, having left it ajar, and invited his grandmother in without more ado. They went straight to Arturu's bedroom where he lay supine and almost senseless, hardly breathing.

"Mother, all of a sudden, in the middle of the night, Arturu fell ill. He got out of bed on his own and I got up with him. Wistin ran for the doctor and he soon managed to get hold of him to bring him here. He came immediately. And I went to fetch Fr. Grejbel. I hurried as much as I could. And I nearly ran. I felt I was losing my breath too, and I was afraid."

"Holy Mary! In your condition!" Katarina exclaimed apprehensively.

"No, no, nothing happened to me and Fr. Grejbel soon came. He left just now. He stayed with us for a long time. He had to leave but he'll be back soon. He gave me his word. When the doctor came he advised us to make arrangements for the last rites. Fr. Grejbel will be administering them early tomorrow morning. Fr. Grejbel also promised he would let the sacristan know so that the mourning bell will be tolled."

They were all gathered around Arturu's bed, repeating a prayer for him, over and over again. He parted his lips slightly and tried to pray with them. He did not have much strength left and when his gaze fell on Katarina he did not recognize her at first. Susanna went closer and gently lifted his hand.

"Take care of Wistin and take care of the baby that's coming, for my sake," he told her, his voice weighed down with exhaustion.

"Don't say that to me, Arturu. You're going to see the baby, too. It won't be long before it's born and you'll still be by my side. And if it turns out to be a boy we'll name it after you."

"And if it's a girl... and if I'm not here..."

Susanna began to weep but tried not to make a sound so that Arturu would not realize.

"Take care of her for me, and remember that I would like to be with you at that moment but I won't be."

"Don't tell me that, Arturu."

"I don't like saying it but it's the truth. Take care of this house. Everything belongs to you and to your children, both of them. I'd like to see Fr. Grejbel, now. I want him. Tell him to come to me."

"Very well," Susanna told him brokenly, against her will.

Arturu never forgot that when Lady was dying, she had asked him to go and fetch Fr. Grejbel from the next village. She wanted none other than him. She had talked to both of them and then to the priest on his own.

Very early the next morning, the sacristan started ringing the mourning bell, to announce that someone was receiving the last rites. The children who acted as altar boys quickly gathered round donning their robes and some men joined them putting on the garments of lay brothers. Someone held up the ceremonial canopy and the eldest boy among them held up the standard at the head of the procession while another big boy took up the hand bell and started ringing it, one ring after another, unceasingly, throughout the time it took for the procession that left from the church to reach Arturu's home. The people who happened to be about went down on their knees and said a prayer in their heart. The women drew a veil over their heads and the men removed their cap or hat.

Susanna too, put her veil on, going to the door as soon as she heard the procession draw near. She could see that the neighbours had lit a candle behind the slatted shutters, to show their respect toward the sacrament being carried along the street and toward the dying man. Fr. Grejbel approached and she opened the door wide and went back inside keeping to one side. The altar boys and lay brothers stopped outside to wait.

Fr. Grejbel went straight in to Arturu. He took up one of his hands and with his other hand made the Sign of the Cross on Arturu's forehead. He then started reciting the prescribed prayers and Arturu did his best to keep up with the prayers being said. Arturu died the next day.

"Now you must put on a black suit and a black armband on your left sleeve jacket, and you must wear a black cap," Susanna instructed Wistin.

"Very well," Wistin acquiesced though half against his will.

"And you mustn't shave today and in the coming days, mind." She continued telling him.

"Very well," he replied again.

"Mother, you've been through this already," Susanna turned to her mother Katarina. "You know what we have to do, how to observe mourning. May I leave it all in your hands? I just don't have a mind for it and neither the strength at the moment. I don't feel like anything."

Katarina lowered her head without a word and hugged Susanna to her. She knew what had to be done. "Mind you don't overdo things, daughter. Remember..." She set about observing mourning customs by first going to the front door and removing the doorknockers. She took some sheets from the linen drawers and draped one over each window that fronted the house. She covered up all the mirrors in the house with cloths. Going into the kitchen she turned every pot and pan upside down. All of them were going to observe a fast for several days, eating only what neighbours brought them to eat. They were not supposed to cook anything themselves in that household for some time. For the next two years or more, both she and Susanna would have to wear black from head to toe, as a sign of mourning.

After the funeral mass, they all set out on foot for the village cemetery. Susanna held Wistin's hand and made him walk closely at her side while Katarina walked behind them, alone. A few people gathered round. The men removed their cap as a sign of respect, and the women kept a tight rein on their children, drawing them to their side and keeping them silent. Some village shops half shut their doors and hung a black band of mourning on their door. The sacristan began tolling the bell that signalled a death, its mournful sound continuing to ring out till the sacristan ascertained that the funeral procession was a fair distance from the church.

As soon as they reached home once more, Susanna told her mother, "Now you must sleep here tonight, Mother."

"No, daughter, it's not my place to do so," her mother replied in a decisive tone.

"But I need you, a woman in my condition!" Katarina was flustered at these words and looked at Wistin as if seeking his permission. Before her eyes, all she could see was the empty space where Arturu had lain on his bed.

"Stay here, Gran," Wistin told her firmly, his voice devoid of any emotion.

Katarina paused to think and then bent her head and said resignedly, "Very well, if that's what you want I'll sleep here, but only tonight. It's not my place to stay here. Tell me which room to take then. I want to turn in soon to have a rest. I doubt I'll be able to sleep. I don't feel sleepy at all. Poor boy! I'm going to pray for your husband's soul."

Wistin did not feel like doing anything. As soon as he saw his grandmother leaving the room he approached his mother and told her, "Well, Mum, here we are again together, just the two of us, just like we were some time ago. We've been alone for a long time, you and me."

"Go to the kitchen and make some tea, son, for you and for me."

"No, only for you, Mum. I don't feel like anything," he answered her in very cool tones. "Tea with lemon, right, Mum?"

"Yes, son, with lemon please. Go down to the garden and pick a lemon."

Wistin went and came back. He cut the lemon in half, slowly raised his head and gave his mother a long look.

"You seem to want to tell me something, son. You know how broken hearted I feel at this moment but I always have time to listen to you."

"No, no, Mum, it's nothing. I brought the lemon for you and I'm going to put some in your tea. And I'm going to join you so you won't be drinking your tea alone. See, I soon changed my mind."

"Thank you, darling, thank you."

No sound broke the silence in the house.

"I think your grandmother must be sleeping, then," she commented.

"Yes, that's what I think, too," he replied, "but what I think doesn't count for much."

"Yes it does, son. It counts for a lot, believe me. You'll see. Hasn't it always?"

"Up to now it counted for nothing."

"There's a time and place for everything, son. The seasons drive life onwards and life is just one step after another. But can you say you didn't have all the love you could wish for here? Didn't we, him and me, love you as much as we could and in the way we knew how?"

Wistin held his tongue. All he said was, "Would you like a teaspoonful of sugar in your tea?"

67

"Just the usual, son, everything just as usual. A small teaspoonful. From today onwards nothing should be changed."

"Everything little by little, right? Everything in its own good time."

Susanna lowered her head to the table bursting into tears, crying her heart out. She tried to be quiet but did not succeed. The silence in that house prevented her. That evening, not even the clocks inside the house would make a single sound with their strokes.

"Susanna! Susanna, dear!" all at once Katarina gave a shout from the room next door, as soon as she heard her daughter's weeping. "Go to your room to rest now. Pray and keep up your courage. There's nothing else to be done. You've done all you could," she reassured her. "At the moment I'm remembering when I too lost your father. But you have to be careful now. Remember..."

"Gran woke up. I think she was asleep," Wistin broke in, as if to avoid discussing that subject in front of Katarina.

"Wistin, you must take care of your mother now, just as before, and even more so," Katarina went on in an authoritative voice almost steely in tone. "Your mother has faced enough woes. You yourself have begun to understand now. And your mother is now a widow, too and not only that but she's also expecting..."

"She's expecting the ship to enter Port, the ship that brings children. Isn't that what you mean?"

Katarina was taken aback and drew in a sharp breath. She did not answer him but her silence spoke volumes, telling him she had never expected him to say such things, and on this particular evening on top of it all.

"The ship that brings children, and also adults. Isn't that what you used to tell me? Now all that remains is for that ship to bring a baby and someone else. I've waited long enough, Gran. I'm fed up."

Katarina came back to the room where Susanna was with Wistin. "What do you mean? Tell me in a way I can understand. Otherwise I'm going back to my own house, right now. After all, this isn't my home. But, but, oh Lady of Mercy!" Katarina went on in a change of voice, as if she was about to start talking to herself, "How can I leave my daughter here on her own in her condition? Can't you understand this at all, Wistin? Don't you think it's too soon to be talking of such things? He's hardly in his grave now, your poor father..."

"My father..."

"Yes, your father is hardly in his grave, yes, that's who," Katarina declared firmly but in a soft voice.

"That's who? Is that what you say? You too now, Gran, want to speak to me this way?" Wistin replied in icy tones.

Susanna went up to Wistin and caught hold of his shoulders, telling him, in a hard voice, "Don't speak to my mother in that way – you of all people! You have no idea what that woman went through for your sake. I'll tell you one of these days. For now you only need to know one thing: I won't let you speak to that woman, my mother, in such a way ever again."

"You too won't speak to me that way again, Mum! I'm no longer the boy I used to be a short while ago and you'll soon find out for yourself as never before. See, I'm leaving then!"

"Where are you going, dear? Where are you going?" Katarina moaned.

Susanna was shocked and she bent her head and involuntarily raised her hands to her face. Wistin left the room and kept going right out of the house.

Katarina ran after him calling out to him. She was afraid of waking up the neighbours at that time, and kept hoping that the sound of her footsteps would move Wistin and make him stop, or at least make him slow down to let her catch up with him. She was convinced that she still had a hold over his affections. He had grown up with her too, not just alongside his mother, and she used to boast that when Wistin, made his first step when he was just a few years old, he left her arms and she had held his hand to prevent him falling down.

In a short while, Wistin slowed down and came to a stop, leaning against a wall.

"Why don't you go back to your mother? She needs you more than ever before, now. Listen to me," Katarina beseeched him.

At first Wistin held out firmly but then he raised his face to hers and told her, "Very well. Today I'll do as you say."

"Oh good, my dear. Come, let's go back," she said in relief, hugging him to her and starting to retrace her steps, coaxing him back to Susanna's house.

"Today I'm saying yes. And I'm saying it for your sake. But from tomorrow onwards, no. Either you welcome me into your own house or else it will be the streets that will serve as my new home. The streets don't bother me."

"Very well, Wistin. As you wish. Everything will be done as you wish." As soon as they arrived, they found the door ajar as they had left it, and just beyond, Susanna stood weeping ceaselessly, a large handkerchief crumpled up and balled between her fists.

"I'm going to close and bolt the door, Susanna," Katarina spoke up.

"Yes, Mother, bolt the door. Bolt it, bolt it, and make sure everyone has come back in," she cried out, breaking into another, more despairing, bout of heartbroken sobs. "There's no one else to wait up for from now onwards. No one else. No one else... Arturu, Arturu!"

Katarina burst into tears as well.

"I had a husband, but he's no longer with me now. I lost him so soon! Who else do I have to lose now?"

"Remember who's yet to come now, daughter. That's life for you."

"Ships come and ships go," Wistin broke in sardonically, standing up straight with his hands in his pockets. "The Port is full of ships. And the ships are full of people."

"Don't you have any feelings for your mother? Not even today? No feelings whatsoever?" Susanna cried out, weeping.

"Your tears don't impress me in the least. I'm not going to feel something more than usual today if I've never felt anything before," Wistin told her cruelly.

Katarina tried to persuade him gently not to talk to his mother in that way. "Your mother, oh your mother! You have her for your mother, my dear."

Wistin took his hands out of his pockets and began to walk towards his room.

"So, you're not going to ask for my forgiveness, at least?" Susanna pleaded. "Just a few words, at least – 'forgive me, Mum' – and you'll lessen the hurt I feel. Isn't this death enough for me to bear?"

"Me? Ask you for forgiveness? For what?"

"You won't even give me one good word before you go off to sleep? Nothing, nothing? Not even today?" Susanna continued beseeching him, weeping and sobbing all the while.

"No, not even today. Actually, today more than ever," he replied coldly, decisively.

Katarina, though feeling hurt as well, thought it was better not to interfere with some stray word, at least keeping Wistin's faith in her. Lately she had been thinking and fearing that Wistin would up and leave, leaving them alone. She used to spend her time rocking on her rocking chair, remembering, wishing and letting her imagination run away with her. With every jerk, backwards and forwards, she saw an entire world before her eyes, turning, perpetually turning, interminably, and her mind would light up and she would feel dizzy.

"I brought you up, I saved you, gave you all I could so you wouldn't just have me, and it all seems for nothing. It's as if it's all been wasted, every step I took for your sake," Susanna moaned in disbelief.

"Maybe each step you took was really for your own sake, not for mine. If you loved me, it's because it suited you to do so," he answered back.

Susanna stopped crying all at once. She made an enormous effort to control herself, drew all her strength and stood up, the large handkerchief still balled in her right fist. "Where did you get all these ideas from? What rotten seed was planted in your mind that grew and spread to your heart? I certainly didn't pass on these ideas to you. Such things never even crossed my mind! You only saw love from me, son, day and night."

"With those stories you used to tell me? Is that how you loved me? With stories you made up to send me to sleep, stories upon stories, and a kite, and a barrel organ and whole days spent out in the fields, and down in the Valley, a stroll along the Valley, how awful, that Valley, do you remember?"

"Yes, son, I remember, the Valley."

"And Fr. Grejbel, always Fr. Grejbel."

"Don't mention Fr. Grejbel. I command you, in the name of all that's holy to you and me. Don't mention him unless it's with the greatest respect."

"With the greatest respect!"

"Yes, with the greatest respect!"

"Very well, I won't mention him."

"At least! Not everything is lost on you, then, if there are still moments when your heart feels something."

Katarina felt glad, smiling at his answer, and she drew near to Wistin to take his hand. He drew back but then regretted his action and rested his hand gently on her shoulder.

"You haven't made me forget what I asked you just before. All these ideas! Where did these ideas spring from?" Susanna asked him again.

"Can't you guess? From books, just like you, Mum. From books. Papers on papers! Folly! Wasn't it you who loved books? Isn't that what you learnt to do? Who taught you to love them? Gran? No, no, not Gran! Gran doesn't have any truck with papers and neither was it..." Wistin said scornfully but stopped just short of naming the priest. "So who else is left? Ours is a small world."

Susanna and Katarina looked at each other, aghast. Arturu's name echoed around each single word Wistin uttered. With a heavy heart and a stricken look in her eyes, Susanna sat down once more and rested her head against the back of the chair, spreading open the large handkerchief with both hands, pulled at it as if trying to remove every crease in it, and then, almost with controlled rage, balled it into her fist once more.

Wistin looked to his grandmother and said, "Bless me Gran," and turned to leave the room.

"Not to me, Wistin? Aren't you going to ask for my blessing?" Susanna asked him, deeply wounded.

"No, not to you," he replied with a short answer in a firm and icy voice. He turned to Katarina and told her, "I'll go with you tomorrow, Gran. If you want me, I'll go home with you..."

"You don't want to stay here? Isn't this your home? Is that what you want to say?" Katarina stammered out, overwhelmed. "Very well, dear, of course, you can make your home with me. I have an extra bed for you, of course I do. I'll leave early tomorrow morning, because this isn't my home."

"Well then, tomorrow morning wait for me before you leave, and maybe I'll be waiting for you at the door already," he declared in a determined voice. "I'm very punctual," he said and left the room.

The two women kept silent in order to hear every sound from the next rooms, his every footstep. They heard him make for the door that led to the garden. Then they heard him open it, leave and slam it behind him. The large garden at the back of the house was a huge mass of inky blackness.

"Lady of Mercy! He's gone, and where is he going to spend the night? Is he going to stay outside?" Katarina wanted to know.

"Yes, I think so. In the garden, and then maybe he'll come upstairs when I'll be asleep. He won't have to meet me face to face then. He hardly looks at me anymore and barely says a word to me. Now that Arturu's gone, I can only expect worse from him. I was half-expecting all this."

"Dear Lord! But since when has he been behaving this way? He was so adorable when he was a child! He was always a very sweet lad. He was always playing, flying his kite, chattering and telling stories. I don't know what's got into him."

"No you don't, Mother, that's true, because in all these years you were at home living in your own house. You haven't been living in the same house with him, day and night, under the same roof as Arturu. His attitude and behaviour have been changing for a long time."

"How does Arturu come into it? God forgive him, he was such a good kind-hearted man!"

"Wistin couldn't stand him. He used to avoid him at mealtimes. He would stay in his room or spend hours out into the garden. And if he sat down to eat a meal with us he wouldn't utter a word. And sometimes, on a whim he would grab his plate and go and eat in the garden on his own. As long as he wouldn't have to eat with us. It's not the first time I called him in the space of many hours. It happened quite frequently and he wouldn't even bother to answer. Maybe he had begun to suspect something; he's been starting to realize the situation for a long time."

Katarina shook her head and closed her eyes, taking a deep breath. "Holy Mary!" she exclaimed beneath her breath. "Those two weren't on speaking terms, then?"

"Wistin rarely said a word to Arturu. Arturu tried everything, always in a sweet and gentle manner though he felt grievously hurt and often came close to losing his temper and all his patience, but he remained calm and didn't cross the

74

line he'd set himself. He never even spoke one word against Wistin. He never hinted to me that he'd like nothing better than to throw him out. He used to tell him, 'Wistin, all this belongs to your mother, and so it all belongs to you, too.' He used to like promising him this. What more could he possibly promise him? Could he have behaved more like a father than that?"

"And what did Wistin use to reply? I suppose he felt glad."

"No, nothing of the sort. Actually, he once told Arturu, 'I want nothing that's yours. You can keep whatever you have.' That's what he told him once."

"Oh poor thing! He bore it out of respect for you, then."

"Yes, I know," Susanna moaned, "all because of me. Arturu gave me everything, everything he possessed."

"And now he's giving you a baby, too. He's gone but he hasn't left you alone. He knew how to work things out step by step, like clockwork. He was a gentleman, God forgive him."

"But Wistin soon started behaving harshly towards Arturu. I never found the courage to chide him. I could see that Wistin had grown up, it hadn't taken him long. Maybe those early years he spent in childhood far away from me taught him many things, and perhaps they made him into a man before his time, too. A young boy who straightaway inherited adult problems. I think that over there, where he was brought up, there were also many other boys who didn't know who their parents were, and maybe this had already become an obsession in Wistin's mind. I used to make up stories for him to show him he was not the only one in such circumstances, and that his father would appear on the scene one day. He just had to wait. And when he learnt to count to ten, and more, he had stretched out his fingers to show me how many years he'd already spent waiting. Learning numbers served him to keep mulling over all the time he'd spent waiting for his father to come."

75

"And his father did come, didn't he, daughter?" Katarina cut Susanna off, forcefully, as if she wanted to put the exact words into her daughter's mouth.

"Come? No, no, Mother! His father never came. Nowadays I tend to think that Wistin never even believed me when I tried to fob him off with stories of ships entering harbour. The time for stories is over and so, a new time had to come, but..."

"Of course he doesn't believe those stories. He's grown up now."

"No, no, Mother. He never believed me from the start. At first he was entranced hearing the tales I made up for him, from the top of my head, in the way I knew how, but he quickly realized that I, too, was expecting someone. And the husband I was waiting for shouldn't have been my Arturu."

"It wasn't Arturu because Arturu was a rich gentleman who lived in this enormous house? Because..." Katarina stammered in bewilderment.

"Because he came late, Mother. My husband had arrived too late for Wistin. And he came from the landward side. We used to go down to the Port and look at the ships entering and leaving harbour. Arturu loved going there. He used to tell me that it all reminded him of his own childhood when his mother and father would spend many a long hour gazing at the deep blue sea and telling him stories."

"Do you mean to say that Wistin kept expecting his father to arrive across the sea on board a ship, from abroad?"

"Isn't that what all the stories were about, Mother?"

"But children's stories are like that."

"And Wistin believed them till he grew up and he believed me as long as I was able to show him that stories and the truth were one and the same thing. It didn't take him long to find out it wasn't so. Now he's angry and is rejecting his whole life, rebelling against the disciplined life in which he was brought up. It's as if he realized that his life was one of those same stories."

76

"How?"

"He came to that conclusion after hearing a stray word here or there. How much I used to rack my brains to find ways and means to make him use his imagination! And how much he loved that! First I'd make up a story and he would listen entranced and then he'd end up inventing something himself. We would fly a kite and then hitch a ride on it ourselves. It was a time for stories, when I'd just found Wistin the first time, and was hoping that it wouldn't be long before I'd find Arturu again. Now I have nothing left, Mother, nothing! I've ended up empty-handed, just like before!"

Katarina was stricken dumb and her cries mingled with her daughter's weeping. She rose and went to the kitchen, coming back a short while later with two steaming cups of tea. She held out one of them to Susanna and Susanna took the opportunity to grab hold of her mother's hand.

"Mother, oh Mother, when will a bright new day dawn for me? When will I see fair weather?"

"Pray for your husband and your husband will pray for you before God. And give Wistin time, maybe he'll open his mind to the truth and see his mistake. One day or another he will learn to love you again just like he did as a little boy, just you wait and see."

"You'd better go to bed, Mother. It's time and you've been on your feet all day long. I don't want to lose you too, now."

"I'll stay with you till the end, daughter. And your father prays for you as well. Now just look after yourself and that baby that's coming to you." Katarina rose and went to the room where she was to spend that night.

Susanna rose as well and went to her bedroom. That empty space in her bed where her husband used to lie terrified her. She lay down on her side of the bed and began to recite the bedtime prayer. Her right hand circled her distended stomach, once, twice, and even more times. She thought she would feel all the usual movements she had come to expect in her advanced state of pregnancy. But a suspicion assailed her

77

and she circled her stomach one more time with one hand, and then with both hands, and her suspicions grew. "Oh! Dear Lord! Dear Lord!" she cried after having passed her hands all over her stomach many times.

"Susanna! Susanna! What's the matter? What's happened? Do you need something?" her mother called out to her from the room next door.

"No, Mother, no," she replied, not wanting to worry her mother. She buried her head in her pillow to stifle the sobs that ripped through her. Her two hands, shaking with fear and premonition, were still slowly and carefully circling her stomach. She could not get to sleep and spent the entire night pressing her hands against her stomach hoping against hope. But there was no sign of life any longer. She tried to muffle her crying and decided not to tell her mother the next morning before she left.

Wistin spent a long time pacing in the garden and when he was certain that the two women were asleep, he went back inside, closed the door behind him softly and tiptoed upstairs. He got into bed, lying face upwards, thinking how very different that night had turned out to be.

The next morning, Katarina and Wistin left as agreed, and they did not call out to Susanna. Katarina was sure that her daughter was still fast asleep and needed all the rest she could get. Wistin was eager to leave that house.

Chapter 4

The coachman arrived exactly on time. Susanna had gone the day before, early in the morning, to find him in the village square, where he and his horse daily spent several hours waiting around for a fare. He did not have much custom because few villagers experienced some urgent need to leave the village requiring the expense and luxury of a *karozzin* ride. Together with that coachman there would be some two others waiting to pick up a fare, and they were all gentlemen enough to agree and share out the trips between them. They knew they could share the loaf together, otherwise hunger beckoned for all three.

"I'm here, Missus," the coachman raised his voice as he arrived in front of her front door and waited to see it open.

"Very well, then, here I am too," Susanna answered his call, closing and locking the door behind her with the large iron key. She patted her hair into place and walked up to the *karozzin*.

"There's no hurry. You can take your time." She mounted and settled herself on the seat edge wanting to look on all they passed during the journey. "To the Port, if you please," she instructed the coachman as she made the Sign of the Cross and then delved into her pockets to set her mind at rest, yet again, that she had enough money to pay him. She knew it was uncommon for a woman to be travelling alone in a *karozzin*, but her self-confidence did not diminish. She had learnt that village customs were there even to be tested to their limit, not merely to observe them in fear of the shadow they cast even when observed to the letter. She had much to say on the subject and now that enough time had passed, she seemed to have acquired some pride as well. Her experiences had made her grow up; even looking at her reflection in the mirror served to make her appreciate herself. All that had befallen her used to make her look with disfavour upon herself, but she had come to learn to trust herself, to trust her judgement.

"Have a good journey!" some neighbours who happened to be passing by called out to her. Others came to peep out of their doors and windows as soon as they heard the horse's steps draw near.

Most of all, wearing deep mourning, swathed in black from head to toe, nobody could forget about the great loss in the family she had just recently suffered, and so her serious demeanour seemed to be more pronounced. As she was carried forwards she remembered the localities she had looked upon long before when she had ridden a *karozzin* and observed the small world around her which made her feel dizzy. Everything was still the same, she thought.

*∗∗

From the few rides she had taken on a *karozzin*, none was still as fresh in her mind as the one she had taken when she had returned to Arturu's house. That day Katarina had felt happy and content, a woman who had won out in the end, and Wistin sat next to her, a young lad full of imagination and curiosity to discover everything during their long journey, the narrow pathways, the countryside and all the rest. At first he had wanted to ride high up next to the coachman and hold the reins, but then he understood that he was too young for this. Katarina had reminded Susanna that her dowry was all gathered in the bundles they were taking with them. All her dowry. She had told Susanna that she must now give all her love to Arturu, in payment for her marriage because not even love came without a price. Susanna had begun telling Wistin another story, about a very large house, far, far away. Three people were riding in a *karozzin* on their way there, a house full of gold and silver, with high ceilings in each room and wide windows, costly furniture and with a garden full of flowers.

In this house, Susanna continued saying, one man lived there all alone. He had ended up alone because one day dark clouds had gathered in the sky and a tempest had raged and carried away all he had. But he had remained there, waiting, always alone, still waiting. Wistin had wanted to know the man's name and Katarina had burst out saying that his name was 'Daddy'. Susanna had gone on to tell him that as soon as those three people arrived at his house, his name was to be Daddy forever more.

Wistin had been very happy that day to be entering that large house and the story had pleased him greatly. Susanna had been certain that now, she and Arturu would begin a long life of happiness together while Wistin, brought up in a house and lacking nothing, would find no difficulty whatsoever to grow up like other children. But seeing it had not worked out that way, Susanna knew that it was only her son's future that was important. She needed to salvage all that was left to her. Widowed early with a son going round in circles trying to find his place in life, she was at least sure that finally she had found her dignity as a married woman.

"Everything works out little by little, slowly," she reassured herself, as if encapsulating her entire life in a few words. That's how Arturu had taught her to think. He had grown up seeing his father always reading and stopping to reflect on the words of that page, with his gaze raised above, up and beyond the book and the rest of the world.

Though years had passed before she could embrace Wistin for the very first time, she had had the good fortune to find him and begin a new life together. Though she and Arturu had spent several years separated from each other, the time had come when she was reunited with him. And when he soon wanted to father a child on her, she had quickened soon after. What had to happen, had come to pass: maybe since Arturu died when she was still pregnant with his child, the baby itself died so as not to be an orphan at birth. Was she, Susanna, thinking straight? The countryside all around was a small world full of sweetness and tranquillity, as far as she could make out whenever she took a peep from between the curtains of the *karozzin*. Greenery all around, which begins to darken and turn black as soon as night draws near.

Now that Susanna had found herself alone once more, she felt something she had never felt before. Not even when she had despaired of Stiefnu, that he would begin to understand and settle down, as her mother had hoped. Nor when she had given up hope that Arturu would ever give an inch and let down his pride by a notch, softening his heart towards her. The experience of becoming a widow was very hard, too, but different, new. Every night she hugged her pillow and talked to herself, waiting in vain for someone to talk to her in return. A double bed was just too big for one person on her own.

Fr. Grejbel had told her she needed to wait. "A change of heart doesn't happen overnight. Everything needs to take its time, and the heart needs a little bit longer."

"A change of heart, Fr. Grejbel?" she had asked him in a tone of disbelief. "Why do you believe that's possible? How long are you going to remain so naive?"

"A change of heart is possible, Susanna, because if you tell a mountain to move, it will."

"As long as you are convinced of it, you mean."

"Yes, that's what I mean. I am merely repeating Someone's words."

"I know that. And do you believe it? I know you've always believed in Him totally, but today, here and now, I'd like you to declare you're not insane or someone who can't think for himself, or someone who can't say no, Fr. Grejbel. Tell me the truth! Did you never feel utterly alone? You've never thought that all you'd believed in over the years would simply collapse on you, block by block? Couldn't a storm have passed and destroyed everything? Tell me, go on, tell me. I have a right to know," she spoke vehemently.

"No, never, Susanna," he had replied calmly, in a neutral tone.

"Not even when the whole village took against you, and each voice of authority spoke against you? When you had no one left at your side? No one, except me, huh, me, oh and my mother, the two of us who counted for nothing then and still count for nothing now!"

"No, never, Susanna! It never even crossed my mind once to think I was all alone. Once is already too much."

"But why?"

"Because there's nothing new in this."

"Should I believe you?" Susanna had been almost afraid to ask.

Fr. Grejbel clasped his hands together, almost as if he was about to start praying, but he had turned to her, smiled and continued, "Susanna, this question teeters right on the edge. Beyond it lies an abyss, the cliffs. What does faith consist of? Say the truth, didn't you yourself continue believing this during all these years? Did your mother ever lose faith in her conviction? Did you ever see her waver and fall? Did you ever know her to turn harsh and lose her temper? Never! Isn't this a great force to be reckoned with? Where did your mother find such strength? Go on, tell me! What makes your mother so formidable? A woman of the fields, who sees the seasons come and go, and the seeds sprouting and growing and flowering, and then withering away. Do you think such wisdom is all wasted? Do you think your mother, in the silence of the fields, never read entire books?"

"She doesn't know how to read. She can't even sign her name. Her signature is a cross. My father had taught her how to sign with that mark."

"Yes, yes. I know that. And you know what I mean."

"Oh very well! Yes, I believe you, I still do, Fr. Grejbel. Yes, yes. But tell me, After all that, why did my Arturu have to die so early? I had already imagined spending many years of quiet happiness with him. My mother was finally happy and content, and she seemed desirous of joining her husband in Heaven. She hardly ever ventured outside the village. She only took a few rides on a *karozzin* in her whole life, and she was always eager to return home in the shortest possible time. She was afraid of getting lost whenever she put some distance between herself and these parts. But in spite of this, she was ready to close her eyes and journey alone far, far away from here, to Heaven! 'Saverju, Saverju! I wonder where my Saverju is now, on his own, without me. I wish I was at his side. Lord, please keep a place for me by his side, seat to seat!' That's what she used to pray, out loud. I myself heard her, and so did other people in church. That's what she used to turn over in her mind, and she felt content, her angel wings already spread out ready to leave and fly up above. I managed to see her content for the first time after so many years, Fr. Grejbel. But it wasn't to last long. Then I lost my baby, I lost a baby again. And then Wistin went on hurting me as much as he could, denying me, denigrating me, after he had already poured scorn on Arturu in his own house. Arturu seemed to close in on himself and couldn't stand it any longer. He was not a fighter. But you know all this. Why, oh why am I telling you all this, dear Lord, when you know all about it?"

Fr. Grejbel inclined his head towards her telling her, "You yourself know none of this is wasted, Susanna."

***

"Would you like to stop at a particular place, Missus? Some exact spot? It's all the same to me. We'll stop wherever you say," the coachman told her when they were nearly there.

"Maybe at the quayside?" Susanna answered with a question of her own.

"If you don't mind me asking, are you going across to the other side of the Port? Do you intend to catch a ferryboat? It's none of my business, but I can drop you off where it suits you best. And the price is still the same."

"No, no. I can stop at whatever point is convenient along the quayside."

The coachman reined in his horse at the first vacant spot and she descended and paid her fare.

Not two minutes passed before two little urchins, barefooted and with tangled hair and wearing an old and rumpled shirt open from collar to tails, were scampering around getting under her feet, begging her for money with cupped hands.

"Do you know where I can find Stiefnu, the trader on a bumboat?" she asked them.

"Yes, yes, I know," each one answered her loudly.

"Well then, where? Tell me!"

Both boys fell silent.

"You don't know who he is, or where to find him, do you?" she told them with a small rueful smile.

The two boys looked at each other, silently admitting their lie, and turned their gaze back on her, slightly ashamed of themselves. "Give us something, Missus," they begged, eager to earn some money. They had spent hours and hours going round the neighbourhood. Their parents would send them out to beg every day and only expect them back late in the evening.

"Let's see now. Which one of you can manage to fetch him and tell him there's a woman who wants to speak to him?"

"Me, me!" one of them cried.

"Me, me!" the other one exclaimed.

"Here, go together to look for him and tell him to come here. Tell him, 'If you please,' politely like that. Well then what must you say?"

"If you please...," they chorused together in one voice.

"Tell him I'm here, someone, waiting for him. That's all."

"We'll tell him that there's this woman dressed all over in black..." one of them burst in.

"Are you in mourning, Missus?" the other boy wanted to know.

Susanna nodded in answer and smiled at them. She thought they were sweet, remembering Wistin at that age, but not barefoot and roaming the streets by day and night, begging for money.

The urchin boys remained with outstretched hands in front of her and she gave them some coins, the same amount to each boy so that they would not quarrel. They snatched the money, closed their fist and ran off.

The Port was a riot of colours, as usual. Ships and boats, people, soldiers and sailors, rich people and beggars, all were full of life.

It was not excessively noisy, in spite of the fact that all kind of work was taking place there. Snatches of conversation between people on board ships and boats could be heard fitfully, coming to one's ears slowly, as if drifting in on the waves right up to the Quay.

"Stiefnu, on a bumboat! The trader on a bumboat, Stiefnu!" the urchins screamed one after another, several times, very loudly to make themselves heard as much as possible. "Where are you? Where are you? Come, come! A woman's here, she wants you!"

At first there was no response. There were only echoing voices, nothing more. But a short while later a voice said, "Here I am! What do you want?" It was coming from somewhere in mid-harbour, close to a ship.

"Come! Are you Stiefnu, the trader on a bumboat?" the urchins bellowed. "There's a woman here who wants to talk to you! She's dressed in black! She's waiting for you here, at the Quay!"

"Very well," the disembodied voice replied.

Susanna kept pacing up and down, waiting.

Stiefnu's boat soon hove into view and was berthed at the quayside. Stiefnu stepped onto firm ground with ease, without stumbling. He tied up the boat and brushed his hands together.

A moment of silence held them in its grip as they looked at each other trying to discern the least movement. It was as if they had forgotten each other's face and were now filled with curiosity to rediscover every feature.

"I see you haven't forgotten the way to come to the Port," he began by saying.

"How could I possibly forget it?" she replied with certainty.

"You can't forget it? Maybe because it's a straight road?"

"No, it's certainly not a straight road."

"Or maybe because all roads eventually lead here, somehow."

"Maybe," she agreed, her thoughts centred on something else.

Stiefnu looked closely at her and then told her, "You're wearing black, from head to toe. Black, all in black. I don't know what's happened but I'm sorry, all the same."

"My husband's died," she replied in a firm voice but without meeting his eyes.

Stiefnu seemed to recoil in upon himself, as if struggling with his feelings and not knowing whether to feel sorry or indifferent. "I'm sorry," he said finally. "I'm sorry, all the same."

"Thank you. And I've just lost his baby too. If she had been born she would have missed seeing him."

"Is that right?" he answered her, his voice betraying true sadness.

"She followed him straightaway."

Another silence fell between them, as if they were both at a loss how to continue.

"I would like your help about something, please."

"My help? If I can help you in any way, of course, yes."

"Wistin has quite grown up now. I don't know how he's going to earn a living. In the village he can only do the round of shops asking to run errands. He hasn't had much luck working in the fields, either. He's looked high and low for work, and I too have asked around, but in vain. I don't know who else to turn to on his behalf."

Stiefnu heard her out.

"If he doesn't find work I'm afraid I'll lose him. A day will dawn and when I look for him he'll be gone."

"But, but you're not short of money! You're not the widow of a lowly trader on a bumboat, who earns his living by sheer hard work and sometimes earns barely enough to eat. You never eat swill, licking up each crumb of someone's leftovers. You don't get filthy after a full day's work or put your life in peril whether on land or at sea."

"No, no, of course not! But what's that got to do with anything?" she cut him short.

"I'll tell you. Let me go on. I don't imagine you frittering away money in taverns. And I must tell that your clothes have class. They show what sort of person you are. You're wearing a very elegant black gown! So, what more could you need, my lady Susanna? What need of a lowly trader on a bumboat could you possibly have?"

Susanna only made a half-hearted attempt to stop his stream of words, declining to make any attempt to appeal to his emotions. She wanted to see the man before her reveal his true nature, without any attempt on her part to make him relent or take pity on her. She raised her head slightly and let him have his say. She could see with her own eyes that since she had last seen him, in that very place many years before, Stiefnu had become a hard man, more brusque and decisive.

"You were lucky, Susanna. Your path crossed with wealth and you married into money. I should think your house contains much wealth and you lack nothing. You own land and riches. Am I correct?"

"But what can I do with all that? Sell it all? Sell up and go to live somewhere else? How will I live in a new home? How will Wistin live? For him, for Wistin I mean, that house isn't his home, and all its wealth isn't his. Do you understand? He doesn't feel at home there, even now, and maybe now even more so."

"Do I have some pressing responsibility to oversee how Wistin lives now, after all these years? How was he living up to a short while ago, when your husband was still alive? What sort of food were you giving him? Keep it up now. Soup today and soup tomorrow. As if nothing's happened, my lady."

Susanna let her head fall in defeat and took a few paces away from him along the quayside, hoping he would follow her. But Stiefnu remained where he was, waiting. He observed her narrowly, from head to toe, giving her a small triumphant smile. She walked slowly back, stopping to face him, arms akimbo.

"You're still beautiful, Susanna. I must say I still find you very attractive."

She remained silent, as if she had not heard him.

Suddenly, Stiefnu stepped forward and opening his arms embraced her and tried to kiss her, once, twice, trying to get a kiss in.

She drew back violently, breaking his embrace, and took a few steps away from him, freed from his arms. She showed him clearly that his attentions were unwanted.

Stiefnu was taken aback by her rejection and felt he had lost face. "You said you wanted my help?" his voice grating, signalling his sudden change of mood. "What can you offer me? We all need one another. Isn't that what you learn in books? And that's what we also do here in the Port. Everything has its price."

"I'm not asking for your help for myself."

"Because you don't need it."

"But I'm asking you to offer a job to your son."

"Sell up all that one left you, that husband of yours, and you can live on it for many years, you and yours. Isn't that a good idea? See? Even someone who can't read or write has a mind that can think straight."

"I know that," she told him repressively.

"No you don't! Sell up."

"How can I sell things I feel don't belong to me?"

"Aren't they yours?"

"I don't feel they are, or that I can do whatever I want with them. You don't know, you can't understand. You didn't know his family. After all, I entered that house as a servant, and found everything laid up for me. By what right can I take apart a story woven by many generations?"

"Then keep looking all that wealth in the face and stay there till you rot."

"I don't want to do that and I don't want your son to fall in that rut, either."

"What do you mean? Doesn't that all depend on you?"

"But that's exactly what he doesn't want. And he doesn't want to be beholden to anyone else, either. I'm not asking for anything myself."

"Only for his sake, then."

"Yes, only for his sake, Mr. Stiefnu. That's why I came here. For his sake."

"You love him a great deal! He must love you a lot, then!"

Susanna burst into tears, and hurriedly scrabbled around in her pocket to bring up her handkerchief and dry her tears which were pouring down her cheeks and soiling her gown. She felt humiliated weeping in front of him and was half-expecting him to begin taunting her any minute.

"For his sake, for his sake entirely! And what's this got to do with me, now?"

"He's your son."

"Is he still my son, after all these years? Answer me!"

"Yes, you know that as well as I do."

"Very well, I'll help him out, but on one condition: that he gets to know I'm his real father."

"No, no, never!" Susanna shouted. "I'll never be the one to take that step," she continued saying, taking to her heels and hoping to find a *karozzin* that would take her back home. A few of them were gathered some way away, waiting to pick up a fare. She raised her hem slightly and went up in the first one she came to.

"Where do you want to go, Missus?" the coachman asked.

"Go, just go, as fast as you can. I'm in a big hurry. Just keep on going straight and when we're out of this neighbourhood I'll tell you where to take me."

"Giddy-up!" the coachman calmly urged his horse on and the horse set off at his usual firm-footed pace.

"She hasn't changed a bit," Stiefnu raged, walking back to his boat and boarding it. As usual, the boat gave a jerk with his habitual calculated jump and soon, a few pulls on the oars had him back out in mid-harbour.

***

"Things look different from this rocking chair, Gran. They seem to move," Wistin told his grandmother jokingly. "And I think that's why you like to stay on it, and almost resist getting up from it."

"But you too have managed to sit down on it, and so much so that you're seeing everything in motion, my dear," Katarina quipped back.

"In a trice! You got up to make some tea and in the blink of an eye I took your place! I grabbed the opportunity without losing any time!" he chuckled. "And now I'm seeing you sway, Gran. The stronger I tap the footrest, the more violently the chair rocks and seems to jump forward and I almost fear that an extra kick will topple it over with me in it! Have you ever toppled over in it, Gran?"

"No, never, up to now, my dear, and this means for many many years. That rocking chair was my father's, God forgive him, and my mother didn't fancy it much. She used to complain it made her dizzy and Father used to scoff at her telling her she was exaggerating. Even the world turns round, he used to tell her trying to convince her, but she didn't believe him."

"That means you've been seeing the world in motion for a long time, Gran!"

"Yes, dear. Even from here, I can see it move."

"You mean to say, you see things changing."

"Changing, moving, it's all the same. This is the most important lesson learnt in the fields. First you have a tiny seed, and then before you know it, it becomes a sapling and then it grows into a tree, and it keeps growing and growing."

"And you water it only a little when it's a sapling but you give it lots more water when it grows into a tree. Actually, when it's a tree you can even rest on it or under it for shade," he continued, spinning out the analogy. "Isn't that what you're telling me, Gran? I think I've got it!"

"I know you understand me, dear. Only a little water for the little one – all for its own good. And a lot of water for the tree – again, also for its own good. Everything for its own good, according to the season."

Wistin rose from the rocking chair and stilled its motion with his foot, drawing his grandmother towards it to let her sit down.

"Thank you, thank you, dear," she told him. Soon, she set it in motion and began rocking. "Oh my! What a lot of happenings I've seen in my life, dear."

"Did you see me being born, Gran? Go on, tell me! I want to know. Did you see me get my first tooth? Did you see me start to walk and say my first word? If I remember correctly, you saw me later than that, certainly not from the start."

"There's one thing for sure: ever since I knew you'd come into the world..."

"By ship." he interjected sardonically.

"By ship, very well, very well, by ship, from that day onwards I loved you with all my might. And not only me."

"Grandpa, too, who was called Saverju, who left me the nativity clay figurines and other stuff, all he had anyway, all stored away in drawers. But Grandpa himself did not move, did he Gran?"

"Move? No, he didn't like sitting in this rocking chair," she replied with a smile, "but he moved in the way he knew how. Slowly, at his own pace, the way everyone moves at their own pace."

"He never told stories?"

"It's mostly women, mothers, who tell stories. I suppose men do tell stories but, but, I don't know. Stories need imagination, sweetness of temper, and loads and loads of patience."

"So you think I can't tell a story, Gran? Just because I'm a man?"

"No, not because you're a man, no, no! It's not because of that, but because you're still young. But if you try telling one, I think it will be a good story in its own way. I just don't know! I never heard your grandfather telling stories, never, to no one, not even to your mother or to me."

"And did you often hear my father tell stories?"

Katarina was startled and she closed her eyes and pushed her head further on the headrest of the rocking chair.

"Once upon a time, Gran, there was a young woman who went down into the Valley, and a young man also went down into the Valley, and then, and then..." he spoke while bending his head and then waited to see her reaction.

"That time has passed, Wistin."

"Listen to this story, Gran."

"Isn't there anything else you could tell me, Wistin?" Katarina objected, decreasing the rocking chair's movements.

"Listen to it, see how well I can still remember it, Gran. Well then," Wistin paused to gather his thoughts. "Everyone was waiting for his turn to come, to get here. I mean, to the village. Because, do you know where we were? In Heaven. From Heaven to the village is but one straight road. That's where we came from, and then one day, as we were walking, we got lost in a wood full of tall trees, towering over us, dense and thick, but then we came upon some kind-hearted people who told us we could wait at their place. They told us a ship had just made port and many people had gone on board to set sail but there weren't any places left for us. We had to wait a while longer. 'But who knows when we can leave?' we used to ask them. They used to reassure us telling us that many more ships would be arriving and we would board them and finally arrive in the village. Empty ships would berth, take children on board and take them to their final destination, the village."

"Well then, you must have felt happy," his grandmother said to him for something to say, closing her eyes wearily and praying he would change the subject.

"We were happy, in Heaven. Ladies wearing white took care of us. A long white gown without pockets. They used to cover their head, holding it bent down, and they would walk holding themselves straight. They wore large rosary beads at their waist, and would occasionally smile, but only a little."

"They didn't smile much, did they?"

"No, not much, because don't forget, we were in Heaven. Even Baby Jesus didn't smile much. He used to cry, sometimes with joy and sometimes with sadness. His eyes would be a bit red because there were so many unwanted children! That meant that a ship would be coming to take everyone but would leave them behind."

"That's nice, a nice story indeed," Katarina commented in the tone of voice which plainly showed her to be affronted. "And this story has a happy ending, doesn't it?"

"No, Gran, the story doesn't end here."

"But why not? I imagine you're telling me the story to put me to sleep. And if I do fall asleep, will it end here? Well then, let me go to sleep as soon as soon can be! As soon as you see me close my eyes, say to yourself that Grandma Katarina is asleep and the story will end there. Alright?" Katarina responded patiently.

"Ships entered harbour every day because the Port is open to the world, and people greet them as they leave and welcome those that arrive," Wistin continued, ignoring her interruption. "And ships brought children and adults. Everybody would be waiting. One after another and nobody could jump the queue. Who do you think disembarked from the ships first, children or adults? That's what I asked, once..."

"I can just imagine to whom you asked that question, dear," his grandmother replied sadly.

"Yes, you're right, Gran. So who would disembark first? Children? Or adults? And the answer was: the first to disembark would be those who had waited most for long. And so I asked, how come I've arrived before my father?"

"Now that's enough, Wistin! I don't want to hear any more of this! Enough, change the subject and talk about something else, for the love of God! After all we've done for you." Katarina burst in, tears welling in her eyes.

But Wistin went on, talking firmly, in a challenging voice. "Maybe there were ships especially for children and others intended for adults. And my father had been waiting for a very long time. Let me tell you how long! I knew my numbers well and I stretched out my hand to keep count. One, two, three, four, and so on. There was a little boy who was always staring out, beyond across the sea, just waiting. He was always asking people he met at the harbour if they had seen someone. 'Have you seen a man?' he would ask. He used to go up to every man he encountered asking if he was the one."

"Wistin, stop right there! Please, for the love of... Stop it!"

"There, do you see Gran how well I can tell stories, just like you!"

"And like your mother, like anyone who loves and brings up someone."

"I want to know who my father is, where he is, what he looks like. I want to talk to him, tell him a story, and ask him to tell me one himself. Do I have a right to this or not? If he's dead I want to visit his grave and I will light a candle and put a bunch of flowers on it, as I did once when you both took me to visit Grandpa's grave."

"You remember that, do you?"

"Yes, I remember it. Even the walk in the Valley with my mother, I remember that, too."

Katarina stilled her rocking chair's motion and lowered her head even more.

"If he's somewhere to be found, I'd like to go and look for him. If he's abroad I want to board a ship and go after him. But, I know where to look for him. Don't children come by ship? And aren't ships to be found in the Port? But the Port is full of people, teeming with all sorts of labourers. Maybe there'll be one amongst them who will answer me when I call him."

"Call him, dear?"

"Dad, Dad, that's how I'll call him. Gran, you're right. I don't know his name yet. I wonder why? For now I'll call him Dad but one day I'll call him by name."

Katarina went up to Wistin wishing to calm him down and soothe him affectionately.

"Come and catch me, Gran! I can fly like butterflies in a story, look! Once upon a time there was a butterfly, and this butterfly, go on, go on, Gran! You too used to tell stories. Don't you anymore?" he addressed her scornfully as he quickly turned about and left the house.

"Wistin! Wistin!" Katarina shouted, in vain. She went to the door and then closed it in resignation. Jumbled thoughts raced across her mind, but she did not want to go to her daughter and alarm her. Katarina had finally realized that Wistin was very different from them and would not change his attitude and behave differently until their troubles were over. "What shall I do?" she said to herself, frowning with worry.

"St. Joseph! Please illuminate me. Could I possibly be cheeky enough to come before you once more and ask for more than ever before? Haven't you granted me enough wishes? And when they all came through I thought I couldn't ask for more. But I was wrong. How could I ever have imagined that Wistin would take against us, too? And if he ever gets to meet his father, what will he feel? Maybe Saverju was right, after all. Is it possible he could see so far ahead? But, no, his eyes were always turned to the past. But how could we ever have imagined that something new would change everything?"

She was lost in her thoughts, wiping away her tears with a large handkerchief crushed into a ball in her right hand. She took up her rosary beads and recited a few Hail Mary's, but did not have the strength to continue. She had no idea what to do. She went to the window and then drew back. The place was deserted, and there was no one she could talk to.

"I'm going, I'm going. I'm going to do my duty, now as well, come what may, St. Joseph. You know I'm not playing some trick. I've always kept my word to you. Isn't that true? Now please, you who have always kept your word to me, hear me out this time as well. What happened before was important but what's happening now is just as important," she gasped, trying to control the sobbing that robbed her of her voice. She went down on her knees in the middle of the room, made the Sign of the Cross, paused to decide how best to word her prayer, and then rose to her feet. "No, no," she decided, "I'd best go and stand in front of his niche. Yes, I must go to him right now."

It was sunset. A few farmers, those who had stayed on last, were making their way home and the shepherds were rounding up the last stragglers to pen them in for the night. Some people were still loitering in the streets. The sacristan was just debating with himself whether he should set off on his rounds with the long candlesnuffer to douse the flames burning brightly on the tall candles. As for the other candles, those small short ones burning in front of niches, he could snuff them out between two fingers. He could feel the weak flame burn for an instant but it did not cause him any real pain and he was used to it. You can get used to anything in life, he was wont to remark, displaying his thick calloused fingers.

Katarina went to the front door and opened it, took out the large key from her pocket and bolted the door shut. She immediately headed for the church, pinching the veil against her face, willing herself to overcome her agitation, and in order not to show any embarrassment should she happen to encounter anybody in the unlikely event that any villager was out and about and could see her go out at that hour. She made a beeline for the church but it was already closed up. She banged on the door with both hands, raised the heavy doorknockers and let them slam back once, twice. She waited to hear the least noise, indicating that at least the sacristan was still inside. But nothing could be heard. She slammed the doorknockers till her hands hurt and started banging on the door with both fists once more.

"Wait, wait! What's happened? I'm coming! I'm coming! Can't you see I've already locked up?" a man's voice could be heard saying inside.

"He's finally heard me! How deaf he's become! I nearly broke my hands trying to make him hear me!" she groused to herself, resting one hand against a doorknocker and gripping her house key with the other.

The large iron key of the church door began turning on the inside till the door opened a crack and the sacristan put his head out, fearful but somewhat angry as well. "Who on earth is it at this time of evening? Who is it? The church is closed. It's been closed for quite a while," he spoke indignantly.

"You're right, you're right! But there's no set time for some things," Katarina countered. "Something urgent has come up. It can happen to anybody."

"Is that you, Katarina? What's happened now? It's been such a long time since I last saw you! Hadn't it all come right in the end, or not?" he asked her, puzzled, opening the door wider to be able to see her face and ascertain that it was truly her, Katarina. "What do you want, at this hour?" he said huffily, annoyance at the disturbance reasserting itself. He was certainly not pleased to be summoned and made to open the door again. Such a thing had never happened before.

"I need to make a vow to St. Joseph!" she exclaimed.

"A vow to St. Joseph! At this hour? Don't you know what time it is? Don't you know that the church is closed at this time? People are going to bed now, and ... I don't know, but... May God overlook my words. Maybe even saints feel drowsy at this time and go to sleep! Maybe it happens, even up above! A vow at this time of evening? No, no! I'm sorry Katarina but this won't do. No, no!"

"If you don't let me in, I'm going to push the door in! I'll show you how strong I am and I'll go straight up to the belfry and ring all your bells with all my strength and wake up the whole village! On my word as a woman! Out of my way! See, I'm going!" she shouted, almost heedlessly.

The sacristan did not belittle her but neither could he believe her. He knew her as a totally different sort of woman from the one he beheld before his eyes at that moment. He knew her as a woman wrapped up in her family, one who had endured much hardship and suffering, who prayed with fervour and who had never let a needless word pass her lips. He could not recognize this new Katarina in front of his eyes. She was a changed woman.

"Are you going to let me in or not?" she asked him with determination in every syllable.

"We were friends, and whether we stay friends or not from tonight onwards doesn't matter. But let you in? No. Wait till tomorrow."

"Tomorrow may be too late," she answered him in an angry voice.

"St. Joseph has become used to waiting. Well then, he can wait tonight too. He can wait for you to come tomorrow morning, as early as you please. As long as I get a decent night's sleep and can get up and open up the church. Then you can come and tell him whatever you want. We were friends before and we'll remain friends," he replied firmly.

"We were friends but we won't remain any longer!" she threatened him. "If that's how you want it, get out of my way! I'm going up to the belfry." she pushed the door open and shoved the sacristan aside and ran as quickly as she could to the corner of the church where a narrow staircase led to the belfry.

"What are you up to? Merciful Heaven! What are you going to do?" the sacristan cried out seriously alarmed, running to catch up with her. "I have been looking after this church for so many years but no one has ever done such a thing before! Are you going to be the one to ruin my life now that I'm nearly at the end of my old age?"

"Either you let me speak to St. Joseph or else I'm going to ring the bells with all my strength."

"But are you sure you know how to ring them?" he asked her derisively.

"I can ring them! And how I'll ring them will be heard far and wide! You can be sure that the whole village will hear them! See?"

The sacristan was in a panic. He was in dread that Katarina might really carry out her threat after all. He had spent many a long year ringing the bells at the appointed time, in the prescribed manner, with the precision he had learnt from his forebears, and according to the long-held aims of the particular hour of the day or occasion. He would ring out the strokes of the *Paternoster*, the prayer to Our Father, early in the morning, prompting some of the villagers to rise from their bed and begin the day's work. At eight in the morning, noon and sunset, he would ring the *Angelus*, when the *Ave Maria*, the prayer addressed to Our Lady, should be recited. And he would also ring out the prayer for *All Souls* at eight in the evening, when the villagers would pray for their dead kin before they went to bed. The same with the bell used for mourning the death of a child, or to announce the administering of the last rites to someone, or to toll for *Lauds* in time of celebrations, and any other special strokes and flourishes. Each stroke of a bell meant a specific call to prayer. The sacristan had never broken this rule and he was not about to see it broken now. The bells were a precise clock for all the villagers, regulating their spiritual and physical daily life.

All at once, the sacristan imagined himself hearing the bells in his belfry breaking that evening's silence, sounding out a loud never-ending flourish, just as he himself liked to ring. He put his hands to his ears, under the illusion that the bells were actually ringing out loudly, crudely, negligently, without rhyme or reason, or pleasure. He imagined people spilling out from their homes in terror, in their night clothes, and he felt he could hear the bellows of frightened animals, and the wails and whimpers of children and babies. He felt horrified and quickly implored Katarina, "Very well, very well! I give in! Katarina, it will be as you say. What do you want?"

"I want to..."

"Wait, wait a bit," he cut in.

"Let me go on. Let me go on," she broke in hotly. "If you only knew how strongly I feel the urge to ring the bells..."

"Very well, very well," he answered her quickly, "but..."

"But nothing."

"But I need Fr. Grejbel's permission. I can do nothing without his express word. I have never let him down, by word or deed. Do you think I'm going to hurt him now, Katarina?"

"Yes, you're right. That's all very true," she said, subsiding, tears in her eyes. "I can never let Fr. Grejbel down. How could I? But what am I going to do? Oh! Dear Lord!"

"Can't you wait till tomorrow? Wait, and come by early tomorrow morning, quietly, and make the vow you wish to make. A new vow. Listen to me, Katarina, wait till tomorrow," he told her very gently.

"I can't wait till tomorrow."

"Well, if you can't wait till tomorrow, then, then... I really don't know what to advise."

"Let me speak to Fr. Grejbel, then. Do you think I could speak to him now?"

"You don't really want to ring my bells, do you Katarina?" he asked her with a smile.

Katarina burst into tears, drew near to him and almost embraced him. "I have no one to turn to! I don't know what to do!"

"But hasn't the storm passed, Katarina? It's none of my business, but, but... hasn't the old trouble passed?"

"The old one has gone but new trouble is brewing."

"A new storm?"

"Yes, a new storm. Just like the seasons of our fields, just the same. A season passes and makes way for the next, and then its turn will come again. Don't you know this ancient rule as well as I do? It's the village law. We ourselves aren't less than the village itself, no more no less."

The sacristan nodded in agreement with her. "Well then, let's go right now to Fr. Grejbel. He has no set time when one can go to him. His house is always open to all."

"There's no need for you to come along. I know the way. Close up the church. Set your mind at rest."

"Well, now, indulge me! Were you really going to ring the bells? Let me tell you, you really had me in a panic!"

"I just wanted you to hear me out, that's all. I'm going straight over to Fr. Grejbel, then. Right now."

"Go on, then. And tell him that the belfry is still in the sacristan's hands."

Fr. Grejbel made her welcome and invited her in to sit down. "Would you like some tea?" he asked her.

"No, nothing, thank you, Fr. Grejbel. I don't feel like anything, not even like living any longer."

"I'm getting you a cup of tea, all the same. Where would we be without a cup of tea, huh? No one would recognize us otherwise! Isn't that so?" he tried to jolly her along to put her at ease and get her to unburden herself.

"I wanted to speak to St. Joseph. I felt I had to speak to him right at that moment. I wanted to make another vow to him, but..." she spoke despairingly but plucked up enough courage to report what had just happened.

"Don't worry needlessly, Katarina," he told her, giving her heart. "You can make your vow to St. Joseph first thing tomorrow morning. He's always there, ready and waiting to hear people out and make things happen. But if you'd like to unburden yourself now and speak, why, go ahead and tell me. St. Joseph knows how to wait. Tell me, tell me."

Katarina told him all about Wistin.

"Wistin is rebelling against everything and everybody. He's realizing how different his childhood was from other youngsters."

"He doesn't want to speak to his mother anymore."

"Yes, yes I know he doesn't want to speak to her," Fr. Grejbel assented, speaking very gently to her.

"Susanna seems to repel him. It almost seems as if, as if... oh I don't even want to say the words! She doesn't exist for him anymore. What shall I do? All that I've left is the hope of making a vow and speaking to you. I didn't imagine I'd be seeing you tonight. Wistin left the house all of a sudden. First he retold all the stories his mother and I used to tell him long, long ago, and then he had the temerity to demand I tell him who was his father."

"That means he did not think of Arturu as his father."

"It seems he realized a long time ago that Arturu was nothing more than someone who loved his mother, a man who tried to fill the place of his real father. It almost seems as if it was our stories themselves which opened his eyes to the truth. We were brought up hearing stories, and by time we learnt to make them up ourselves, using our own imagination, and tell them. We put in all that we know of our village. This is where we took life, everything! Our whole world is here, in this village."

Fr. Grejbel was mystified with these words. "Wistin is searching for everything," he told her after a pause. "His roots, those that are hidden beneath the soil, and on which everything depends."

"His father. He's searching for him, that's all there is to it."

"No, Katarina, not only for his father. He's looking and trying to find himself, his mother, and even you. He's walking on a path and feeling lost. Like when he said he was walking in a wood and found himself someplace he didn't know. Do you remember that story?"

"Yes, of course, of course I do. Susanna had told him that one."

"Well, now that he's growing older, the moment has come for him to start questioning things, and to look for the truth. Why should this upset you, Katarina?"

"Should he know the truth?"

"Why not? Why shouldn't he know it? The law is there for us to follow, but there's also love."

"I didn't use to think so, a while ago. Between the law and love. Do you remember, Fr. Grejbel? Who should win? You talked to me about this. Should it be love that wins?"

"Yes, because in the meantime the law is no more."

"I don't understand you, Fr. Grejbel. You know I can't read or write. My memory isn't what it used to be."

"In the meantime, Arturu is no longer with us," he spelled it out clearly to her.

"May God have mercy on his soul! Arturu was a good man." Katarina had recovered all her courage at this point and she looked at the priest from below her brow to show him she wished to know more.

"Wistin has grown up, Katarina. This is something new, both for you and for Susanna. In life, whatever happens the

104

first time is always new. But it's nothing new in itself. The second and third time round it starts losing its newness, maybe, but it can also remain feeling new, perhaps. That's why we make so many mistakes! And do you want to know how truly grown up Wistin is?"

Katarina remained still, gazing back at him, waiting.

"Wistin is fond of a young woman."

"Then, he told me the truth. He wasn't making it all up, or making fun of me. And where does he meet this young woman?"

"Where do you think?"

"In the village square? No! In the backstreets of the village? Neither. Maybe in another village close to ours? I don't know."

"I'll tell you, Katarina, because he himself gave me permission to tell you. If he hadn't, I wouldn't say a word to you."

"Of course, of course. He talked to me too. But he himself told you to tell me?"

Fr. Grejbel nodded his head in assent, remaining silent.

"What did he tell you, Fr. Grejbel? Since you're allowed to tell me, you can speak out. Right?"

"Yes, you're right. In the Valley."

"Is that where he's meeting his girl? He's got the Valley imprinted on his mind! He's always going on about it! That place has a special significance for him. Between ourselves, it's the cradle."

"Well that's where he's meeting her. And he often says that one day he'll just up sticks and leave this place to go far, far away. Leaving everything and everybody behind. Start anew, that's what he often says. He also told me to tell you all this."

"To me? His grandmother?"

"Yes, to you, to his grandmother."

"Meaning, not to his mother."

"No, not to his mother."

"That means he doesn't want anything to do with her."

Fr. Grejbel bent his head as much as he could, almost as if he wanted to hide his face, and remained silent.

"Fr. Grejbel, you're duty bound to tell me. And do you know why?"

"Why? No, I don't know."

"Because you're the only hope we have left this time, yet again. Our world is tumbling down around our ears again, and the only support we can cling to is you. We have nothing and no one else. Even our love has turned bitter. A bitter love. Why is life like this, Fr. Grejbel?" Katarina wailed. After a pause she continued in a changed tone of voice, firmly, "I'm going to ask you something. And you must answer me! Do you truly believe all that you preach from the altar and when you climb up to the pulpit?"

"I will answer you. But will you believe me, Katarina?"

"Yes, I will believe you, even at this moment. I will believe you till the end. That's why I wanted to hear all this from your own lips. And I know, I know what you're going to tell me. You're not a weather vane, turning wherever the wind blows. But I need to hear once more the certainty you feel."

"I believe every single word I preach," he told her with a happy lilt to his voice. "And do you know why? Because I've already tasted the bitter dregs in life myself, too. Otherwise I wouldn't have the right to speak for others."

"I can't contradict you, Fr. Grejbel. Time has made me a grandmother. My daughter made me go up the hill of sorrows, even though she never intended it. First she went courting in the Valley, without Saverju's or my knowledge, then she fell pregnant and Stiefnu abandoned her, and then she gave birth to a baby whom she wasn't even allowed to see, and then she finally found her son after many years and brought him up, and just look, now what's happened...She gave him a father, a home, and meanwhile he wants nothing of that. Nothing! Not even his own mother! And she is now a widow, too, having lost her baby, the baby of her dead husband."

Fr. Grejbel held his tongue.

"Say a word, just one word, Fr. Grejbel! That's what I want from you. I don't know how I've plucked up the courage to ask you these things, now that I'm old. Maybe this is the time when I need to find out whether I can still stand on my own two feet. Times are changing, from what I can see."

"And if I do tell you, will you listen to me?"

"Don't you know that I will? When have we ever not listened to you? Me, and Susanna, and even Saverju. We all took your advice, maybe at different times, but we listened to you."

"Well then, if that's so, Katarina, let me speak plainly to you. Wistin needs to have what he wants and to learn who his father is."

"No, no, Fr. Grejbel, no he can't," she replied in a very decided tone of voice. "Everything has its own time. The seasons, the rule of the seasons, the forecasts, Fr. Grejbel."

"What do you mean?"

"It means when the right time comes."

"And when is the time right, Katarina?"

"I don't know. You tell me."

"Very well, I'll tell you. It's now."

"Dear Lord! Now? What shall I do? Help me!"

"Of course I'll help you! I will."

"Shan't I make a new vow to St. Joseph, then?"

"Of course you must make it if you want to. And I hope that both of us will agree on it. I hope he'll prove I'll be doing the right thing."

"What are you going to do, Fr. Grejbel?"

"Oh now, that's a secret between the two of us. Set your mind at rest, Katarina. You've always done your duty according to the times you've found yourself in."

"According to the season."

"That's right, according to the season. This time round, too."

"Will you keep close and talk to our Wistin?"

"Yes, don't worry at all."

"Don't leave him to flounder about on his own. And how will you be certain that he'll listen to you?"

Fr. Grejbel smiled but did not reply.

"You don't want to tell me. Never mind, I'll ask St. Joseph now and he'll tell me all about it. He's never let me down so far, and I don't think he's going to start now."

The priest simply looked back at her with a smile on his face.

Katarina nodded to him and left. She went straight back home, but Wistin had not yet arrived. She remained in a great worry not knowing where he could be at that time of night, and with whom, maybe down in the Valley, maybe somewhere at the other end of the village, or maybe he had even gone beyond the village. She was only certain that he had not gone home to his mother.

***

That same evening, the four men who used to spend a few hours late in the evening at Baskal's wine tavern, were also waiting for the priest to turn up. After many years, always in the same place with a glass of wine before them, and perhaps drinking a cup of coffee with a dash of orange blossom water right at the end, Baskal's friends remained the same, living out their life in the same unchanging manner. This served Baskal well, giving him the means to keep his tavern going since the few clients he served had nowhere else to go and nothing else to do. And for his patrons, this situation served them well too because it allowed them to go through life without wondering what to do with their free time. Not that they had empty hours on their hands. They would wake up early to hear mass, repeating prayers they had learnt by heart ever since they were toddlers at home, and would hear the mass celebrated in Latin, all the while trying to keep up with the words being said by the priest, repeating them as they heard them. Since they could not understand a single word, their distortion of Latin did not worry or surprise anyone.

The priest finally arrived on the tavern's doorstep, removed his hat, smiled at them and entered.

"You came late today, Fr. Grejbel. Usually we expect you here earlier. But never mind. The main thing is that now you're here," Baskal told him as he welcomed him inside.

"I've arrived now. I promised you I'd come, and so here I am. Whenever I can come, I will."

Fr. Grejbel used to spend much of his time in the confessional. The villagers used to queue up in a corner of the church, the men on their own and the women in a separate queue at some distance from the other, all of them waiting for confession time to come and take their turn. First a man would go up to make his confession and then a woman from the other queue would go, and they would alternate like this till everyone was done. Most of the villagers felt the need to go to confession on a daily basis and consequently the priest did not feel comfortable about leaving the church before making sure that everyone who wanted to go to confession had in fact done so. Even children, with their arms crossed in front of their chest and with downcast eyes, would approach the confessional to confess their minor sins, as their mother would have instructed them beforehand. Even the old, kept away from all vice and mindful only of their prayers, would approach to register their presence and declare the least transgression to make sure of their state of grace. Otherwise they would find no peace in their heart and quite possibly worry themselves to death, needlessly. Fr. Grejbel wanted to make sure that nobody would remain troubled because of him. Consequently he used to spend the day going in and out of the confessional, as and when the need arose, as long as he served the queues that gathered from time to time. Finally, he would be free to dedicate some time to himself. He felt he needed to stop and have a rest, especially now that he was getting on in years, but he did not know how. Between over scrupulous old people and innocent young children, when everyone crowded around the confessional he felt he could never say no to anyone.

"How can I say no?" he used to ask himself, certain of the answer. "I can't!" he would repeat in his heart of hearts. It was in this way that he felt happy and content, even though he would be suddenly overcome with fatigue like the sunset colours that descended daily all of a sudden on his village. "Your life isn't your own, don't forget," he often admonished himself. "A time will come to rest for a long time, a very long time, a time without end, but it's not now. It's too soon for that, too soon." That's what his mother had taught him.

For some time now, especially since he had started discerning signs of old age in himself, the priest had taken up the habit of dropping in on Baskal and his loyal patrons in the wine tavern to spend some time in their company. Not every day, but whenever he could manage it. He realized how much they appreciated it. It did not take him long to learn of their great wish to learn. They were men who had never been to school, and who had never had someone to teach them. Slowly, slowly, Fr. Grejbel realized that in this way their talk did not always turn to gossip.

Ġwakkin, Ġamri and Kieli rose slightly from their seats around the table and greeted him. A glass of wine stood before each of them, but they did not take another sip before they learnt what he would like to drink. Now that the priest had arrived, none of them dared to continue their old custom of gossiping about the village and its environs. He had told them right at the very beginning that there were other things they could spend their time discussing.

"Tell them, just tell them, and what you'll tell them to do I will order it done," Baskal told him.

Fr. Grejbel returned Baskal's look and by a slight shake of his head in his direction invited him to continue speaking.

"Well then, no word about the other villagers, no gossip about our neighbours, huh?" Baskal concluded.

"But then, what shall we talk about, Fr. Grejbel, if not about people? What else can there be?" Ġwakkin asked, perplexed.

"And what's this about the other villagers and those in our neighbouring village? People we know well and those who live only some little way from us? What can be better than talking about them?" Ġamri intervened.

"And not only that! There are other people too! Aren't there those who lived before and lie in the cemetery now? And those still living, here in the village, men and women?" Kieli objected too.

"No, nothing more about them!" Fr. Grejbel had insisted, in a gentle voice but giving a command, nevertheless. "From now onwards, there's to be no gossip at all."

"But if we stop any tittle-tattle about the rest of the villagers, will you come by more often?" Baskal wanted to know.

"Rest assured, Baskal. I'll come whenever I can."

"And will you still have a drink with us each time you come?" Ġamri asked him.

"I will, I will, Ġamri. I get thirsty too, you know."

"And will you still talk to us and teach us things?" Kieli wanted to know.

"Of course I'll talk to you, about all sorts of things. There are many, many things we can discuss, so many you can't even imagine how much!" the priest replied.

"So what shall we talk about? What more can there be left to say about this world of ours? How can that be?" Ġwakkin was still in doubt.

Fr. Grejbel gazed back at them, an indulgent smile on his lips, but vouchsafed no answer.

111

"We're only simple villagers, Fr. Grejbel," the four men spoke with one voice.

"And aren't I a simple villager too?" Fr. Grejbel responded. "It's a truly wonderful thing to be a simple villager, my friends. To be a villager means you're bound to the land, where there's life, the beginning of everything. There can be no town without a village."

"Is that what you still think, even though you spent so much time abroad?" Baskal wondered.

"That's what I used to think before I went away and even more so when I saw other countries, countries that are so very big, but, always before my eyes I kept this tiny village of ours, set at the very edge of the world."

"Very well, we're villagers. But we don't know how to read and write!" they exclaimed, appearing unconvinced of what he was telling them.

"Never mind. You're still villagers. You have a good memory. You carry everything up here. Your mind is like a thick book, full of stuff."

"Our mind is like a thick book?" they chorused in astonishment.

"An archive! That's what we call it!" Fr. Grejbel affirmed, twinkling at them, no irony intended.

"Then we're an archive!" the four men said in one voice, preening. "An archive, an archive. What's that exactly?" they went on repeating amongst themselves.

"What a difficult word that is, Fr. Grejbel *an-ar-chive*! And what a lovely sound it has! It's like the name of someone you don't know," Baskal commented.

"Teach us to write one of these days, Fr. Grejbel. We don't know how to write even one word, not even our names!" Gwakkin interjected.

"Why, of course! Whenever you want," he replied heartily.

"We want to! Right now!" they exclaimed together.

112

"All we need is a piece of paper and a pencil. That's all! A blank page with narrow or wide lines, whichever, and a sharpened pencil. Once you get them we can begin writing *a, b, c*, and you'll see how quickly you'll learn to read and write," Fr. Grejbel said encouragingly. "A whole new world will open up in front of your eyes, wide and beautiful."

"Is that right? How so?" they all asked him together.

"Oh yes, it will, wait and see. If you want, next time bring paper and a pencil with you, that's all!"

"But where can we get paper and a pencil?" Ġamri asked him.

Kieli and Ġwakkin reiterated the same question.

"Very well, my friends. Next time round I'll bring everything with me. It's hardly a bother. Four blank pages and four pencils, sharpened well, with a point!"

"Thank you, thank you!" they shouted happily.

"But how is it possible for us to learn all that, now that we're grown up?" Ġwakkin wondered aloud.

"It's never too late. We remain alive till our last breath. Children or old ones, we're all still here, waiting to pass on, but for the moment we're here, all the same," the priest declared.

"But you know all this because you're a priest," Ġamri told him, gazing respectfully at him, scrutinizing the priest's black cassock, an entire gown, before him.

"Ġamri, I'm a priest, the son of a village woman, a woman like any other. She's dead now, she's been dead for a long time, and she doesn't lie too far away from other mothers. My mother, too, didn't know how to read or write," Fr. Grejbel answered him.

"Your mother didn't know how to read or write? How can that be?" Baskal wondered. "Would you like something to drink?" he asked in a lower tone of voice, meaning it as a compliment.

113

"Not yet, not just yet, Baskal. Later," Fr. Grejbel answered him and then continued. "No, my mother didn't know how to read or write, but she knew how to remember things. Everything was stored up in her mind. She had a great memory, a huge store where she saved up all she knew, and all the lore of her folk, whether of only a short while ago or from many years back. That's the secret, one's memory. And if you think about it, you'll realize that our forebears never had paper and pencils, as far back as we can go. They only had a very good memory and they succeeded in doing everything, so much so that here we are this evening, the five of us here, now! All through their efforts."

The four men gaped back at him, eager to hear more.

"Your mother could remember everything?" they all wanted to know.

"Yes, she remembered everything. Just like you, no more than that. You too save everything in your mind, my friends," he told them.

"We do, Fr. Grejbel? But we're too ignorant!" Ġamri exclaimed in disbelief, certain that his mates would agree wholeheartedly with him. "That's how we were born, turnip heads, and that's how we'll have to die."

"But what can be better than a turnip, Ġamri, when you know how to cook it well?" the priest quickly took him up on his words.

"Our minds are like a slide, like a slope. Everything rolls to the bottom, nothing stays up. We can't remember anything," Kieli said glumly.

"Just try, and if you try you'll soon see that you can learn," the priest encouraged them.

"Could we really learn to read and write, Fr. Grejbel?" Baskal intervened. "I've been here all these years, in this tiny place, selling wine, tea, coffee and some *biskuttelli* and *galletti* and pieces of toast, which sometimes get burnt on that capricious kerosene stove, that ancient contraption, look, look, there! And I've done all this without ever knowing how to sign my name and surname. I've always signed with the mark of a cross. And now you come along and tell me that."

"I'm telling you, from now on, you can start to write as much as anybody can," the priest affirmed.

"And so, you think I can learn to read the newspaper? I'll be able to know what's happening outside our village, too?" Baskal asked, pathetically eager.

"Of course, you'll be able to know what's happening out there beyond our village."

"Without having to go there myself?"

"Yes, of course."

"That's interesting, mates. What a lot of things there are to know about, huh? We never knew any of this," Ġamri declared happily.

"The thought never even crossed our mind!" Kieli remarked.

"If only we'd known that before, what a pity!" Ġwakkin complained.

"We'll make a start. Whenever you want we can start," Fr. Grejbel assured them.

"From today?" they all pleaded together.

"Yes, we can start today, right now in fact, in the little time we have left before the night draws in," the priest approved.

"Really?" they said. "But we don't have paper and pencils here this evening. We didn't know we had to bring–"

"It doesn't matter. Did you bring your memory with you?"

"What? Oh dear, what's that?" they asked him with one voice, flustered.

"I didn't bring anything with me, except a few coins to spend on drink," Kieli observed. "I've been doing the same thing for years on end."

"You can remember things, you all have the ability to remember things, don't you? That's all I'm asking from you so that we can start," the priest replied reassuringly.

"Of course we can remember things. Everything, we can remember everything, and wonder of wonders, the older we grow, the more we can remember! How come? Did it ever happen to you?" Ġwakkin wanted to know.

"Of course it had to happen! Did you ever grow old some other time? Isn't it the first time you're getting old? You're a brand new old person!" Kieli teased him.

"When are we going to make a start then?" Baskal asked impatiently.

"Let's begin tomorrow, after I'll have given the blessing and have finished confessing people and seen to all my duties at the church," Fr. Grejbel told them.

"And what shall we bring with us?" they asked.

"A piece of paper, one or more, maybe two or three if you want but not more than that, and something to write with. A pencil or a pen or a dip pen or even a feather!" he replied with a laugh. "Actually, no, don't get anything. I'll bring everything with me."

"Shan't we get a rubber, either?" Kieli asked.

"Are you all set to make mistakes?" Ġamri mocked him.

"We'd better have a rubber, just in case. Anyone can make a mistake," Ġwakkin defended Kieli.

"I'll take care of that. One should be enough," Baskal put in. "Here's the rubber friends, look!" he added, opening the drawer under the counter and fishing out a rubber.

"That's a brand new rubber, Baskal," they all commented with one voice, pretending to be astonished but with a hint of disparagement.

"Yes, it's brand new. Maybe I've never made a mistake and never had to use it," Baskal defended himself with a smile.

"Or maybe you don't know how to use it," Kieli made fun of him.

The next day, Ġwakkin, Ġamri and Kieli went some time earlier than usual to Baskal's tavern taking a blank piece of paper and a pencil with them.

Fr. Grejbel began teaching them the alphabet, *a, b, c,* and the rest. He raised his voice as he enunciated every letter, teaching them to do the same and how to write it down, and they painstakingly wrote down each letter as he directed onto the page before them. He taught them to recite the letters of the alphabet in a sing-song manner, the way young children learnt them in their first years at school. At first, the men found it hard to remember all the signs but then he made them practise the chant by repeating it after him. They quickly mastered the chant and were able to repeat his recitation. In this way, he sang through all the letters of the alphabet and they stared back at him, open-mouthed in astonishment, as if looking upon some great wonder for the first time. He continued teaching them on subsequent evenings at the tavern and before they knew it, the day came when they could read an entire sentence.

They were overjoyed, feeling as if they had discovered an old world that had been staring them in the face all their life but had been completely unknown to them.

Chapter 5

Except for birdsong and the soughing of the trees whenever a strong gust buffeted them, the silence down there was profound. Nothing existed but nature, clean and free from all interference. In those hidden depths, as always, plants and creatures could grow and multiply without hindrance. Antonja and Wistin continued running after each other, happy in the knowledge that they were alone and all that open space was theirs to enjoy. They passed under the arches of the old bridge that spanned the Valley and hid in every nook and cranny they came upon, as if they were still children playing hide-and-seek. Then, she went to hide under the low branches of a tree with a thick trunk and he ran about trying to find her. He passed between trees, parted the tall reeds, jumped from rock to rock, and finally found her, opening his arms wide to reach her, telling her he had won their game, and then he hugged her fiercely to him.

"Ouch!" she cried but embracing him once more.

"Do you think you'll stay in love with me?" he asked her.

"Yes, yes! Why are you asking me?"

"Time passes and perhaps, who knows..."

"It's still too early to say. But, yes, I believe so. At this moment, here, I imagine I'll love you forever."

"Promise me?"

"Yes, I promise. That's what I feel, so that's what I'm telling you. There, are you satisfied now?"

"Yes, I'm happy, Antonja. If we get married, will you come away with me, somewhere far away from here? Somewhere far more beautiful than here, where the flowers have a sweeter fragrance..."

"How can that be?" Antonja wondered in disbelief.

"Somewhere where even the fruit is tastier?"

"That's impossible, Wistin."

"And where the valleys are far larger, with rivers and ponds, and where there are mountains, and never-ending forests... There, Antonja, you can play hide-and-seek with me and really hide yourself away, and I won't be able to find you in all that enormity. Don't you want to go?"

"Do you want me to get lost, Wistin?"

"Antonja! No, no, Antonja! Nothing of the sort, my love." Wistin gazed long at her, all the while holding her face gently between his hands, and once again he asked her, "Will you come with me somewhere far away from here?"

"I don't know. But what are you thinking of? We're still far too young to concern ourselves with such things," she replied to show him she was not taking him seriously. From the little she knew of him, she supposed him to be a decent lad, but he was prone to let his mind wander, his thoughts flitting here and there like the many colourful butterflies that chased each other up above their heads. He changed his mind from one day to the next, and he was fit to burst with dreams and desires, even with wishes that were far too grand for such as him. She was certain he wanted to grow up without waiting for time to pass at its usual pace.

"Don't you wish our life was in our own hands and we could live in a house where only both of us could command?"

"I don't know, Wistin. All I know is that I'm fed up living with my parents. My mother wants to know everything I do, and possibly even every thought that comes to mind, and she wants to direct my every step. If it was up to her, I wouldn't even set foot outside, till she herself finds some young man who she thinks will do for me. She wants me to get married, but in the way she wants, to whom she wants, and when she wants. That's how she herself was brought up. And my father agrees with her because he's more afraid of her than he is of me. Whenever he dares to say something she pounces on him and belittles him as if he were her son. I think that whenever I have an argument with my mother he takes my side, but I can expect no help from him. He's too weak."

"So, don't you want to go and live somewhere where no one can interfere anymore?" he asked her again. "Just imagine it, a world away from here, the way we want it to be, just the two of us."

Antonja felt happy hearing these words. Nothing could be more beautiful than that, but at the same time she knew that Wistin let his imagination run away with him. It was not the first time he came out with such a proposition. She did not like to dampen his enthusiasm because she enjoyed hearing all about his flights of imagination, though she always cautioned him against running too far ahead with his ideas. All in all, in spite of everything, her wishes matched his.

"You can say that, Antonja, because you haven't spent all your life waiting for someone. It's no fun at all having to wait."

"Waiting for whom? What do you mean?" she asked him but in a disinterested sort of way.

"One day I'll tell you," he declared.

They strolled around the little puddles of water that had formed along the valley bottom, occasionally taking off their shoes and wading in since the puddles were shallow. They enjoyed feeling their feet explore the bottom, and each stone that lay there pressed against their soles without causing any hurt. They picked up stones and threw them, making them skim across the surface till they sank.

They rested between leaps and runs and finally they held hands and strolled slowly on, swinging their hands.

All of a sudden, like a bolt out of the blue, it started raining heavily. At first they only felt some fat drops of rain, heavy isolated spatters, but then the drops became a sheet of continuous rain that quickly made everything wet, filling up all the holes and cracks. It grew steadily stronger and kept up an unbroken rhythm for a long time. The sky was completely overcast and thunder approached from afar with an occasional clap, rather like an embattled navy drawing near. Antonja and Wistin had heard the thunder but it had sounded so far away that they had imagined the storm would take a long time before it came there. But it had not been as far away as they had thought. It came upon them before they knew it.

"Run, run, Antonja," Wistin cried, taking her hand and pulling her along. "There, didn't I tell you to come away with me somewhere far, far away?"

"But you didn't tell me a storm was brewing!"

"We should have realized before that a storm was coming. Let's go in that cave, look, and mind your step. It's become very slippery now. Just look at all these puddles! They've formed in the twinkling of an eye!"

"Oh no, we'll be caught out! We're soaked to the skin! Sopping wet! Look at me, I'm wet through! Oh dear Lord! My mother will have something to say when she sees me like this! I don't even want to think about it. I'm really frightened. She'll create a real fuss, I'm sure. What excuse can I give? Think! If you have any idea, tell me."

"Stop thinking about that for now. Let's shelter in that cave, quick! We can stay out of the rain in there, waiting for it to stop, and maybe we won't stay as wet as we are. Maybe the sun will come out soon and we'll dry as quick as can be!"

"You must be joking, Wistin, or pulling my leg! Don't you know that such a downpour doesn't stop suddenly, just like that? And the sun isn't going to come out this evening just for the two of us. It's time for sunset by now."

Wistin and Antonja kept running hard but Antonja slipped suddenly and fell straight into a small puddle. She hurt herself and whimpered. Wistin helped her up and tried to lift her but could not. He also slipped and slithered, finding himself sitting next to her in the puddle. He drew closer to her and snatched a kiss. She smiled happily after the kiss but wanted to show him that there was no time for love at that moment.

The rain, sheeting down as hard as ever, did not dismay them as much as the darkness that reached out from the clouds and began to spread everywhere.

"You'd better crawl to that rock there, look. Don't try to get up before because you'll slip again," he directed, helping her to suit the action to his words and helping himself to get up. As soon as he stood up he felt on firm ground and was able to push her towards him with the palm of his hand against her back. She rose and scampered to a spot where she felt able to stand firmly and walk on.

"We'll soon be there, you'll see," he encouraged her.

She looked back at him admiringly, and for a few moments forgot her fear, but only momentarily. She had been drawn to him by his ability to climb trees, to jump from branch to branch, and to jump over dry stone walls and find the most roundabout paths without ever getting lost. As soon as they entered the cave they wrung out their clothes, ridding themselves of the excess weight of water, shook off water from their hair, and smiled, well-content with each other.

"That's better," he told her, glad to have made it inside. "We can see the rain falling better from in here."

"I want it to stop, but I know that even if it does stop raining we'll still be soaked to the skin. Oh dear Lord!"

Wistin embraced her fervently. "Now I know that you truly love me, even though you wanted to leave me."

"Don't you know that wasn't my doing? I'm not the one who wanted to leave you. It was my parents who pushed me to do it, and they still feel that way. Maybe because our two families aren't friends, maybe..."

"Maybe because I'm Wistin."

"Because you're Wistin?"

"Susanna's Wistin," he elaborated.

"You're my Wistin, I still love you," Antonja declared in a decisive tone of voice. "Can't you see I'm beginning to love you more than ever?"

"And why's that? Because I'm good-looking?" he asked with a laugh. "Because I'm lively? Because I like to talk? Because I can climb trees?"

"No, no! Well actually, yes, yes, for all those reasons too, but most of all, because you're brave and stand your ground. That's how you are, firm, and you don't give in easily," she told him, burrowing further into his arms. "Not like me..."

"Is that why you love me?"

"Yes, because I'm not like that. I get frightened and quickly lose heart, give in easily. I'd already given in, in actual fact, and I still don't know whether I'll manage not to give in once more. My mother and father are always on at me, repeating the same words, so much so I've learnt them by heart... Ohh! I'm so fed up of hearing the same words over and over again!"

"Against Wistin, right?"

Antonja held her tongue.

"Yes I know; they've taken against me. But I don't want them. I want you!"

"Wistin! Wistin!" his name burst from her lips as she pressed him more closely to her.

The rain was still sheeting down but the thunder had abated.

"Let's go, Wistin. We can't stay here anymore. With such a dark menacing sky overhead."

"What! In all this rain? How can we? We're already sopping wet. We just have to wait some more."

"But, but, what am I going to do?"

"Didn't you say you trusted me?"

"Yes, yes I do, my love, but if we're soaked to the skin, what can you do? How can I go home and face my mother? Maybe my father would already have gone to bed and I'll evade him, but my mother? No! She'll be lying in wait for me somewhere, with wide-open eyes, behind the window left ajar, or perhaps at the door. The door won't be locked and bolted, and the crossbeam won't be put across the door – all because of me. She'll be there, hands on hips, standing up straight, a challenge in her very stance."

"Can't you think of some way of getting into the house in secret, without her noticing?"

"How? From where? Are you having me on? I'm not a butterfly, you know!"

"You're as beautiful as a butterfly."

"Which one? There are many kinds of butterflies! Red admirals, swallow-tails, the common blue..."

"An angel butterfly!" he interjected in clear tones, with a smile.

"I love you darling. I feel as if I'm falling ever deeper in love with you," she declared, wanting to show him what pleasure his words had given her.

"Then stop thinking about other things. Just imagine, you're a butterfly and you're flying, and from here you're going straight home and getting in through the half-open door."

"In this rain? As if! Can a butterfly fly in the rain?"

"No, no of course not, it can't fly in the rain. But just imagine the rain's stopped and the leaves are already beginning to dry out, and the clouds are all clearing up. Fine weather is on its way. Can you use your imagination?"

"Of course I can use my imagination, but it's still raining. Wistin, I really don't know what I'm going to do. Look, we have to leave. It's time to go. But, when my mother sees me like this! Sopping wet! Mother of God!"

"Can't you tell her you were with me? Blame me!"

"What are you saying, Wistin? She's not supposed to know I'm still meeting you! When I go out I don't tell her where I'm going. I just mention friends. You're a friend, after all. It's not a lie. But nothing's changed between us after that last time. She doesn't want me to be with you."

They waited till the rain lessened and then stopped. They walked hand-in-hand till they came to the end of the Valley and climbed up. The streets were deserted. No one was about, and not even a dog's bark or a cat's yowl broke the silence. The small lamps at street corners were the only sign of life, shining enough to light their way at that dark hour. A strong gust of wind could snuff out their flame at any moment and increase that stark darkness.

"Wistin, what am I going to do?"

"Leave it to me. You said you trust me. Well then, leave it to me," he declared as he walked on determinedly, though with a hint of anger that had been absent before.

"Where are you taking me? Wistin! Home! I need to go home! But how can I in this state?"

The church clock struck, as it did every quarter of an hour, and Antonja was startled.

"You must get used to that clock. You must get used to it as you have to abide by life's rules and regulations."

"Yes, yes, I must get used to it. But I can't take notice of anything now. I don't even know where I am."

"You'll soon find out, never fear," he reassured her, and wanting to show her he was in control.

They walked on, hand-in-hand, keeping to each other's hurried pace.

"Home, I can't not go home. But how can I, like this?"

"I'm taking you home; we'll be there soon."

"What? Home? And then, what's going to happen?" she turned to him trustingly, but with fear in her voice, too.

"Now don't worry about a thing. Let me do the talking. We're going home and nothing's going to happen, you'll see."

"How can that be?" she asked him in disbelief. Admiration mixed with an equal amount of uncertainty overwhelmed her. "Where are you taking me?"

They arrived in front of his grandmother's house.

"Where have we come?" Antonja wanted to know.

They stood there and he waited to see his grandmother come to the door. He was certain she was waiting for him, probably in her rocking chair, holding her rosary beads tightly, pressing them ever more strongly against her hands the more she worried and turned distressing thoughts over and over in her mind.

Although the door was closed, the dim light of the candle burning in front of Our Lady's image could be seen flickering through the curtains at the window. His grandmother was still up and about.

Wistin knew Katarina through and through. "She's a very devout woman, fervent in her beliefs," he used to say to himself. "She's a good woman, a religious one. The rule by which she lives is to love, at whatever cost. She can't bring herself to let me down, and neither will she prevent me from doing whatever I want because she knows that otherwise I'll just up and leave. And if she lets me down and is hard hearted with me, she herself doesn't feel happy doing it. It doesn't suit her to be unkind to me. Her whole happiness rests on me. I know where to draw the line, neither more nor less, one way or the other. She attends mass every day, prays constantly, kisses every holy statue she sees, loves Fr. Grejbel dearly, forgives others, has a kind heart... yes, I know her well. And if she starts behaving differently to me, why, I'll just change my attitude to her in return. I have a good pair of legs that can take me wherever I want, on land and even at sea." He was certain of all this and it fuelled his stubbornness.

"Wistin, where did you stay out, dear?" his grandmother called out to him as soon as she perceived him in the dim streetlight. "Come in, come in, quickly now."

"I'm not alone, Gran," he told her in a firm and decisive tone of voice.

Katarina had not noticed Antonja. She stared harder but in her confusion she barely understood him. "You're not alone?" she repeated, bewildered but curious.

"No, I'm not alone. Look who's here, Gran! This is Antonja, and she's soaked to the skin, like I am."

Antonja, terrified and embarrassed, held her head down as far as it would go and tried to hide behind Wistin.

"And this is my gran, Grandma Katarina," Wistin told Antonja, all the while looking at his grandmother and noting her astonishment, writ large across her face. He looked at her hands, crossed across her stomach, and saw her rosary beads clutched into a ball. "We've interrupted you saying the Rosary I think, haven't we? Sorry Gran, you were right in the middle of your prayers. You're always praying, you're such a good soul."

"Of course I prayed, dear. I've prayed very hard for you. Mostly during these troubled times."

"Did you pray just for me, Gran?"

"I pray for all those I know."

"From today onwards, Gran, pray for two."

"For all those I know."

"Tonight you'll see I'm not alone."

Katarina stared back fixedly at him, lost for words, and then said to him, "Never mind, never mind. Our Lady has become used to dealing patiently with me. I start the Rosary and leave off half-way, and then take up the prayers again when I find time. She would be waiting for me wherever I would have stopped. When you love someone, you know you need to wait and sympathize, my dear. Isn't that so?"

"That's right, Gran!" he answered her. "See what a kind-hearted grandmother I have, Antonja?" he said, turning to the young woman.

Antonja ducked her head, tried to smile, but unwillingly, and kept silent. She was still not sure what to make of the situation, though she felt certain that Wistin's grandmother could not possibly be pleased to see her there, even if she looked to be the sort of person who did not cause trouble.

Katarina did not know what else to say.

"Can we come in, Gran?" Wistin asked, wordlessly motioning to Antonja to step forward to the door and enter the house.

"Come in?" Katarina stammered in consternation. Those words came as a complete surprise to her.

"Can we come in?" he repeated with a smile. "Let's do that, then. Here we are, we're coming in!" He caught hold of Antonja's hand and accompanied her inside.

Katarina stood staring at them, speechless, more confused than ever. "You're completely soaked; it was such a heavy downpour! I imagine you were caught in it outside with no shelter in sight since you're sodden," she went on to say, biting her bottom lip in an effort to appear nonchalant and disinterested in their whereabouts at the time. "Such a torrential downpour coming all of a sudden, can take you completely by surprise, it's so unexpected. But there wasn't any kind of shelter at all?" She was realizing where they had been at the time but she held her tongue. An internal struggle was raging in her breast and she was torn between wanting to say yes and giving in to him and wanting to say no and sending them away. "Holy Mother of God, help me! Tell me what I should do! I don't know what to do, truly I don't! I've never found myself in such circumstances. Oh Wistin! Wistin!" she moaned soundlessly. She was about to tell him that it did not please her to welcome an outsider in her home, at that hour, in such a state. And with him! She was afraid that Wistin would lose his temper and threaten to leave her house, just as he had already done when he left his mother's house. At the same time, she was unwilling to tell him that they were both welcome in her home. It all went against tradition, the customs she had been brought up with and which she herself had inculcated in her daughter. She thought of Saverju and this was enough to make her withdraw within her shell whenever she felt she was losing courage and being feeble enough to give in.

"Stand firm, woman! Don't even back down one step from what you believe in! If you give in, what sort of woman

128

does that make you? Not my wife, that's for sure!" she could hear Saverju thundering in her heart. She remembered how long before, Saverju had hardened his heart against Susanna and never gave in to his love for her till the day he died. She recalled Susanna approaching his deathbed and asking, for the last time, to know where her baby was. Katarina brought it all to mind, as if it was happening once more before her eyes, on this rainy night, though the heavy downpour had now passed.

Wistin and Antonja came inside and stood waiting.

Katarina, too, waited to see what was going to happen next.

"Antonja is the girl I'm courting, and she's staying here tonight," Wistin told his grandmother in a bantering tone. "I don't suppose you'll refuse. I know you're too kind-hearted for that." He turned to Antonja, telling her, "I'm not just saying this to her face but you won't find another woman like my gran, really! She's too kind-hearted for words! She's got a heart of gold and she can tell stories too..."

"She's going to sleep here? Your young woman?" Katarina exclaimed, unwilling to believe her ears.

"Yes here, to spend the night, my young woman. You heard right, Gran."

"But, but, how can you? You know very well dear, this thing just won't..." Katarina replied brokenly.

"It won't do, you mean."

"No, dear, it won't do," she replied, suddenly changing her tone of voice and plucking up the courage to show him plainly that she did not want to.

Wistin simply turned to Antonja and continued, "I was saying that my gran, amongst other things, knows how to tell a story. She used to tell me many. Listen to this one. Once upon a time there was a young woman looking for shelter to spend the night, and she knocked on the door of a kindly priest..."

Antonja looked at him, wanting to tell him that she knew that story because he had already recounted it to her.

129

"If, if this young woman, your young woman..." Katarina stammered.

"Antonja, Gran, that's her name, Antonja," Wistin cut in abruptly.

"If Antonja's going to sleep here tonight, her mother and father must be quite distracted with worry! They don't know what could have happened to her, at this time of night, and after such a storm as we've had. Isn't it better...?"

"No, better nothing, Gran!" he stopped her flow. "The best thing is for Antonja to sleep here tonight. Don't worry, she'll sleep in one room and I'll sleep in another. The important thing is that she'll have a roof over her head."

"Her parents' roof, dear, that's best for her. Actually, it's the only roof that will do."

"Once upon a time there was a young woman, and this young woman was with child, and she looked for someplace where she could find shelter..." Wistin began once more, assuming the tone of one telling stories.

"Once upon a time, Wistin, once upon a time indeed," Katarina interrupted him in the tone of one who has taken umbrage. "God understands everything that happens, only God does, dear. We can only see the surface of things. It's the roots that matter, the roots under the soil, and only God sees those."

Wistin drew closer to his grandmother and hugged her to him, kissing her fondly.

Antonja had remained silent meanwhile, but all of a sudden she burst into tears. She dragged her hands through her hair, tugging it so hard it nearly came out in clumps, and screamed, "What am I going to do? What am I going to do?"

"Someone must go to her parents and... I don't know. I don't know what comes next. God will tell him what to do and say," Katarina suggested. She was still feeling bewildered and could not think of another option.

"And who can go and tell them?" Wistin asked.

"Don't you know who, you too?" Katarina replied.

"Yes, I know to whom you're referring. But he'll be asleep now, or about to turn in."

"Yes, yes, that's true, but, but for a priest like him there's no such thing as prescribed hours for doing anything. Go, just go to him Wistin, and see what he has to say, so you too will find out what it means to be a man of God."

***

Tumas and Ester were sitting at the kitchen table, staring vacantly into space, dumbstruck, worried to death, waiting to hear a knock on the door and seeing their daughter enter, and hoping it would happen any time soon. The expression on their face could be better seen in the *chiaroscuro* light of the lamp that stood between them where a fly was buzzing around because it too was not sleepy and was drawn to any light. Sometimes it descended to the table and Antonja's father would swat it away angrily, displaying more anger than usual. Time passed but Antonja did not come. During the storm, they continually asked themselves where she could have gone and with whom. Sometimes they reassured each other that she was a sensible girl and knew how to take care of herself when she found herself on her own, far from home, or with her friends. They had always warned her to choose her friends wisely, other young women who were good girls and she would then ask them how she could discern who was a good friend or not.

"You can always see clearly in the light of the lamp, daughter," her father would always warn her. "Good friends are those who don't steal away all the goodness of your upbringing. Those are truly good friends."

When Ester had discovered Antonja's love for Wistin, she had immediately told her that she wished her to court some other young man. She warned her off without any prevarication. "It's only puppy love, that's all, my dear daughter. It's like a gust of wind that blows itself out, leaving you with nothing. Listen to me, and listen well! I'll make you see it my way, by hook or by crook! I'm the only one who knows what's good for you, not you! And your father thinks exactly the same. Isn't that so, husband?" she had gone on, turning to her husband and expecting him to answer her in support.

"Yes, yes of course you're right," Tumas had replied half-asleep, with his head down on his crossed arms across the kitchen table, under the dim light of the lamp.

His wife instantly realized he was half asleep from his tone of voice. "Do you know what I'm saying or not? Are you awake or asleep? Huh! Some support you are! Things would come to a pretty pass if I had to rely on you!"

"Didn't I say yes? Do I need to make myself hoarse to agree with you?

"Is that all the interest you can muster in our daughter?"

"She's old enough to know what's what. She's not some silly naive little girl. She knows what's good for her and also what's wrong for her. You can tell her once, twice, but then she must fend for herself. That's what I think."

"Well, you're wrong to think so! Is that how you were brought up? Some upbringing you've had!"

"I was brought up in the same way you were, wife, in these same village streets, at the very same time as you were. We're much of an age, you and I. Am I right?"

"You're half asleep! Go and sleep the other half then, and don't mention how old the two of us are, because you'll add on several years to me in a trice!"

"I'm off to bed then," Tumas had declared, "and as for you, Antonja, take care of yourself. Don't let your heart rule your head because – do you know what will happen? The same thing that happened to me!"

"Aren't you ashamed of yourself, saying such things?" his wife's voice was shrill with anger.

In spite of all this however, both her mother and father were in agreement that Wistin was not the young man with whom their daughter should fall in love and later marry. They did not want him.

"Now mind, as soon as Antonja comes, be careful how you speak to her. She made a mistake, a big mistake, and she knows it as well as we do. That's what I think," Tumas told Ester. "But it will do no good if you deal too harshly with her."

"Give in to her, then? Is that what you're saying? Let her come back home as if this were a hotel open all hours, and let her go to bed just like that, as if nothing has happened?" his wife told Tumas, enraged.

"She must be sopping wet!" he exclaimed.

"There, you see, when it suits you, you can use your head! Just keep thinking along those lines and you'll soon find out how right I am."

"Meaning?" he asked her scornfully.

"Meaning I'll soon not leave her in any doubt that she won't get away with it. This won't happen again. That's what I'll tell her."

"And then?"

"And then...," Ester repeated in bafflement, pausing to think. "Then... I don't know. But at least I'll have done my duty."

"So what?"

"So what? I expect her to heed my words. That's all! I know Antonja through and through. She'll give in, sooner or later."

"I hope she'll give in."

There was no sound, no movement. The time that had elapsed now served to slowly dissipate their anger and have it replaced with worry.

"Do you think something's happened to her?" moaned Ester.

"There, do you see? Maybe all that's happened hasn't been her fault."

"I'm going out to look for her," Tumas' wife declared, making up her mind. "I can't keep waiting here on tenterhooks."

"Where are you going?"

"I don't know, but I can't bear to stay here waiting impatiently. I'm going to leave the door ajar. And as for you, mind you don't fall asleep."

"I'm very worried, too, even though I don't show it. I suffer but bottle it all up inside, that's the way I'm made," he whispered to her, letting his head droop down once more onto his crossed arms across the kitchen table.

Ester made the rounds of all the main streets and drew near to the church as well, but there was no sign of people anywhere. She was reluctant to peer inside the wine tavern, the only place still showing a light, where the usual patrons could be heard talking and drinking wine. She was quite certain that her daughter would not set foot inside taverns. With her heart pounding and her breath coming in short shallow gasps, she turned tail and went back home.

The door was closed.

"She must have come back!" she thought. "I left the door ajar." She knocked on the door and waited. As soon as the door cracked open she shouted, "Antonja!"

Her husband met her in the doorway, telling her not to shout. The night was fast drawing in.

"Has Antonja come back?" she asked him.

"Fr. Grejbel's here." He whispered back. "He's just arrived this minute."

"Fr. Grejbel!" Ester called out, going to the kitchen and taking a seat at the table. "Tell me! Tell me what's happened to her! What is it? Where is she?"

"Now calm down, calm down and set your mind at rest. Nothing's happened to her," Fr. Grejbel reassured her.

In the meantime, her husband had gone back to his seat at the table with a cup of coffee steaming in front of him in an effort to avert sleep. After a few moments he rose again and made another two cups of coffee, for his wife and the priest.

"Then tell me, please tell me, Fr. Grejbel."

"If I tell you what's happened, are you going to berate her?"

"There, see what the priest told you?" Tumas sneered. He was glad that the priest seemed to be vindicating his position. "See how we agree on this, him and me?"

"Stay out of it, you," his wife replied angrily.

"Calm down, calm down," the priest urged her. "For now it's enough to know that nothing's happened to Antonja."

"And what about the storm?"

"Well she got thoroughly wet caught in a downpour! That's what happens when you're caught in a downpour!" Fr. Grejbel tried to pass it off with a smile.

"Oh dear Lord! And where was she?"

"Now if I tell you that, are you going to heap censure on her?"

"Oh, Fr. Grejbel, you're beginning to confuse me. I'm glad that nothing's happened to her. And that's why I feel I don't want to censure her in any way. But, but, I don't know how it's going to end."

"Where was she, where do you think she was?"

"Don't tell me my daughter was down in the Valley! Holy Mother of God!" Ester cried out. "Everywhere but there! Not the Valley!"

"Many beautiful flowers grow in the Valley, and there are also many ancient trees, and there are ponds and caves dating back to prehistoric times," her husband interjected. "The Valley is a beautiful place, wife. One day I'll take you down there, would you like that?"

Ester did not want to acknowledge her husband with a reply, in order to show her disparagement, but she could not keep back a sneer, "The Valley, huh? What do the likes of you know about the Valley?"

"I know, indeed I know. Wasn't it in those parts that I met you for the first time? Don't you remember?" her husband replied.

Fr. Grejbel paused and smiled, and then he went on talking soothingly to Ester. "Yes, she was down in the Valley."

"Oh dear Lord! Dear Lord!" she exclaimed. "Then ... if she was down there in the Valley, she couldn't have been alone."

"In the Valley there are birds, frogs, and sometimes mosquitoes, swarming above the surface of the ponds," Tumas interjected scornfully once more. "Pesky mosquitoes, always circling around trying to bite you. Everyone says they're the greatest insect pests. Mosquitoes from those parts."

"Just like you, a pest," his wife spoke contemptuously, her tone deliberately cruel.

Fr. Grejbel smiled ruefully again. "We're only human, that's how we've always been and how we'll always be. It's nothing new."

"So she wasn't alone, then," she stated once more.

The priest shook his head in agreement.

"So she was with him."

"With him," the priest assented.

"With Susanna's Wistin, then. No and no! It cannot be! I don't want her to stay with him. Understand?"

"I'm trying to understand why."

"Why don't you thank the priest for his pains, leaving his house at this time of night and coming here to reassure us?"

"Thank you, thank you very much, Fr. Grejbel. Of course I want to thank him a lot! But, but... I say, did Katarina welcome them in her own home?"

"Did you want her to turn them away?"

"I don't know, I don't know! Maybe she should have sent Antonja home, to her parents' house straightaway. This is where she should be, only here."

"Antonja wanted to come home, but she was afraid. There was nowhere else she could spend the night."

"I had no idea Katarina was the sort of woman who could come to this."

"You can say this after she welcomed her in her own home and gave her a bed for the night?" Tumas was astounded.

"Don't you interfere, you! Let me do the talking! I'm her mother, no other!"

"Katarina is a mother too," the priest observed calmly.

"A mother! Katarina is a mother. Susanna's mother. Need I say more?"

"I've told you all I had to say, and I was at liberty to do so. And do you know why? Because up to now, there are still those who have faith in us," Fr. Grejbel told her gravely.

"Faith in you, you mean," she was quick to respond.

"No, no. Faith in you two, as well, and this means that all is not lost. Just think it over now, decide for yourselves and then, if it pleases you, tell me. If one loses faith, one loses everything. Let me say one thing," Fr. Grejbel went on, addressing Ester directly. "If your daughter loses faith in you, it will be you who will lose your daughter and she will lose her mother."

Ester rose from her seat, smouldering but trying to control herself, standing straight with both palms pressing against the table's surface, and facing the priest she declared, "Fr. Grejbel, if that happens, I'll lose everything. Don't I have full rights over my daughter? Or is it my daughter who can command me? Who is the mother and who is the daughter? If my daughter wants a fight she's welcome to it! If need be, if she doesn't bow her head to me, she will have to leave this house!"

"As for me, I will hold my peace. I pray that you and your husband will see fit to leave the door ajar. It's still not too late. If the door slams shut though..."

"If the door slams shut..." Ester repeated.

"Well then, whoever's inside will be safe inside and whoever's still outside will be left out in the cold."

"Meaning I'll lose my daughter?"

Fr. Grejbel bowed his head and clasped his hands in front of him, on the table edge, and remained silent. Then he told them, "They sent me here to you. I came immediately. I've done my part and will continue to do so till the end. I'm going to try and keep the oil lamp burning. When it starts flickering and dimming I'll begin to have some fears. And when it goes out, oh then, when it goes out I'll have to admit that it's gone completely dark."

"What Fr. Grejbel? The lamp oil that's left? What are you saying?"

"The faith that's left. Not much is left. Antonja can remain here and you won't lose her if you accept Wistin."

"Wistin isn't far away from the Port's doorway to the world, Fr. Grejbel. That's where his thoughts keep turning to – he wants to take ship and leave these shores. And he'll take our Antonja with him, carrying her far, far away from here," Ester burst in, her voice full of anger and fear in equal measure. "Holy Mother of God!"

"If you two can shift your position slightly, I'll be able to convince Wistin to think again. Wistin truly loves your daughter. That way, both of them will be able to stay here. Think well on this!"

***

Early next morning, Ester rose from their bed and invited her husband to accompany her.

"Where are you going, so very early in the day?" Tumas asked her in surprise.

"Go and get dressed and come with me, and I'll tell you. Anyway, can't you guess?"

"You're joking!"

"Come, let's go. That woman, his grandmother, needs to learn that she shouldn't have let Antonja and that one sleep at her house. The storm has passed and Antonja can't wave that excuse anymore. A new day has dawned and she should have returned home by now. I should think she's no longer soaked to the skin this morning! If she made a mistake yesterday, she needs to suffer the consequences today."

"Maybe they're still asleep. Don't forget, it's still early."

"It's still early only for lazy people. I'm referring to you. Come on, let's go."

"I'm not going with you."

"You're not coming? What sort of father are you?"

"I don't want the oil lamp to go out. Didn't you pay attention to those words, yesterday?"

"Oh, so you understand things when you want? How well you've learnt to speak!"

"No, no, wife, I've learnt to listen."

"But I, if you must know, don't want to listen to anybody. I don't need anyone's advice. I know what I have to do and what to expect my daughter to do. Antonja has made a mistake and I'll forgive her. She spent the night out of this house, and I'll try to forget and to forgive her. She went down into the Valley, oh... I don't know, I don't know if I can bring myself to forgive her. And she continued loving that lad. No, no, things can't keep going on like this now. I can't forgive her this time."

"Well then, you must go on your own," Tumas spoke with decision.

"I'm going on my own. It would be good to have you along but without you it will be even better!"

"At least we seem to agree on something."

Ester was not sure where Katarina lived. She asked for directions, mentioned Susanna's name and people told her where to go straightaway. She knocked on the door once, waited for a few moments and then knocked again. No one answered the door. She looked around in the hope of seeing someone who could tell her where Katarina would be at that time. It was far too early for a female villager of her age to be out and about outside her home. Unless she had gone to the church, to hear daily mass and maybe stopped to chat to people near the market. Some street hawkers would already be doing the rounds to serve those patrons who only slept for a few hours and would start the day early. She went back to the door and knocked again, once, twice, harder than before.

"She's not at home. She went out," a neighbour told Ester, opening her window when she heard Ester knocking loudly next door.

"She went out?"

"Yes," the other woman answered shortly, closing her window again.

"Where do you think she went?"

"I don't know though I can imagine where. Where do you think? To her daughter, of course!"

"She's at Susanna's house, then."

"Yes," the neighbour's voice came from behind the window, plainly cutting short the conversation.

Several thoughts chased each other in Ester's mind. A mixture of rage and fear kept her company as she walked all the way to Susanna's house. "As soon as I find her I'll give that granny a piece of my mind. And her daughter too. And him. To all of them. And Antonja too, ninny that she is, throwing herself on a good-for-nothing! She too won't escape my tongue-lashing."

She knocked on Susanna's door and looked up to the balcony, expecting someone to come and peek out. She knocked again and then saw Katarina in the doorway.

"Come in, come in," Katarina told her.

Ester made her way in but stopped and waited just inside. She looked around vacantly. The silence in there startled her and her bewilderment grew when Katarina did not speak and, as Ester noted, merely crushed a handkerchief in her hand. She was crying.

"Come in, please, come in," Katarina invited her in again.

Ester stood still, not moving an inch.

A few moments later, Susanna came out into the hallway from another room. The two women gazed long and hard into each other's eyes, without exchanging one word. Susanna's eyes appeared to be red from weeping, even at that distance.

All of a sudden, Susanna drew in a deep breath which sounded loud in that silence, and Katarina burst into tears.

"What's happened? Mother of God, what's happened?" Ester cried out in fear.

Susanna walked forward, plucked up her courage and drew closer to Ester. After a few moments she embraced her, with tears coursing down her cheeks.

"What's happened? Mother of God!" Ester kept crying, taken aback by Susanna's action.

Susanna embraced her harder and kept sobbing.

"They've gone, they left early this morning. I don't know where they've gone. It was early," Katarina babbled brokenly, her voice hoarse with crying. "I spent half the night on my rocking chair, staring into space and praying hard. When I could not bear to sit there any longer I went to lie down on my bed, staring at the ceiling unable to sleep for a long, long time. Then I finally nodded off. When I woke up the next morning everything felt normal. I went to wake Wistin up and then Antonja. I'd already set the kettle to boil to make tea and had prepared some *biskuttelli* for them. But then I realized I was alone in the house. They had left."

"They left? Both of them?" Ester interjected.

Susanna wordlessly nodded assent.

Katarina went on. "I started shouting and screaming on the threshold, I don't know why but I needed to do something. Then I went out into the street and walked and ran, calling out their names, 'Wistin!', 'Antonja!' I didn't even feel embarrassed, I just didn't know what to do, or what I was doing! I only knew one thing, wanted only one thing: to see them again." She paused and then spoke again in a changed tone of voice. "I welcomed them into my home, took care of their every need before they went to bed, and prayed for them, but see what's happened now."

"They left? Together?" Ester asked again.

"Yes, together."

"But how do you know for sure?"

"Because they looked so very much in love with each other."

Ester appeared to be less than pleased but she tried to hide her feelings as much as possible.

Katarina saw her reaction and was about to say something but she quickly bit her lip and bowed her head.

Susanna and Ester walked towards the dining room together. Katarina walked slightly behind them, between them, with her hands resting on their shoulders. None of them could muster any strength to talk. Katarina wished she had enough courage to tell them to make it up and go to church and make a vow, the same vow, to St. Joseph. She imagined Ester going first, on her own, quietly but rather unwillingly, with some shreds of anger still simmering inside her directed at Susanna and her son. And then she imagined Susanna, also going on her own to make her vow, her heart free of any trace of anger. She imagined them meeting each other unexpectedly, arriving in front of St. Joseph's niche at the very same moment, and looking upon each other's face in astonishment. The two of them would be wishing for the very same thing, Katarina was envisioning.

Street noises, the usual sounds first thing in the morning, could be heard already, heralding the start of another ordinary working day.

Chapter 6

"I heard right! I thought so!" Katarina exclaimed in a loud voice that could be heard from the room next door. She shut the window and pulled the curtains closed, leaving only a narrow gap between them to allow some light to enter the room.

"Mother! Mother, what is it?" Susanna asked her.

"Fr. Grejbel is at the door. He's just got down from a *karozzin*. Go and open the door! He must have brought us some news, then! Dear Lord!" Katarina still spoke loudly. Against her will, she was still staying with her daughter after Wistin and Antonja had left her own house and had not returned. Ever since Arturu and Susanna had separated shortly after getting married and had then become reconciled, she had hoped that her strenuous efforts had proved successful and there was nothing else to be asked of her. She had felt certain she could now live quietly at home, glad to have served as an exemplary grandmother who could mend things, demonstrating how one should live, by word and deed, and by holding her peace. St. Joseph had supported her at every step and she had remained grateful and beholden to him. It was in front of a crowd of people at the celebration held for Arturu and Susanna that she had shown everybody that St. Joseph had never abandoned her. She had addressed him in prayer: "Today you have granted me contentment, and I am completely content. Now I've finally walked all the way down my allotted path. There's nothing more I can expect in this world. When it pleases you, call me to you. Over there I can continue my story." That had been her prayer and it had come to pass since at the time it looked as if the storm had passed. She had ended her prayers saying: "If you can, please save me a place next to Saverju in Heaven... so that I won't be alone." From that day onwards she had been convinced that her daughter's family could walk down the rest of their way without any obstacles till it came to a natural end.

Some time later, Katarina had changed her tune and her prayers to St. Joseph ran on these lines: "Some time ago, when all was plain sailing, I told you that you could call me to you whenever it pleased you. I never imagined that storm clouds would gather and threaten everything once more, several times over. If you please, have patience with me and ask Our Lord to leave me down here a while longer to see if I can mend more of all these broken lives. How can I come to you if I can't set my mind at rest that I've left everything in place behind me? Though I'd be in Heaven, my mind would still be down here! I'd be up there and my mind would be down here! No, no! If you can, please see to it. I don't want to see all my happiness evaporating even in Heaven! I had thought it was all settled but see, all of a sudden there's thunder and lightning and now the storm is raging."

"Mother! Mother! What's happened?" Susanna exclaimed again. She took off her apron, wiped her hands clean since they had become messy with kitchen chores and went quickly to the door. "Lady of Mercy, let it be good news!" She opened the door and looked at the priest but then her head drooped. She waited for him to enter and then closed the door behind him. He walked on alone towards the dining room and stopped to wait for her. She followed him, approaching him shyly as if she felt embarrassed walking in her own house.

Katarina was waiting for him, standing straight in the centre of the room, a stricken look in her eyes, and with her rosary beads dangling from her hands which were clasped together. She went up to him, kissed his hand and without a word motioned with her hands and head, inviting him to sit down.

Fr. Grejbel pulled a chair from around the table and sat down, rearranging his cassock and dropping his hat in his lap.

"We're like two souls in Purgatory, me and my daughter, look. Two souls waiting for prayers to be said for us, hoping for an early remission. Two statues staring vacantly, praying for mercy, like those statues you see along country lanes. We've spent all our time looking at each other, waiting and praying. Nothing else, nothing but that. Two souls left only with a flicker of hope."

The priest looked at her and leaned forward to squeeze her hand in sympathy.

"I pray, Fr. Grejbel, I pray. I've never stopped praying. And I made Susanna keep praying with me. Isn't that how I brought her up? But then the children's children... The branches spring from the tree trunk and the tree trunk is joined to the roots. But it seems every branch grows its own roots! But there, I'd better keep my mouth closed before I utter some sacrilege! Lord forgive me! We've prayed hard but as you can see, we're still here, alone. I'm mostly sorry for her, look at her, poor thing, she looks like Our Lady of Sorrows. My poor daughter!"

Susanna remained in the doorway as if too shy to approach him. He read her mind and rose, going up to her in an encouraging manner. She walked by his side and took a seat around the table. Silence fell for a few moments.

"Antonja has returned to the village," he began. "She went back home. And needless to say, her mother and father welcomed her and made much of her. They themselves asked me to come and give you the news. She told them all that had happened and they understood her. Antonja and Wistin spent all that time going from one place to another without knowing where to go. At first she agreed to follow his thoughts through and escape with him. But she became frightened and lost heart and told Wistin she wanted to return home. And as they were walking on, she stopped and turned back. He wanted her to continue on the road with him..."

"So it was all Wistin's idea, wasn't it?" Katarina questioned him though she was sure of the answer as well.

The priest nodded assent.

"Did she know where they were going?" she insisted.

"She knew, but... perhaps... well, perhaps not. Let me tell you all I know," he replied.

"Then Wistin must have had a plan all along," Katarina burst in again.

"Antonja didn't want to go on with him but then she gave in and they went on. They arrived in the Port area. It was neither an easy nor a short journey for them. But Wistin does not give up easily and he wanted to get there."

"So he got her there then, in the Port area," Katarina interjected. "It seems that's where his heart lies now."

"And they looked for a hotel where they could stay for a few days."

"Then Wistin was carrying money. He took money with him," Katarina observed.

"He had enough money to stay in a hotel but they ended up not staying in any."

"So he must have saved up some of the money he'd managed to earn, to fall back on when he needed it. He had a plan all along," Katarina affirmed.

"They didn't stay at a hotel and it seems they slept outdoors, here and there, and they spent their days wandering around until Wistin noticed that amongst the boats teeming in the harbour there was one that had been tied up for a long time, lying apart, as if it didn't belong to anyone. Suddenly he became convinced he could take it. He could use it to make the journey he had long made up his mind to undertake, there and then, with Antonja to accompany him."

"He had made up his mind to make that journey from a long time before?"

"Yes, Katarina," Fr. Grejbel answered her straightaway. "I think Wistin wanted to leave here, once and for all. But then

146

Antonja made him think twice about it, even though she herself was not averse to leaving."

Susanna, in the meantime, still had her head down on the table weeping into her large handkerchief in silent grief.

"He told Antonja, 'Look, let's take this boat and leave the village behind, and all those people who didn't want us to come here. You'll soon see how happy you'll be, happier than you've ever been. All your wishes will be fulfilled, all your dreams will come true, all of them, just wait and see. But you'll have to wait a bit.' Anyway, he told her something like that. Antonja kept insisting she wasn't up to it but he kept on at her. And they approached the boat and he pulled it in close to the quay and helped her climb aboard. She was frightened and he held her hand and helped her get down in it. The sudden sway of the boat as she got in terrified her but Wistin took up the oars and quickly rowed the boat away."

"They left the quay? They were leaving? Going out of the Port?" Katarina was astounded. "And then what?"

"And then they both rowed the boat. 'Row, you row too Antonja. Every pull on the oars you make is like a breath of fresh air,' he told her. And frightened as she was, Antonja took up an oar and rowed as best as she could. But all of a sudden she decided she didn't want to make this journey but she was too frightened to tell him, and she rowed on. 'The Port, the open doorway of the Port is there, we'll soon get to it,' he coaxed her, 'and from there onwards we'll be free. Row on, just row on, and don't look back anymore. From now onwards, their village is no longer ours. In fair weather we'll row together and when there's bad weather about, leave it all to me. I can weather storms on my own. I'm used to it. I was born in the middle of one. Don't you trust me? Didn't you tell me you had great faith in me? From today onwards no one will interfere in our lives anymore. Our life will be our own, all of it, all the time. We'll have our own home and we'll be in command, just us. And you'll be able to stay beside me from morn till night, just like it is now.' That's what he told her."

147

"Is that what he told her? But how could he?" Katarina mourned.

"This doesn't surprise me at all, Fr. Grejbel," Susanna spoke up. "This is wholly his father's character. Brave alright and adventurous, but scornful of the village and wanting to show he could achieve something none of our forebears had accomplished, neither his nor much less mine. Wistin resembles Stiefnu right down to the ground. Isn't that what people always told me? How much he resembles his father! He's not mine. I have my shortcomings of course but they're not that sort. They're different, and have nothing to do with the sea and ships. Dealing with the land, the Valley, that's where my shortcomings lie."

"Don't speak like that, Susanna. You've done the best you could. And all is not lost," Fr. Grejbel sympathized and tried to bring her comfort. "All that's happened means they still love each other."

"Oh, my dear daughter! Imagine your father hearing you speak now!" Katarina exclaimed, cutting her short.

Susanna gestured to silence her mother. She hungered to hear more and had many questions to put to the priest. She had begun to fear that she would never set eyes on her son anymore and would never have the chance to speak with him again. Wistin had kept up his extreme reserve with her, had remained hurt and offended, withdrawn, almost embarrassed in front of her, and he was curt when he spoke to her, all his words devoid of any mannerly aspect. He did not even want to look her in the face on the few occasions he needed to address her. He avoided her gaze.

Fr. Grejbel went on with his account of events. "Antonja didn't want to go on. 'I want to get off the boat! I want to get off! This very minute! Get me out of this boat! Turn back!' she cried. He tried to calm her down and give her some courage, telling her, 'We're there, look, we're nearly there! Look there, that's the other side of the harbour, the other side of the world!' But she went on shouting, "Let me out, Let me out! Otherwise, I'll jump into the sea, that's what I'm going to do, jump in right now,' Antonja screamed. But Wistin kept on rowing ahead all the same. He was sure Antonja wouldn't carry out her threat: she admired him and was fearful. 'I'm going to jump into the sea if you don't take me back to the quayside,' she threatened him once more. 'Can you swim at least? The sea is very deep you know. There are many large fish at the bottom ready to eat anyone,' he answered in return. With these words he reassured himself that Antonja wouldn't jump overboard, and he continued rowing out to sea. 'If you're going to keep rowing out to sea, I'm going to jump in,' she warned him again. 'You can't jump in, Antonja,' he called her bluff, rowing harder than ever. He grabbed the oar she still held and rowed faster on his own. 'I'm jumping in!' she cried. 'Don't forget you can't swim!' 'I'm still going to jump. See if I don't. You'll see if you don't turn back. I want to go.' 'You want to go back home? How can you?' he challenged her. 'I want to go back on land, and I'll decide where to go afterwards. I want to go where I want, Wistin, I want to decide for myself!' Antonja's cries carried clearly across the water and people on board ships in the vicinity and on the quayside heard her, thinking they were hearing an argument where a ferryman refused to let people disembark where they wished to or that an argument over the fare had arisen between the ferryman and his passengers. All the ferrymen knew that their livelihood depended on the goodwill of each other. Every spot of trouble encountered by one of them involved them all, too. That was what they were used to."

"And so Wistin had to turn back," concluded Katarina, as if she was making up and telling a story to try and imagine what could have occurred. "He had to turn back, against his will. Didn't he?"

"Wistin had to stop and turn the boat round back to shore, taking Antonja to the quay, and from there she found her way back home to the village. The two of them parted ways over there. She had triumphed over him."

"Wistin! Wistin! But where is Wistin, where is he?" Susanna wailed.

"Now don't worry Susanna! Wistin will come back one day, and you'll be quite content," Fr. Grejbel soothed her.

"But I want to know where he is now, that's what I want to know! To set my mind at rest," Susanna explained. "Tell me, tell me, Fr. Grejbel."

"I would like you to believe every single word I said, Susanna," he affirmed. "Won't you rest assured, take my word? I'm telling you everything, and all I'm saying is true. You'll see."

"But this isn't enough. I'm the only one who knows what my heart is feeling. A mother can only be a mother alone. Every grief hurts you but the grief that comes from inside is overwhelming, immeasurable! A grief striking you from within is endless. Please try to understand me this time too, Fr. Grejbel, understand me please! You were the person who saved me up to now, and I'm pleading, save me this time too! I'm drowning in the Port, me too..."

The priest did not try to stop her flow but wanted to hear her out.

"In my own Port, I feel I'm also drowning." She paused, crushed her handkerchief between her hands and gathering up all the strength she had left, faced him, "Fr. Grejbel, I want to know where Wistin is. I want to know."

"Not like that, daughter, not like that!" Katarina remonstrated with her. "Merciful God, you shouldn't speak to him like that!"

"I need to know! You know where he is, don't you?" Susanna demanded, ignoring her mother.

Fr. Grejbel remained silent. He had learnt, from a long time before, that his pastoral work depended on his skill to speak when there was a need to do so, with carefully thought out words, and to keep silent when the need arose. Just one mistake, once, and it all went wrong. His was not an easy job and sometimes he found it hard to sleep when his mind kept turning over the thought that he could have said more than he should, or the opposite, that he could have said less than he should. Ever since the Bishop had summoned him, before he had to leave the village, and the country, he had learnt a lot. Meanwhile, he strived to remember all he had ever learnt. Perhaps the Bishop had served him well indeed and he had reminded Fr. Grejbel that the world was not as he, Fr. Grejbel, knew it. However, in spite of that he remained the man he always was and he wished to remain so till the end.

"I pray you, Fr. Grejbel, on all my faith in God, and on my great faith in you. Tell me. Do you know where Wistin is or not?"

"Susanna, I'll answer you: yes, I know."

"I believe you. As I've always done," she spoke in a very decided tone of voice. "So then, tell me where he is." Unbidden, the scene played out at her father's deathbed rose before her eyes, and she saw herself approaching his side, frightened but holding on to her last shred of hope, asking him to tell her quickly where her baby was. And her father, drawing his last breath, had refused to tell her.

Fr. Grejbel bowed his head and remained silent.

"Tell me! Tell me if you don't want to see all that you yourself have built in all this time, come tumbling down about our ears! Tell me!"

"I can't tell you," he answered her gently. "The day will come when I'll be able to tell you, but for now..."

"It's still too early then, too early," Katarina interjected suddenly.

"For now I can't speak out," the priest affirmed.

"In the meantime, did he come and speak to you?" Susanna insisted.

Fr. Grejbel remained silent.

"Don't ask him anymore, daughter. Show some prudence. What more can this man do? He's a priest. And he's human after all, just like us. He's not more of a man just because he's a priest. He's got God at his side but he's not God! Not God Himself! Why do you expect him to have more power than he commands as a man and as a priest? You're tempting him to overstep his duty. And if you're tempting him you're sinning! Just believe him, that's all, believe him," Katarina lamented with great conviction. She spoke harshly to her daughter in a tone of voice she had never used with her before. Then she turned to the priest and told him, "I'm not going to teach you patience. That's the best thing in the circumstances and so, if you please, have patience with my daughter in this instance too," she pleaded. "Maybe she doesn't know what she's saying in her state at the moment. Please, forgive her."

"Wistin was born to grieve me and only make me worry. Even before he was born he was a source of great unhappiness for me. A whole sorry tale with Stiefnu that began in the Valley where he was conceived," Susanna spoke mechanically, as if reciting a story whose details she did not want to forget. "I recall the exact hour, time and day, as if it was yesterday. I remember what the weather was like. I was still young. All that I had written down for me was to bring Wistin into the world at the appointed time, and then not set eyes on him again, not even knowing who he was, and to spend many a long year dreaming about him, far away from me, imagining what he looked like, wanting him by my side! And then, after my father died, we found him, brought him up, and gave him everything, everything we owned and desired. Perhaps... well maybe after my separation from Arturu, I ended up getting together again with my husband also for his sake. I wanted to give Wistin everything, even the father he didn't have, and I wanted to make it up to him, all that he'd lost out on as a child. I spent many years with him, till he grew up. And then my husband died and Wistin's father still kept his distance. I had long suspected that Wistin hadn't remained my boy. He was wholly mine – except in his heart of hearts."

"One day he'll come back, he'll be the little boy you had once more, Susanna," Fr. Grejbel comforted her. "This season will pass."

"Was there something, Fr. Grejbel, you must tell me, was there something I had to do and I didn't do it? Was there something I messed up? Is he being bad on purpose? After all that I've done for him, when did I ever let him down? He's sick of me now? He's unhappy that it was I who brought him into the world? From the open spaces of the Valley and the rooms in the orphanage where he spent his childhood, I was able to provide him a home like everyone else. My mother welcomed him, and what my father failed to do was done by her, when the time was ripe. My mother more than made up for everything! So, after all this, don't I even have the right to know where he is, know right here and now?" she demanded hotly.

"You do have every right, but, but..."

"It's too early, daughter, the time has not yet come. That's what he's trying to tell you," Katarina tried to pour oil on troubled waters.

"That's it," Fr. Grejbel confirmed with a relieved smile.

"So Wistin made his escape from here, and he'd been planning it for some time, meaning to take that young woman with him, wanting to escape from the village and getting to the Port. He's been drawn to something there for a long time. Like an enormous magnet which we lack over here. There's nothing we can do about it, then." Susanna paused to think, her forehead creased in worry, and coming to a decision she announced, "I'll go and look for him at the Port. I think he's escaped from here to stay in that neighbourhood." She looked at Fr. Grejbel as she spoke, trying to catch the reaction that would flit across his face, since he knew where Wistin was to be found.

The priest was careful not to let his expression change.

"If you go after him you'll lose him for sure. You'll just make him harden his attitude and distance himself further from you. Don't go, don't go anywhere. Just wait and pray," Katarina was quite adamant with her. "And anyway, who told you that's where you'd find him?"

"I think that's where he is," Susanna answered.

"Be careful! Don't risk it! Don't forget, the Port is a wide open doorway. Do you want him to leave you by going through that doorway, daughter? If you find him and he sees you, that's what he'll do. You can't bring him back home against his will."

"We made him sick of us then, Mother, with the hoe and the rake, and with our traditional singing. The fields no longer smell fragrant to him. Going to church no longer appeals to him and we make him fed up when he sees us holding the rosary beads in our hands. He can't stand the way we dress. He can't stand the way we cook. We've managed to make him sick of us all! More than that! So I brought him into this world—"

"Our village, lying at the end of the world. Isn't that what you're saying?" Katarina tried to cut her short.

"So I brought him into this world to make him feel sick of it. How cruel! How cruel of me, wasn't it? But tell me, how could I have loved my son more? What more does this lad want?"

"Stop right there, daughter, stop it!" her mother scolded her. "Stop it! This kind of talk is beneath you. It ruins everything we've done till now. Why are you blaming yourself, and us? Let your father rest in peace forever now. And allow me to live the rest of my life at peace with God and with myself. If you're trying to find somewhere to lay the blame of all that's happening, blame the entire village, and beyond it too, but not here, no, no, my dear daughter, not here!"

"Don't worry, Katarina, don't worry, leave her alone. Let her have her say. It's a good thing she's speaking out, very brave of her. And it will relieve her too," Fr. Grejbel declared.

"Wistin wanted more," Susanna continued. "That's where children come from, we used to tell him. And that's where his father was, somewhere in the neighbourhood. He lives his own life, because that's his. And I don't want to have anything more to do with his life. What's happened is over and done with and whatever happened down in the Valley can remain in the Valley. But I'm just realizing, Fr. Grejbel, how much the Port is proving an attraction for Wistin, far more than I've ever been, with my house, my husband, and all the things I could offer. But he didn't want any of that," Susanna spoke with icy rage in her voice. "I have to admit it. I, too, have to surrender now."

"What do you mean, surrender, daughter?" Katarina snapped at her.

"Listen to me, Mother, and understand me properly – Wistin isn't ours!" Susanna shouted, and crossing her arms beneath her chest she laid down her head on the table, as if she was about to nod off.

"What are you saying? What do you mean? What's happened to you, daughter?"

"He's not ours, not yours, not your husband's. And he's not even mine."

"See what she's saying, Fr. Grejbel? What's happened to her, lately? I know she's grievously hurt, but where on earth did she find such things to say?" wondered Katarina. She paused and with a quick motion turned to face her daughter, drew in a sharp breath as if gathering all her strength and went on, "Look here, I'm your mother and you're my daughter. I'm ordering you to stop this nonsense. Don't let me start thinking that all I've done for you was in vain. Both I and your father did our best for you at the time, according to our lights. Every season has its own dictates. After all, Susanna, it was you yourself who grabbed life a bit too early!"

"Don't condemn me, Mother! Not now, not in my present situation!"

"Me condemn you? My Saverju walked on his allotted path according to what he believed in and did his best to mend matters."

"Mother, Mother! Wistin is Stiefnu's son," Susanna replied firmly. "He is mine, but at the same time he does not belong to me."

"I don't understand, daughter."

155

"Then it's still too early for you to understand, Mother. That's all," Susanna responded hastily, her tone plainly betraying her umbrage.

***

As soon as Wistin realized that people could hear all their shouting, streaming in waves from the boat, he hastily took Antonja alongside the quay and helped her off the boat. No sooner did her feet feel solid ground than Antonja took to her heels and sped on her way. She did not utter another word and Wistin was certain that it was all at an end between them. He was regretful and angry, and not a little hurt, but now he was aware that people had seen him coming back in the boat. It was quite possible that they would realize that the boat did not belong to him. Had he stolen it? Had he taken it without the owner's permission? Had somebody lent it to him? And who was this somebody? Over there, in those parts, everyone jealously guarded their boat. The boat was female, they all said. Who was Wistin, a new face in those ancient parts where a face was known for an entire lifetime? The boat which Wistin had grabbed, and on which he had taken Antonja in the hope of impressing her, had been tied up there like many other boats. Several men were employed as ferrymen and they used to tie up their boat there, day and night, without fear of having it stolen. No boat could be handled without every other ferryman learning of it. Every boat had an owner and it followed that it belonged to them all. They had all learnt, from a long time before, that their life in the Port was one integral whole. They could all succeed together but they could all, in the blink of an eye, fail together, too.

Wistin left the boat where he had found it, tied it up securely and hastily put in as much distance as he could manage between him and it. He roamed around the Port as if discovering a world he had never even dreamt of, but following an instinct that seemed to reveal he had long known it. Somehow, he felt the Port was home, and it had ever been thus. He loved it because it was the exact opposite of the Valley. His feelings towards the latter vacillated between love and hate. He peeped inside wine taverns but did not set foot inside them, wishing he could dip his hand inside his pocket in the sure knowledge that he had enough money to enter and drink a bottle of beer and stand someone a round. But he was uncertain whether he had enough money to eke out for the coming days though he had spent a long time secretly saving up the few coins he had managed to earn by running errands in the village.

He continued roving around, and then came upon a sheltered corner where the local beggars congregated at night, appearing in the gathering dusk and spreading the sacks and blankets they had on the ground, to sleep the night away. This was the only home they had. Some men carried sacks holding all they possessed in them. They used to trawl through the dustbins and throw anything they thought might come in handy into their sacks. Beggars who owned nothing could find something wherever people threw away their surplus, things they no longer had any use for.

After wandering around the entire neighbourhood and coming to the decision that it would be the utmost folly to risk sleeping in the boat he had used, Wistin concluded that his best option was to strike up a friendship with the crowd of beggars and become one of them. At least, in this way, he would not feel all alone. He needed to have company during the night, and he wanted to feel at ease in letting himself sleep away the night in the company of those who shared his circumstances. They may not have been true friends, but at least they were not enemies. And he was certain he would not be dossing down with them for long. Now that his dream of escape had ended in disaster, he had no hope of clinging on to anything else and only needed to spend the coming night. He liked the Port and it held a fascination for him, but it began to frighten him too. However, in spite of all that had happened to him, it was not long before he found a quiet corner to himself and flinging himself down and stretching out, he slept soundly.

157

The next morning he woke up early and roamed around. Thoughts crowded and jostled around in his mind, easily making up a chain of events as if they were following a fairy-tale, one of the countless tales he had heard in his childhood. He remembered that the Port was the place where ships carry people on board, both children and adults. Many people worked there, all of them considering the sea as part of their land. Some of them worked as ferrymen, others as traders on a bumboat or even as ship chandlers. There were also stevedores carrying loads of coal, a man's job. Somehow or other, this place meant a great deal to him even though he had been born and bred among the fields.

"The village is lovely, but this place is lovelier," he told himself.

He strolled along the quayside, as if he knew he had to look for something which he would eventually find. All the stories he had ever heard led to this conclusion. Now that Antonja had deserted him, and all the plans he had laid to build their own little world had vanished, he had nothing left to do except grab the opportunity to remain in that place and search for that something. He only had the vaguest hint what that something could be. Everyone arrived at the village after a long sea journey on board a ship. That is how children came, and also adults, men and women. People would go there, at the Quay, and wait and watch for other people to arrive and disembark. His mother had told him that even Fr. Grejbel had once arrived on board a ship and had disembarked to find a big crowd of villagers waiting to welcome him. Ships left and entered harbour every day, always full of people. The Port did not go to sleep, neither by day nor by night. There was always something going on, on land and at sea. Men and women sang and drank and danced in endless celebration. There was none of that in the village.

Many boats were tied up to the Quay. Wistin walked slowly along, keeping his eyes peeled, always on the lookout.

"What are you looking for, lad?" a man who happened to be passing by asked him. "Have you lost your mother, by any chance, and you've come to look for her here?"

That was something that would have been better left unsaid and it roused Wistin to a fury. "Hey, are you talking to me? Where did you spring from? Who are you?"

"Keep looking, keep looking! You never know, you might strike it lucky," the man replied in a muddled sort of way.

Wistin was about to answer him back by giving him a piece of his mind but he soon realized that the man was drunk. He was swaying from one side to the other, as if his legs could not support him and he needed a walking stick to walk, and at times he approached the wall and stretched out his hand to it to lean against it and rest. He was not the only man who appeared to be drunk. Other men, holding a beer bottle in their hand, could be seen walking, stopping to gaze vacantly, talking to themselves and waiting to see if anyone would stop and talk to them.

There was no clue that there was the boat he had in mind somewhere around that place. The boats looked all the same to him and yet they were all different from each other. How could he possibly look at them all and recognize it? Maybe it would give off some signal? Now that he had come to know a little about the Port, free as he now was, yet he still needed to arrive in the place he wished to be. But how was he to achieve that? There was nothing he could hold on to but at least he had already learnt that every boat had some element bonding it to its owner. He approached the Quay and noticed that at that time of day there were not many people about. Everyone was absorbed in their own work, after all. He took hold of a boat line in both his hands, pulled the boat closer, untied the rope and got down into the boat, snatched the oars and started rowing out. He skimmed between the stationary boats, not knowing what he was looking for. He had already observed that on the hull, every boat had its name painted elaborately with swirls of paint. The names were all those of men or women, or of saints, or of some town beyond the Port. All those names represented a bouquet of the tastes, loves, and devotions of the ferrymen and traders on the bumboats who plied their trade and earned a living by rowing boats.

Wistin wended his way between one boat and another, looking for something but unsure of what that something was. He read all the names of the boats he passed but did not give them a second glance. He marvelled at how different the boats were one from another. He was also pleased with himself in succeeding to read the few letters of the alphabet that made up the name of each boat. Sometimes he became confused and stopped midway, going back to the beginning. He was only sure he was reading the name correctly in a handful of cases, seeming to know how to spell these by heart.

All of a sudden, as he was rowing slowly by, he came upon one particular boat, and he found himself reading its name, 'Wistin'. Overjoyed that it bore his own name he repeated to himself, "This boat's name is Wistin!" But of course he was not the only person who was called by that name. He read the name again, several times, feeling proud not to encounter any difficulty and pronouncing it without a single error. W-i-s-t-i-n, there was no doubt he had read it correctly. The name, painted on the hull, was drawn with bright paint strokes, standing out boldly against the coloured background of the boat. He stopped to gaze at it and his eyes were drawn to another part of the boat, aft. He observed it closely and noticed the painted image of St. Joseph. There were other boats with the image of the same saint painted on them. He drew closer and it seemed to him he knew that particular image very well indeed. He gave a swift glance around and noted that no one was in the vicinity, aboard the nearby boats. He jumped from the boat he was in into the one bearing the name 'Wistin' and went to study the image, closely observing the painted face.

"This is the face of the statue of St. Joseph we have in our village. It's him! It's precisely the same! The statue in our village," he said to himself in amazement. "This is the statue to whom the vow was made!" He was absolutely certain of it.

160

Hastily jumping back into the boat he had borrowed, he began to row back to land as fast as he could. In his haste he hit another boat. The sound it made was loud and the splash made some people look in his direction.

"Hey! You there! What are you doing? Look, look! There he is men! Someone's stealing that boat!" somebody shouted.

On hearing these words, the others took up the shout.

Wistin could not escape now that he was close to the quay. He dropped the oars and jumped into the sea, swimming strongly to another part of the quayside where he hid behind some boats, waiting till the boat's owner turned up and took it back to its usual berth, and the story ended there. It was simply another adventure, one of the many that occurred on a daily basis, and to which the people working there had become inured. Usually, it was naughty children and precocious lads who were the culprits and people would generally pour oil on troubled waters by giving them a few coins and getting them to leave without any more fuss and bother.

Wistin continued mulling over in his mind thoughts about the boat with the name 'Wistin' painted on its hull and about the well-known face of St. Joseph painted aft. He could not bear to sit still with these thoughts troubling him. He decided that in the coming night he would not go to sleep in that place where beggars congregated but on that boat. As dusk fell, he found ways and means to climb back on board that boat, making sure he was not seen. He was very tired and sleep soon overcame him. The gentle splash of the sea that evening did not upset him. He slept soundly till morning and when he opened his eyes, a beautiful blue sky and the sparkling sea around him met his gaze. He felt sure he could remain in that boat as if it belonged to him.

A new day had dawned and the entire Port was waking up and greeting him.

***

Ester was waiting for Susanna as she was leaving church, and approached her. Susanna came to a stop, and removing the veil from her head and folding it slowly, she waited to hear what the other woman had to say. "I'd like to have a word with you, please," Ester said.

"Of course, yes of course. I can imagine what you're going to tell me," Susanna replied ruefully and not a little shyly, but pleased that now the approach had come from the other woman.

"My Antonja and your Wistin are still meeting. Did you know? It seems they really do love one another. My husband and I have discussed it a lot, and I'm not ashamed to say we've had words over it too! We've quarrelled with Antonja about it as well but she's standing firm on her position. She's promised us she won't leave the village, whatever happens. As long as we give in. She won't leave on the condition that we, my husband and I, won't hold out against her choice of husband any longer."

"Is that what she said to you both? Truly?"

"Both my husband and I told her we would accept her choice if in return she agrees not leave this neighbourhood."

"And she agreed?"

"Yes, she said yes."

"Thank you for telling me all this. In my situation, you have no idea how happy it makes me. It's been a long time since I received such glad news."

"I should have thought the priest has already been to see you, Susanna."

"Yes, yes he has, but that man is carrying too heavy a burden. I have no way of knowing what it is that Wistin wants, at this stage. That's why your words, on behalf of Antonja, mean so much to me."

"Antonja told Wistin very plainly that she doesn't want to leave here. At first perhaps, she too, thought she could up and

162

leave with him. But not anymore. Let me tell you something, Susanna. Did you know that Wistin is riding a bicycle?"

"No, I didn't know. I've never even seen him on one! Where on earth did he get it from?"

"I have no idea. Antonja told me he bartered it for something. And it's on the bicycle that they often go, him and Antonja, far, far away from the village. They can go very fast on it and wander around far away, putting in as much distance between them and the village as they please. I very much fear that the bicycle is just like a boat on land. What do you think? Both can go fast and both can take you wherever you wish to go. Some time ago, your son told Antonja, 'I'm taking you to see the other village. Only a little further away from here. Riding on the bicycle you'll see the world in motion.' That's what he told her. He waited for her on the outskirts of the village and she went to meet him there, punctually. They rode to the other village, I don't know what it's called, and they spent their time roaming the streets and seeing the church, and then they came back."

"And how do you know all this?"

"Susanna, how would I know if it wasn't Antonja herself who tells me everything?"

"She herself tells you?" Susanna marvelled. "How lucky you are, Ester!"

"Yes, she herself tells me, of course. We don't want to lose her. We don't want her to leave us. There was a time when both my husband and I thought she'd got fed up staying with us and there was nothing about the village that pleased her any longer and made her want to stay. We were afraid that the first squall that came would blow her away. And, please forgive me Susanna, but at first we thought that this squall was no other but your Wistin. But we were wrong. We wouldn't have realized this on our own, no. It had to be someone else who made us see that."

Susanna did not want to dwell on the subject of Wistin. "I hope Antonja too learns how to ride a bicycle, and she can then bring him home. If he remains the only one who knows how to ride a bicycle, I very much fear he'll never find his way to my house. That's what I think. Maybe if he remains in love with Antonja..."

"He's not riding that bicycle on his own. Don't you believe me?"

"But are you happy with this situation, Ester?" Susanna asked her, doubtfully.

"Up to a little while age, no. But now I see it in a different light."

"Was there someone who helped you see it differently?"

"Yes, Susanna, and you know very well who. God knows what we would have done otherwise! With his help I didn't stay set against you any longer. I'm very sorry for what happened before."

"It doesn't matter. Time brings changes and heals wounds."

"If I can set your mind at rest, even a little, I'll make amends for my behaviour towards you, in front of the entire village. If Wistin remains in love with Antonja, his heart will lead him back here. That's it in a nutshell. You're afraid the sea will manage to lure him away. Susanna, if that happens, I'll do my utmost to make my daughter leave him. And I have my husband's full support in this. We gave in to her on the condition that she won't spread her wings and fly away. If she tries to spread her wings, she'll soon find me and my husband coming down on her like a ton of bricks! She still fears us."

Susanna was taken aback. The sudden change of mood was completely unexpected. She was speechless, in dread. But then she had to admit to herself that she wanted that very same thing.

"You can be sure of what I'm telling you! Susanna, I'm not holding back anything. You and I are both mothers. Wistin is yours and Antonja is mine. That's how they must remain, forever. That's the way we were brought up and that's how they have to live. Susanna, Wistin truly wants a wife, one

164

who'll always stay by his side, who'll always remain his. He told our daughter so, speaking plainly."

"So he wants something his mother and father never gave him. Me and his father. Isn't that what you're telling me, Ester?"

"I don't know, Susanna. But there's one thing I've learnt: Wistin wants to have something he's never had before."

"Meaning?"

"Meaning, I think he really loves my daughter. He needs her. He needs to hold on to something solid, in his hands, his life. If that weren't so, I wouldn't be trusting him now, and I wouldn't have changed my mind."

Susanna was at a loss for words. Ester's words wounded her, but in some strange way they also brought her comfort. The woman appeared to be utterly convinced of what she was saying, and it was quite clear to Susanna that the thoughts Ester was expressing were not entirely her own.

"I'm not going to risk anything where my daughter's concerned," Ester reassured her. "I have faith in your son. Look about you and see how you can try to convince him to stay here."

"Hmm, convince him to stay in these parts. And will that satisfy you and your husband?" Susanna paused to gather her thoughts and then continued, saying, "It appears you know my son. Did you speak to him?"

Ester smiled back at her and inclined her head, pressed Susanna's hand and left without saying another word.

Chapter 7

Like most women, Susanna used to go out early every morning, first to go and hear mass, and then to buy food and other necessities. It was a straight run from home to church and then on to the street where the open air market was held and thence back home, on a daily basis, without variation. On her way, she, like all the other women, stopped to chat with others, discussing prices, what sort of things were to be bought that day, the current weather, whether it was hot or cold, raining or dry, and most of all, about the work going on in the fields. The life of every villager depended on everything that grew in that soil. There were four seasons and each held out the promise of gifts, stored away in the soil. One of the hawkers from whom Susanna bought something every day was called Pawlu. He had always been known to everyone as Pawlu *tal-Ħaxix*, the vegetable seller. He owned several fields, inherited over and over again by many generations of his family, and he continued to cultivate them diligently using the skills he had learnt in his boyhood, and he was also able to employ a few field hands of his own. Every morning, he loaded his cart with an array of fresh vegetables and took them to market, stationing himself in his usual place, long held, and he would fuss over the arrangement of his produce to attract the attention of potential customers and call out as usual: "Lovely vegetables, fresh from my own fields, good value for money, come and taste it and see for yourselves." Everyone knew his call, chanted in a sing-song manner, with pleasure and pride, and many women bought from him or at least scrutinized all the produce laid out on his cart to compare his prices with those of other hawkers. No one could go to market and say he had not come across Pawlu *tal-Ħaxix*. He had such an attractive voice, such a winning smile and so much to sell! He lived only for this.

Pawlu used to hear mass every day, too. And then, as soon as he left church, he would go straight to his farmhouse, take out his cart and take it to market, loaded with vegetables. He used to push it effortlessly as if he was still a young man. Working in the field kept him hale and hearty and the years went by sparing him illness and he never tired of his work on the land.

"Some vegetables for your *minestra* soup, Susanna?" he told her that day.

"Yes, a few vegetables, as usual, Pawl," she replied.

Pawlu began to search amongst his vegetables, choosing the very best produce for her. He had long become used to Susanna. He knew she always bought her vegetables from him without haggling over prices, or grubbing about the items or disparaging them. She would tell him at once what she was going to cook that day and with his usual enthusiasm, pride and satisfaction, he would plunge his hand in his display and, almost with his eyes closed, would bring up what was required, meanwhile raising his head and observing the people all around him and then delve once more amongst his vegetables. One reason people would stop and buy was because he had a knack for selling.

"The hawker's cry counts for half a sale," he used to like saying, perhaps also to attract attention. "And do you know who the other half is? Who could it be? Pawlu *tal-Ħaxix*!" He frequently burst into song, singing a short sweet melody after calling out his known chant which people had come to identify him with.

"Some vegetables to make *minestra*," Susanna told him with a preoccupied air.

"What sort of *minestra* are you thinking of cooking? *Minestra* with rice and celery? *Minestra à la Prête* or *Minestra Milanese*? Tell me and I'll give you whatever you need to make it. I have every kind of vegetable here," he told her with pride but very politely too. He gave a glance around and lowering his voice went on, "And anyway, I can provide the very best vegetables to be had, for certain people. I'm going to choose the very best for you, because you're you!" When he noticed that other people were gathering close he raised his voice again, "Look, to make *Minestra* with rice and celery you need large-leaved celery which you need to bring to the boil in broth before putting in the rice. And as for *Minestra à la Prête*, see how good this will taste! You'll need a turnip, some celery, potatoes, an onion, pasta beads, some *ricotta* cottage cheese and a little oil, and some cheese and eggs. Oh and some pumpkin, I nearly forgot! How could I forget? And then get your pot and start. Listen..."

Susanna stared back at him, her thoughts miles away. Her black dress, unrelieved black, made her a serious looking figure, and made her stand out from all the other people.

"And if you want to make *Minestra Milanese*, well then, listen, you will need some ham, which you can't buy from me, but there, you need it. And you'll also need onions, and I, folks, have onions of the finest quality, and garlic and parsley," he went on.

"How much do I owe you?" Susanna asked him, putting her hand in her large skirt pocket and bringing up money.

"Goodbye, Susanna. Good day to you," he told her, gazing back at her with a long look, admiring once more her beauty.

Susanna went on her way wishing she was safely back at home. She had just caught sight of someone gazing fixedly at her, waiting to see her leave Pawlu tal-Ħaxix. She pursed her lips tightly, bent her head and walked on, quickly increasing her pace. She did not want to come face to face with him. "Lady of Mercy! What is he doing here?" she whispered to herself. She knew she was being followed. As soon as she left the market street, teeming with people, she instantly felt a hard hand pressing against her and making her come to a halt.

She realized that at any minute he would try to stop her forcibly.

"Susanna!" he cried loudly.

She continued walking. She was only a few paces ahead of him.

He kept pace with her till it pleased him to do so. "Su-san-na, what sort of *minestra* are you going to cook today? What good recipe did Pawlu give you, huh? Mr. Pawlu knows how to season *minestra* very well, what say you? As if he's never cooked *minestra* before you went shopping from him. Maybe he's even thought up a new recipe just for you? Go on, tell it to me, tell me don't write it for me because, don't forget, I don't know how to read or write. Ahh, I have to remember everything. I carry everything up here, in my mind, look. Tell me, go on, tell me."

She did not look back. She was startled when she felt his hand on her and his voice grated in her ears. "What do you want from me? Stiefnu, please, go away, go away," she exclaimed, holding her heavy shopping basket tighter.

He was quick to snatch it from her and he kept walking holding it.

"What do you want from me?" she cried, staring fearfully at her basket and trying to get it back. She knew it was hopeless to try. He had a hard grip, holding it roughly.

"I'm going to carry your shopping basket for you. That's the right thing to do for a woman like you. Walk on, walk on, I want to talk to you."

"What do you want to say? Whatever it is say it here and now, and make it short."

"I'm not going to tell you here and now, and I won't make it short either. I will tell you where and when I please. I will decide and I'm in no hurry."

"Give me that shopping basket. I need to go home and start cooking."

"You, cook? For whom? Don't you just need to cook for one? Who's there to wait for you at home? Nobody!"

169

"How cruel you are!"

"Isn't it true, all that I'm saying?"

"That's why you're cruel."

"Just go on home now, put your full shopping basket on the table, take out all the vegetables, look at the recipe and start cooking. *Minestra* for one. That's all!"

Susanna lowered her head, trying to wrench her hand out of his grip, but without success. Then she brushed down her black dress because every particle showed up on it. "You've managed to learn to hate me."

"Me, hate you? Well, nearly. If you want, I can still love you. I'm my own master! There's no mother at my heels, interfering in everything. I'm master of my own heart. Shall I show you? Here and now, if you want. I have a kiss for you, a big, big kiss, deep and long. I brought it with me on purpose. Do you want it? Maybe it's the last kiss I have left – for you."

Susanna, pursing her lips in annoyance, instantly recoiled. "I don't hate you, Stiefnu. I've managed to control my own heart in this matter, up to now," she replied, backing further away from him.

"Is that so?" he said with suppressed anger, putting even more distance between them. He felt humiliated but did his best not to let her know it.

"But I don't love you, either. I can't. You don't exist any longer for me. You used to once, but not anymore."

"But I do still exist, Susanna. And I will continue to exist. Here I am, look. Instead of Stiefnu from the Valley I've become Stiefnu from the Port," he sneered at her.

In the meantime, their steps had taken them out of the heart of the village to a deserted area where no prying eyes could see them. The noises from the market, the hum of the crowds, the sounds and bustle of daily life, all were muted, heard faintly from where they now stood.

"Since you want to have a word with me, we can talk here," Susanna declared. "Go on. But first I want to know where Wistin is, tell me. I have a right to know where he is. I can't live without him any longer."

"You'll have to."

"Where is he?"

Stiefnu was full of glee as soon as he heard those words. He felt he had won a complete victory. "At least, now I've won completely. I've managed to hurt you where it hurts most."

"Have you become so very cruel meanwhile?"

"No, not as much as you think but even more than that!" he answered her defiantly. "I can show you just how much if need be."

"But do you know where he is? Tell me, tell me!" she moaned.

Stiefnu made her wait and then told her, "Yes, I know where he is."

"Is he well?"

"Yes, he's fine. He doesn't need anything. I'm not going to tell you more than that."

"Cruel!"

"This is the time when I have to be cruel. That's what the sea taught me. The sea taught me to be hard-hearted. And I'm going to be even more cruel. Much more. Listen to me. Wistin needs to live. I can't support him. You have to look about and find the money for him."

"Do you mean he's going to stay on with you?"

"Maybe. Probably. I can't tell you for sure."

"In the Port?" she questioned him full of curiosity. "Where are you going to put him up? Where do you want him to live in the Port area?"

As soon as she spoke Stiefnu instantly saw red. "Don't you dare show your face there! That's no place for you! Don't forget, the Port has a wide-open door. Many people pass through that doorway. People come by ship, but they also leave that way!

"Very well! Very well!" she replied disconsolately.

"And since the Port has a wide-open door, do you know what can happen?"

"I understand," Susanna acquiesced against her will.

"I need money to be able to support Wistin. You have money. You have loads! This is the second time I'm telling you."

"I don't have money. I wish I had. Didn't you tell me your trade was flourishing and that you were becoming something else? You told me you weren't going to be a trader on a bumboat for long but was getting richer, a ship chandler. Do you remember?"

"Hold your tongue, Susanna! I'm not a ship chandler yet. I'm still making ends meet. And I still have to eat swill quite often, or else go to sleep on an empty stomach. Is there something else you want to know now?"

Susanna ducked her head, knowing she had no choice but to listen.

"Hand me the money, my fine lady! See where you can lay hands on it."

"From where? Is that what Wistin wants then?"

"I have to say, yes, that's what Wistin wants."

Susanna could not say another word, feeling large tears slide down her cheeks. She did not want him to see her crying but she could not help it. She did not want to stain her black dress, either. Her mourning gown should always appear smart, out of respect for the dead.

"Cry all you want. I'm used to your tears by now. But see what you're going to do about the money."

"This means you came here for the money, only. If I remember correctly, you brought a kiss with you too, but I didn't want it!"

Stiefnu advanced on her intending to assault her. He raised his hand and curling it into a fist he nearly slammed it into her face but lowered it and shook his head penitently, his blind rage evaporating as quickly as it had come.

Susanna ducked and ran below his upraised arm, coming to a halt a few paces away, standing still with shock, her hands to her face.

"I came here for the money," he repeated, his voice still full of anger.

"Very well, very well. I'll do everything for Wistin."

"You'll do everything for Wistin? That means handing money over."

"Yes, I still want to do all I can for him."

"Well then, from now on I'll be telling you: hand it over! But he isn't ready and willing to do everything for you," he sneered back at her.

"You said that deliberately to hurt me, to wound me deeply."

"You know what you feel. Each to his own."

"You've hurt me greatly, really. But it doesn't matter. I will do my part, all of it, till the end."

"Why not make another vow, Susanna? Your vows, those you and your mother make, seem to be granted. You've found a very patient saint who's ready to grant your every wish!"

"At least, tell me you know where my son is. Tell me he's well."

"Money. Money. From now on my conversations with you will only concern money. You can lay your hands on it. Get it. For Wistin, not for me. But you'll have to hand it over to me. Get hold of it, let me know and I'll come and get it, and then pass it on to Wistin. And everybody will be happy."

Susanna did not utter a word. She stared back at Stiefnu and waited to get back her shopping basket.

"Here, take your shopping basket. What sort of soup are you going to make today? Do you want me to give you the recipe? Don't forget, I'm a villager like you, when I want to be."

"When it suits you, you mean."

"When it suits me. Yes. For now it suits me to see you make amends. Hand over the money, otherwise you're going to stay having your meals alone, right till the end."

"And if I bring you the money and be sure that Wistin is alright, well, in that case I can see him again?"

"I can't hold out any promises, My Lady Susanna! All I can say for now is that Wistin's future depends on you. Decide." He turned his back on her and left.

She stared at his retreating back, getting ever distant and shook her head in disparagement. More than ever before, she was certain not a trace of love for him remained in her heart. "Even if I were to try and love him, I couldn't manage it," she told herself.

***

Antonja and Wistin kept courting, as if nothing had happened. Their love for one another grew and blossomed, and both of them were content. The village remained far enough away from them not to be a burden, though they knew very well it was only a few steps away. Sometimes Wistin felt himself free of any ties to his mother and father, though he was still sad to see the great rift between them. He had been born in that no-man's land and had come to realize that that was where he had grown up, as well, a land resembling one of the fields in the neighbourhood that lay fallow and untended. An abandoned field surrounded by cultivated fields, one more beautiful than the other. All this served to nurture rebellion and rage in his heart, but, paradoxically, a wish to love someone and build a nest that could withstand the gusting of the wind. But he sometimes felt a great need to be at their side. In his heart of hearts he knew he loved both his mother and his father, and wished he could be closer to them. Now he was old enough to know that those two, whatever else they did or could do, were unable to give him something they themselves lacked. But he was not suffering a good deal because he was living apart. Up to now at least, he was convinced that his young woman could fill the void he felt.

He felt lucky to have found her; that is what he often told himself. Their story had begun from an exchanged look to an exchanged word; it had begun and was continuing. All the trouble their courtship had caused seemed to be something outside of themselves, something distant. Being face-to-face, in one embrace, it seemed as if their world, contained in those precious moments, felt beyond the world of others, of old people who could not understand. Wistin had her and his bicycle. With both of them his, he felt he had found his freedom. The fact that he had spent a good part of his childhood, from the day he was born, apart from his mother in an orphanage together with many other children, made him come to feel a new-found freedom, detached from a bond with a closed-in house. But now he was feeling the need to build a closed-in house for himself.

"I want to have what I've never had," he had got it into his head.

On her part, Antonja was realizing that her mother and father were no longer as strict as they had been, dictating everything. Her father had long made it plain that he did not want to interfere in her private life as much as he used to. Truth to tell, he had never been the sort of man to dog his daughter's every footstep because it seemed he had long felt that his daughter was entitled to take her own path in life. For some time now, even her mother had softened her approach.

Antonja often heard them discussing her with lowered voices in the room next door, but she used to pretend she was fast asleep and never betrayed that she knew it, let alone have it out with them.

"She's still seeing him, that lad," Ester told Tumas. "I know it for certain because someone told me."

Her husband stared back at her but made no answer.

"Did you hear me?"

"Yes, I know. She still sees him."

"So, is that all you have to say?"

"Let her choose her own path. She's old enough, Ester, and if she's drawn to some lad from these parts, so much the better. You're lucky!"

"I'm lucky? Is that what you call it?"

"Yes, you're lucky. A lad who knows the land."

"Don't you know that her young man is also familiar with the Port?"

"If he was born and bred among the fields, his heart will remain here, for sure. His beginnings will draw him back. When it comes to a choice between the field and the Port, at the end of the day he will choose where he was brought up. If he's used to the hoe, he's not going to get used to the oar in a flash."

"But who told you that? Where has all this wisdom come from?" she answered him with a taunt in her voice.

"Ester, I keep listening to you first and then say to myself: look, one and one makes two. And that way I sum it all up, as if I've gathered up a treasure, always listen to you first and then save it all up, penny by penny."

"That's a good one, Tumas! What a very clever husband I have!"

"If he's grown up here in the fields, he'll return," Tumas insisted, wanting to end the discussion.

"I hope that if they do stay together, and get married, they'll want to set up house in these parts."

"Are you already thinking so far ahead? You're letting your thoughts run away with you."

"No, I'm not thinking ahead of myself. Wistin comes from a decent family."

"Has all your anger against his mother gone, then?"

"Every mother is always on the lookout for any mistake her daughter makes. And every mother can make mistakes. If you think I was wrong before, say so. Yes, I was wrong.

You're the only one who doesn't make mistakes, because you don't care enough to make any move."

"Yes I do, I care a lot as it happens," Tumas defended himself. "But without making an almighty fuss like you, wife."

Ester turned to face him, wanting to know more. "Maybe, if I understand you correctly, you went to speak to that priest?"

"You certainly can put two and two together," he applauded her with a smile.

"What did he say, what did he say?" she questioned him eagerly.

"First of all he told me that it would make matters worse if we interfered needlessly. Secondly, that Wistin is a good lad. He was well brought up. And most important, that it was Antonja herself who approached Fr. Grejbel, behind our back, asking him to talk to us both and make us try to understand her better so that, you know, we won't continue dictating to her in the least thing."

"The priest told you she asked him to tell us all this? Did I understand you well?"

"Yes, you've understood."

"So couldn't Antonja have told us all this herself, here, to our face? What is she shying away from? Since when has she been so afraid of us?"

"Antonja couldn't bring herself to tell us. Maybe she feels too shy, too afraid."

"She's afraid of me?" his wife's jaw dropped.

"Yes, I think she's frightened of you. Even I feel afraid of you, sometimes!" her husband replied, half seriously and half-jokingly.

"You're afraid of me? You?" she cried, rising from her chair at the table and making a run for him, all the while trying not to bump into objects.

Tumas walked quickly away and out of the room, slightly apprehensive but scornful at the same time, bumping into things as he went. "No, no! It's not true, I'm not afraid of you! I'm simply ter-ri-fied! I'm sha-king!"

"Where's the rolling pin? The rolling pin I use when I prepare *ravjul*? Where is it? It must be in the kitchen drawer! At him! At him with the rolling pin! Afraid of me, you said?"

"No, ter-ri-fied!" he repeated mockingly. "Only a little bit!"

She used to intimidate Antonja with the rolling pin when she was a little girl, and armed with that round antique wooden implement Ester now tried to make some sort of impression on her husband.

Tumas managed to reach the roof and lock the door of the little room up there behind him, putting up the crossbeam as an added precaution. From the roof he could see an unbroken vista of roofs, all decked with clothes hanging on washing lines to dry.

That same evening Antonja came home and went straight up to her room, without saying a word to either of them. Her mother followed her up and stood in the doorway. She smiled at her daughter and waited for her to speak.

Antonja remained silent. Then she wiped her eyes and her mother instantly realized she was crying. Advancing into the room, her mother took her in a fond embrace.

Antonja's father appeared in the doorway a few moments later and he stood there with clasped hands in front of his chest as if asking for mercy. "Here I am! I came to take control of the situation. If you need any help, Antonja, call me. You'll find me at your side straightaway. Your mother can't do much faced with the two of us. I'll be downstairs, waiting to see what's going to happen this evening."

"There's nothing to wait up for," his wife told him in a huff.

"Well, that's very good news, already!" he was quick to reply. "Antonja, it seems your mother's mood has changed. There's a great change about in the air! Do you understand?"

"Really, Mother?" Antonja wondered, gently disengaging herself from her mother's arms.

"Daughter, I only wish you to be happy and content. Tell me, tell me, what is your heart telling you? Can't you tell me? I want to reassure you, I'll listen to you with great attention."

"And you won't get angry with me?"

"No, I won't get angry with you. My word on it."

"And you won't go and take it out on him?"

"Take it out on whom?"

"Don't you know who, Mother?"

"Ahh! With him, then, dearie, with him."

"With him. Don't laugh at me, Mother. At the moment, my whole world contains just two people. Are you going to rage at him?"

"The one you love? Do you love him, Antonja?"

"Yes, Mother. I love him."

"Are you sure?"

"I realized I loved him only lately. We were on the sea," she went on with a tremor in her voice.

"On the sea, daughter? Far away from here?"

"I realized I loved him then, and also that he loved me."

"How do you know he loves you?"

Antonja started telling her mother about the long hours they were spending in each other's company. They walked in the open countryside holding hands, in step with each other, and sometimes they chased each other, smiling but not saying a word. Other times they stood still, gazing at trees and clouds. At times like these, it dawned on Antonja that her beloved's heart was still bound up with that area. Though he was searching for another distant place, something was holding him back, reminding him that those green spaces were

179

still his for the taking, and that perhaps he still had a duty towards them. Wistin never actually expressed these thoughts in words to Antonja but she understood his feelings. All that was needed was a gentle push from her, in some form or other, to make him have second thoughts about leaving that rural environment.

Wistin and Antonja frequently went down into the Valley, whenever they managed to find the time. Once he told her that his life had begun down there and that he disliked the area when he was young. He could still remember when his mother had taken him for a walk down there one day and he had been bored stiff. He had not liked the place at all. The fields up above, only a little distant from down there, seemed far more wonderful and he used to like flying his kite up there while his mother and Grandma Katarina spent the time talking to each other. They used to bring a picnic with them. They would sit down on the grass, with their wide skirts spread out all around them like a big carpet and he would be able to sit and rest on it, and even have a nap without feeling the grass prickling beneath him. Sometimes, the two women would send him off to play further away whilst they talked about things between themselves, things he was unable to understand.

Whenever they talked about the future, Wistin used to tell Antonja, "You'll see how happy you'll be with me. We two will never part from each other, and even if I had to go far away to find work, I would still come back and bring all the money I would have earned. I'll earn enough to support us, and the children we will have."

"But how are you going to earn a living?" Antonja would ask him, worried.

"Either with the oar or with the plough. I'm still not sure," he had replied. "Either with one or the other, don't worry." He paused and then continued. "But what do you want me to do?"

"Don't you know what I'd like?" she answered him, collapsing on his chest.

"And if I don't manage to do what you'd like?"

"I'd still love you, all the same."

"Are you sure?" he wanted to know.

Antonja did not know how to go on. "I think so, yes, yes, I'm sure. At least... that's what I think at the moment."

***

Susanna did not know where she was to find the money. She wanted to support her son, but all the worldly goods she had inherited from Arturu could not offer him more than a hot meal every day. Stiefnu had appeared on the scene again, a menace, expecting wealth he could take hold of on behalf of his son. Wistin was unwilling to touch another's riches for which he had no feelings, but now that the opportunity had arisen to share in some wealth, he wanted his share of it. After all, Susanna had everything fall into her lap. Stiefnu himself had once taunted Arturu that he had inherited much wealth without putting in a day's work. All that wealth belonged to Susanna, too, and if it was hers, well then it belonged to her son as well. But how could Susanna support Wistin when all she had was enough to go to market every day with a few coins in hand and buy her daily food and other necessities?

"When I die, you won't have any problems. I've thought of everything. You'll be able to live on the money I'm leaving you," Arturu had promised her, since he had not wanted her to go out to work when they were living together once more. His family's customs and traditions did not waver from this precept. One's wife should never go out to work unless exceptional circumstances prevailed. Almost never. Part of a man's pride lay in the fact that his wife had no need to go out to work and earn money. He had enough in hand as well as some saved up. "I inherited enough to be able to live without having to go out and earn a living. That was Lady's wish," Arturu had told Susanna, "and that's what she told me just before she died. And I too, Susanna, don't wish you to go out to work for a living, till this money is at your disposal. If you're thrifty and only spend what you need every day, you'll have enough to see you through many years."

Arturu's forebears had lived in this manner and he wished Susanna to continue in this tradition during their married life and even after his death. It was all safely kept in a trunk, a kind of large suitcase, heavy and scratched on its sides but tough and secured with a lock that was opened with a little key. Ever since it was no longer used as a suitcase, the chest was not moved from its place in a dark corner under the bed, pushed in the farthest recess, and it became a treasure chest full of money. Whenever Lady required money, she used to ask Arturu to get down under the bed to pull the chest forward enough so that she could unlock it and lift its lid and then she used to plunge her hands down and bring up a few coins, all that was necessary for that day. Only a few coins, as usual, and they would serve and be enough for the entire day, from dawn till dusk. Susanna kept up this traditional custom ever since Arturu had first broached the subject. In this way she learnt to judge the correct amount necessary for each day and never brought up an extra coin when the daily expenses were normal. And if an extra coin happened to be left over from the day, lying about on the table, she was in the habit of putting it into the cupboard drawer to join the rest of the coins brought up from the chest the following morning. Arturu had always been in the habit of repeating his father's words, important advice he had dinned into him a thousand times: "This isn't stinginess, but discipline." That household held to this rule for a very long time, and Susanna came to realize that it was a rule held for entire generations of villagers. She had no wish to be the first person to break this rule. Out of respect for her husband.

But now the situation had changed immeasurably. Stiefnu was demanding a large sum. Many thoughts crossed her mind as to how she could raise such a sum. One possibility she considered was to have a quiet word with Pawlu *tal-Ħaxix*. The moment had arrived when she had to swallow her pride and ask for a favour. That is what other women had to do for their own sake and for their children's, and now it was her turn to take this step.

"I'd like to have a word with you in private, please," she asked him.

"How can I say no to you, Susanna?" Pawlu responded.

"Umm... I don't know how to say this, what I have in mind," she faltered, overcome with shyness.

"Tell me, tell me. You're too beautiful for me to deny you!"

Susanna felt overwhelmed. She ducked her head but felt a tingle of pleasure to have Pawlu gaze at her in admiration. She had become aware of his interest for some time.

"Tell me, tell me how I can be of service to you."

"Do you need any help in your work? May I work for you? I need employment."

Pawlu was silent for a few moments considering her request. "What sort of work do you have in mind?" he asked her in a decided voice.

"You tell me. Whatever you think is best. I'll do it. I need some money. I don't want it for free. I want to earn it, I want to work."

"I can guess why you need it," Pawlu observed, all the while running through his mind a list of jobs which women usually performed. "In the fields, at the farm, where would you prefer?"

"Wherever you say."

He paused and with a note of satisfaction creeping into his voice told her: "You can begin tomorrow. Come to my field early tomorrow morning and pick some flowers. There are always many varieties for you to choose from and pick, all the time, depending on their season for flowering." He spoke happily.

"Really?" Susanna exclaimed. "Sell flowers?"

"You can sell flowers! There, would you like this job? There are daisies, asters and winter daisies, and there are carnations, dahlias, tulips, stocks and buttercups, there are violets and yellow lilies or white ones, and water lilies. And there are also the pink roses of Our Lady and damask roses, blue passion flowers and sunflowers, and lilies of St. Joseph, and apothecary roses and white roses too. Everything in its own season. And there are other varieties too, you'll see. But not everyone buys flowers. So don't come to market with only flowers to sell. Pick some bunches of celery and parsley, mint and marjoram and sell them together. You can come with two baskets, one with flowers and the other with herbs and seasoning plants. Tell people the price and if they haggle give in but not by much, and not straightaway. See who's going to give in first, whether you or the buyer. Otherwise we won't earn anything!" Pawlu told her with a smile. "The main thing is that you sell them. Don't return with a full basket. It's better to have earned only a little rather than have you come back with nothing, only wilting flowers and plants which have to be thrown away. Flowers lose their bloom very quickly. Afterwards we can agree on the wage between us."

"Very well. I'll do that," Susanna nodded assent. "But what if I don't manage to sell anything? What shall I do?"

"I think you'll manage to sell enough each day. People will definitely buy from Susanna!" he spoke with admiration. "But let me make you a promise: If you don't sell anything, I'll still pay you a day's wages all the same. Can I be any fairer than that?"

"Thank you very much! You're so very kind!"

"I'm very kind and you're very beautiful," he responded.

Susanna was speechless.

"Aren't you going to tell me anything?" he wanted to know.

"I hope I manage to sell your flowers, and the herbs too of course, more than you've ever sold before."

"Susanna, you have the job I've promised you, starting tomorrow. Set your mind at rest."

"Starting tomorrow!" she repeated, relief washing over her, and she turned to leave.

"Someone came looking for me, on purpose, for your sake," he called out, wanting to delay her departure. "If you hadn't come asking me for a job yourself, I myself would have come offering it to you."

Susanna was astonished. "You yourself were going to offer me a job?"

"Someone came along urging me to give you a job. I wanted to approach you myself but he convinced me it would be better if I left you to make the first move. And that's how it's come about!" He stopped there and then looked archly at her: "And do you know who came to tell me?"

Susanna smiled. "Someone wearing black..."

"Someone dressed entirely in black," he assented and then added, "like you."

Susanna was still in deep mourning, wearing an unrelieved black gown. As she walked back home she imagined herself between two large baskets in some corner of the market, the target of many curious eyes, with scores of people looking on in amazement to see her, Arturu's widow, Lady's daughter-in-law, reduced to selling in the street to earn a living. And it wasn't as if she were selling her own produce. The older villagers remembered her working as a servant in Lady's large house and they also recalled that Arturu had ended up being drawn to her and marrying her. She felt that in her new circumstances as a flower-seller in the street, she was returning to her own station, the world of her own sort of people. All this helped her take heart and to look at her new job with interest, not to see it merely as a necessity. It was a job that appealed to her immediately. In which part of the market should she station herself? She felt light hearted, knowing that Pawlu would take care of everything.

"You sit here now, look. Not far away from my post. From today onwards, this place is reserved for you," Pawlu declared on the morrow.

Susanna put down the two baskets in front of her in the place indicated by Pawlu which was right opposite his own post on the other side of the street. He chose that spot so that he could get on with his own work without any interruptions but at the same time he would be able to look at her and admire her to his heart's content.

**

It was sunset but the Port was still bustling with life. Fr. Grejbel arrived there in a *karozzin*, descended, paid his fare and left. He sauntered from one side of the Quay to the other, feeling nervous and anxious. Sometimes he felt embarrassed at standing out in that environment, a priest, alone, distinguished from others by his long black cassock. He recalled that time when he had been summoned by the Bishop, having to answer for something he had done out of duty, all in good faith. A good deed that had been transformed into an accusation, he mumbled to himself. But he felt certain he was doing the right thing again now and he was determined to carry out his mission. He did not want to return to the village without having pushed matters forward a little. This time, the Bishop would understand his motives, for sure.

"My friends, do you know where I can find Stiefnu at this time?" Fr. Grejbel put his question as he stepped lightly on the doorstep of a wine bar, waiting for an answer.

"Oh, Reverend, come in, come in," some men invited him in, though they did not know him. His appearance commanded respect. He too did not know them. A strong smell of toast and cigarette smoke assaulted his nostrils.

"Gladly, gladly," he answered them.

"What would you like to drink, Reverend?" the landlord promptly asked.

"Let me have a little drink with you!"

"At the moment we're drinking tea," the men said.

"Oh good, I'll drink some tea with you," he replied cheerfully. He could well imagine that in their heart of hearts the men were wondering what he was doing at that hour in those parts.

"Your tea, will you have some lemon with it?" the landlord spoke up again.

"A slice of lemon and a teaspoonful of sugar, please," Fr. Grejbel replied. Then he turned to face the others. "I'm looking for Stiefnu, the trader on a bumboat."

"Stiefnu doesn't stay in these parts at this time of day," the landlord answered his query.

"So, if I were to wait a bit, will I find him?" asked the priest.

"Yes, you'll find him," they chorused.

"But no one really knows where he comes and goes," the landlord observed.

The priest drank his tea and put his hand in his pocket to draw up some coins and pay. But both the landlord and the other men refused to allow him to pay. He thanked them and left, continuing to stroll from one side of the Quay to the other, his hands crossed behind his back.

Stiefnu came on the scene a short while later and as soon as he saw Fr. Grejbel a little distance away, he greeted him with the appearance of surprise, saying, "Fr. Grejbel! What brings you here? Have you come looking for a lost sheep, by any chance? Here and at this time of day? Here's your lost sheep. It's called Stiefnu."

Fr. Grejbel smiled back at him, approached him, and taking his hand tried to show him how very pleased he was to see him.

Stiefnu drew back his hand. "What has changed between us, Fr. Grejbel, for you to come along here now and shake hands with me and make out you're pleased to see me?"

"But why not?" the priest replied. "Haven't I always been pleased to see you whenever we met? It's been a long time since we met and so I'm that much more pleased to see you."

"Should I believe you?"

"Not believe me? Why ever not? I admit, it's a bit hard for you to trust me but you'll soon see you need have no qualms.

187

If people don't believe in me any longer, I'll have nothing left. And you know this very well."

"What do I know, Fr. Grejbel? All I know is that throughout this saga, you have always taken Susanna's side. Right from the start, when she fell pregnant and was kicked out of her parents' house and you let her sleep at your place, and when you found her a job as a servant with Lady and Arturu and she later married him, and even after that, when she found her son and brought him up. Anyway, it's always been like that, always, and now too."

"Don't you think, Stiefnu, that in all this I've only done my duty? Nothing but what I was duty bound to do, don't you agree?"

Stiefnu stopped to gather his thoughts. "Yes, you've always done what you had to do. But you never came looking for the lost sheep."

"There was no lost sheep. There was only a sheep that sought different paths. It knew what it felt."

"So, I was never a lost sheep, Fr. Grejbel. Thank you, thank you! At last! This is good news."

"You said those words, not me." The priest paused and then went on speaking in a different tone of voice. "It seems you want to say things you've been meaning to tell me for a long time. However, I can never forget, my dear Stiefnu, that one day you went to speak to the Bishop about me, and had many a good word for me. That meeting you had with the Bishop for my sake, was of great service to me. Thank you."

"Finally, Fr. Grejbel, I too decided I had to do my duty. I admit, I could have done so, gone to the Bishop I mean, a long time before that. Don't ask me why I didn't. Now, I can't tell you why I didn't go before. Maybe my heart had hardened in the meantime. Maybe I didn't find someone to help me take that other step. I had to walk on all alone, for a very long time. I couldn't depend on my mother and father, or on you. A whole village was able to depend on you, but not me."

"If in all I tried to do, I made a mistake in this as you say, well then, I really am very sorry Stiefnu. Even with the best will in the world, people still make mistakes. Mistakes can also happen out of good intentions. That's the way things are."

"Well, then they're wrong, Fr. Grejbel. Can't they be righted?"

"They will be, but not in this world."

"Not in the village, you mean to say?"

"Not in this world, Stiefnu. All of it. The village is no different from the rest of the world in this case. In all other cases, well, the village is even better than the rest of the world."

"Are you saying that because you went far away or because you think nowhere is more wonderful than the village?"

"There's nowhere more wonderful than the village, Stiefnu. But things that are wrong will remain wrong. That's how they are everywhere."

"We must wait then, mustn't we? We must wait. But set your mind at rest, Fr. Grejbel. I don't know what more you could have done. But, but, I have to say this. Have you never, but never, favoured this side? Is it possible you never found anything good to say about this side?"

"Your side of things, you mean?"

"Of course, my side of things. Here, where I am, a trader on a bumboat. Stiefnu the trader on a bumboat. You're a priest and I'm a trader on a bumboat. What a difference!"

"You say that to me, Stiefnu? Have I ever made out I'm any different from you?"

"Maybe you're right. But, in any case, there's a great distance between us."

"No, there's no distance at all."

"Then I could have been a priest and you could have been a trader on a bumboat. Is that what you mean?"

"We're not so very far distant from each other as much as you think."

"Sometimes Wistin asks me why people are so very different from each other in so many ways," Stiefnu cut him short. "I never know what to tell him when he asks why some people are born with a silver spoon in their mouth and other people are born in dire poverty. He knows what it is to live in a luxurious house as well as what it means to live outside in the Port area. But let's leave it."

Fr. Grejbel was struck by these words and he quickly raised his head and promptly lowered it once more. He did not want to pass any comments.

"Well then, what brings you here?"

"I have something very important to tell you, Stiefnu." The priest paused and glanced around. "But not here. I can't talk properly here."

"Where then, Fr. Grejbel? Don't you know that for us, folks from these parts, the land and sea, noise and quiet are the same?"

"Wherever you say, but not here."

"How about on board my boat? Shall we go there?"

"Yes, if you want, the boat will do fine. Why not?"

Stiefnu welcomed him aboard. "Go on, say what you have to say. No one will overhear, only the waves and the large fish in the depths. Go on, go on."

"I want to begin by impressing on you that Wistin isn't only yours. You have as much right to him as his mother. You both brought him into this world, the two of you together. There can be no mother without a father, and no father without a mother. Either both together or nothing at all. A sole mother cannot exist and neither a sole father. Nature dictates this."

"I know all this."

"Very well, you do know it but you seem to be forgetting it!"

"Father and mother, the two of us. What do you know about what we did, Fr. Grejbel? Wasn't that something between the two of us?"

"Nature. Something between the two of you, in the same way I was created by my mother and father both. Aren't I a man just like you are, Stiefnu? I was born as a baby not as a fully-fledged priest."

"Yes, just like me, except that you don't know that I didn't make Susanna pregnant and a mother because I wanted to."

"Because you could."

"Yes, because I could. I was man enough to do that. And I don't regret it now. Wistin is a boy to be proud of."

"Very good! Now all that's left is for him to be proud of you. He's your son, but he's not only yours, Stiefnu. Nature divides everything between two parts."

"Listen to me, Fr. Grejbel, and if you want to repeat what I tell you to someone else, that's your business. You're standing in the middle between us, after all. Without your presence there would have been too much distance and an endless silence. Wistin isn't just mine. But tomorrow is a new day when Wistin might belong to no one. Do you take my meaning? In these parts there are too many things to urge one to gather up one's belongings and up and leave. And there are too few things to bind one to this place. His roots are too weak. There, do you see Fr. Grejbel? Even I, an unlettered man, can think things through. The roots, Wistin's roots, are at breaking point."

"Then, we must do something."

"Who?"

"Let me go on. We must do something, you and I together, to prevent your son's roots from breaking off. Otherwise, without any ties whatsoever, to places and people, what will become of him? Don't you worry about this? You spend your entire day among boats and you know very well that there's no boat without a lifeline."

"I do worry, a bit, sometimes, not often mind you and not much. And to forget I go to a bar and drink beer. One bottle after another. Beer is men's milk. After eating a meal of swill, I drink beer. And you have no idea how fast the hands of the clock go! That's the beauty of time – that it passes! Hurray for time, because it passes!"

"So you do worry that you might lose your son one day, Stiefnu."

"Fr. Grejbel, let me tell you something. The village was at one end of the world. And let me tell you something else. The Port is at the other end of the world. Meaning..."

"Meaning?" the priest was prompt to interject and cut him off.

"Meaning we're all on the edge."

"Where did you find all this wisdom, Stiefnu?"

"It seems you want to pull my leg, Fr. Grejbel. I didn't study books like you did. I walked all alone on my path from that Valley down there to this place here, and I kept everything stored up here in my mind. I have nothing but my memory."

"Which means, if I understood you correctly, you don't want Wistin to leave."

"No, I don't want to lose him, at any cost. Now that I've come to know him, I don't want to lose him."

"And you do know you're in danger of losing him, don't you, Stiefnu?"

"The Port's doorway is open, look, it's open wide, night and day. Children come by ship through that doorway and adults leave by ship from the same place. And it won't surprise me in the least if I wake up tomorrow morning and search for Wistin on land, along the Quay, in the bars, on boats, in the streets, and don't find him. There are too many strong winds blowing from this direction. Even women can carry him off, it only takes one of them to do it. A smile, a wink, a waggle of the hips and off he goes, and I won't see him again. Maybe I'm to blame for all this. But the wind blew me to these parts."

"Well Stiefnu, that means Wistin needs someone to bind him to here, someone who won't let him disappear."

"That's what I've been doing so far. If it was up to him, Fr. Grejbel, he'd have taken a boat or a ship and left by now. With my blessing or not, according to the rule of law or not. If it was up to him he'd have left everyone behind. First he got fed up of the village and liked the Port, and now perhaps he's fed up of everything and everybody."

"But he's still here. Right? Stiefnu? Please, tell me, is Wistin here or not?"

"Set your mind at rest, Fr. Grejbel. And you can deliver this piece of news to whoever. I won't interfere because I know that whatever you do, you do for someone's own good. I may bring myself to quarrel with you, but I know that it's your kind heart that leads you on. However much I try, Fr. Grejbel, I cannot condemn you. Yes," Stiefnu said, pausing to change his tone of voice. "Yes, Wistin is still here, up to now. He wanted to escape though. Even though he came to know me, his real father, as he wanted to. Sometimes I looked for him to no avail. He was a stowaway on board a ship. But now I've convinced him it's not in his best interests to do that. He's still far too young to leave. And I told him that even in other ports, far away from here, he would find it hard to make a living. But maybe he doesn't even know what he's doing at the moment. Up to now I've managed to hold him back from leaving. But I don't know if I'll be able to keep him from taking that step in future."

"I suppose it's no use asking you where he is, is it?"

"No, don't expect me to tell you. If you don't mind, Fr. Grejbel, I'd rather you didn't ask me again. You know I won't tell you."

"Very well. I won't ask you again. The main thing is that he's still here."

"You have my word."

"He's here, at the Port, right?"

"The Port covers a large area and don't forget, it's open all the time. Many people live here and they don't always know everybody else. I've been working here for many years but I can't say where the Port begins and where it ends. There are no surrounding walls or hills here. There's only water."

Fr. Grejbel was afraid to say another word. All that Stiefnu was telling him seemed to be the very opposite of what the village stood for.

"Well anyway, what did you want to tell me? What news have you brought me that I don't already know?"

"Even if you do know it already, Stiefnu, and can hazard a guess where it comes from, pay attention to what I'm about to say. Susanna will do her utmost and will start sending you money for Wistin."

"Very good."

"It's going to mean a great sacrifice on her part."

"That's a very good thing, too."

"She's going to have to go out and find work. And she's going to do it to be certain to fulfil all your expectations. Can this poor woman do more than that?"

"Everyone needs to work for a living. Time will tell. Everything depends on someone else."

"Someone else?" the priest wanted to know, taken aback.

"On Wistin. If he's happy, well then... Then there's no problem."

"But what if he isn't?"

"Fr. Grejbel, please don't ask me any more questions. This time I won't give in."

"You're asking too much, Stiefnu."

"Fr. Grejbel, I'll have you know that up to now I've lost every battle, starting with the very first one. This is the very first time, after all these years, that the wind is beginning to favour me a little. After all I'm his father. I still have a right to bend his will to mine. Do I have that right or not?"

"Up to now, yes."

"Up to now, true. But there's something very much in my favour."

Fr. Grejbel brought to mind the whole sorry tale, from the moment when Susanna found herself to be pregnant and did not find anyone to come to her aid. "There's something in your favour?"

"Wistin has now discovered his real father and it seems he gets on very well with him. We agree on things and we're alike."

"This is good news."

"It is for me. But not for you. And even less for her. Wistin is convinced that all the stories they used to tell him served only to cheat him. Stories upon stories, so that he would lose himself in a world that doesn't exist, with dreams and fantasies which would make him forget. But it couldn't go on when he grew up and began to realize what was happening. At that moment he wanted to know the truth, and that was something they had never told him."

"They couldn't tell him the truth, Stiefnu."

"Because it wasn't in their interest to do so. The stories served their purpose. It was still the time for fairy tales." Changing his tone of voice he went on saying, "But Wistin knew it was simply a game to keep him happy without questioning it, to keep his thoughts centred only on ships and a port, somewhere far away from him, and on people who had to wait..."

"If you want, Stiefnu, I could tell Wistin the whole story myself and he can set his mind at rest. All you have to do is tell me where I can meet him."

"No one knows the story of Wistin's birth better than you. If you manage to tell him everything, and win his trust, well then, Fr. Grejbel, it would be a grand achievement. But I have my doubts how far you'll succeed."

"I'm going to try."

"I hope he'll believe you. He hardly believes me. He needs confirmation."

A few days later, Fr. Grejbel met up with Wistin. "There's a story I'd like to tell you," the priest said to him.

Wistin smiled and Fr. Grejbel embarked on a narrative...

"Once upon a time, there was a maiden who lived in a village, and she loved everything about it and one day she met a young man and fell in love with him. It so happened that one day they went down into the Valley, far away from anyone. He wanted to show his love for her. Some time later she found out that she was with child. Her parents couldn't accept it. Her father, especially, took it very hard because it went against all he had ever believed in. So he came up with a plan whereupon his daughter would give birth in a place unknown to her and the baby would immediately be taken away as soon as it was born to a place where it would be brought up, without anyone ever knowing where. At one point, the pregnant young woman was turned out of doors by her father and she found herself out on the street without knowing where she could spend the night. She was in her fourth month of pregnancy. She went and knocked on the door of a priest who had already turned in for the night, but he opened the door and invited her in. When she told him she didn't have a roof over her head and nowhere to sleep, he made her welcome in his own house. It was unseemly to spend the night sleeping outside. She was very apprehensive and reluctant to accept his invitation but he put new heart into her. But that's how all the trouble began, both for him and for her. When her time to give birth arrived, her father accepted her back into his house but he had laid all his plans and her baby was taken away as soon as it was born without even allowing her to know whether it was a boy or a girl. When her father lay dying, the young woman went up to her father's sickbed together with the priest, imploring him to tell her where her baby was. He refused to tell her. In the meantime, the baby was well looked after. The young woman's father had once let his wife know where the child was being brought up, on condition that some time would be allowed to pass after his own demise for the child to be restored to its mother. He was adamant he would not break with tradition. And that is what came to pass some years later, and the child, a boy, was found and brought up by his mother. The boy passed from the orphanage run by nuns into his own mother's hands," Fr. Grejbel said, heaving a sigh and falling silent, his head bowed down with remembered cares.

"Meaning the child passed into my mother's hands," Wistin said, wanting a full clarification of all he had listened to.

"That's right, Wistin," Fr. Grejbel hastened to reassure him.

"And that pregnant young woman was Susanna?"

"Yes, it was Susanna."

"You mean my mother."

"Yes, your mother."

"And Susanna's mother was Katarina?"

"It was Katarina, your grandmother."

"And Susanna's father was Saverju?"

"Yes, he was Saverju."

"I remember, once they took me to see his grave."

"Yes, that's right. He was your grandfather."

"You knew my grandfather well, didn't you?"

"Yes, Wistin, I knew him well."

"And the priest was called..."

"You know his name, don't you?" Fr. Grejbel said with a smile.

"Yes, yes, I know. I've realized most of this through the years. A little from here and a little from there, sometimes thinking it through and sometimes dreaming it up, alone, without any word being spoken, and suddenly it all came together. But I could never bring myself to believe it entirely. Should I believe you, Fr.Grejbel?" Wistin spoke in a very firm voice.

"There's too much love in your story not to believe it, Wistin. Whatever happened, happened out of love, with the love they knew how. And above all, from amongst all of them, there's your mother."

"My mother? Do you think my mother loved me? Or, truth to tell, she didn't want me? How do I know my mother didn't abandon me because she didn't want it known that she was my mother? She didn't want it known she'd given birth to me and so..."

"Can you bring yourself to think that?"

"So, in this whole sorry tale, the blame can be put on her mother and father. One who is a good, kind woman, devout and pious, and the other who was an arrogant man but is now dead. Who can contradict all this? Her mother counted for nothing, she had no say in anything. And her father kept sole command. And my mother, Susanna, that poor, poor girl was the innocent victim of all this," Wistin spoke with barely controlled rage. "And the true victim, in actual fact, was none other than me."

"To a lesser or greater extent, Wistin, the victim in these circumstances was everyone. Your grandfather died in a storm of worry estranged from his daughter. He was unable to marry love and duty as a father right up to the end. He remained feeling torn apart between the two, even though he was convinced he had done the right thing. I was there Wistin, by his side on his deathbed."

"You were there, by his side?"

"Your mother pleaded with him for the last time, but he remained adamant."

"And what about Grandma?"

"Your grandmother remained beside herself with worry for a long time and didn't find peace till she found you. When Saverju died, she did her utmost to resolve the situation, she and Susanna. Both of them were now free to take their own steps."

"But not before Grandpa Saverju had died. Before his death they could do nothing!"

"No, Wistin, before his death they couldn't do anything."

"A neat story, Fr. Grejbel. A very interesting one. But what proof do I have that it is the whole truth?"

"Don't you believe it, Wistin?"

"No I don't! How do I know there wasn't a place in an orphanage all ready and waiting for me even before I was born?"

"And who do you suppose thought up such a plan?"

"My... my mother."

"No, no! Wistin! Your mother always wanted you, from the very beginning, up to now, this very day!"

"And what proof do I have of this?"

"There's no proof except for one thing. You have to believe me. Do you believe me, Wistin?"

"Please forgive me, Fr. Grejbel, forgive me, but I don't know! Maybe it's because you're such a good man! You might have been duped! I can't just take your word for it."

"You don't believe me?" the priest was stunned, doubting whether he had heard correctly. "I don't have proof, I don't have any other proof but what I'm telling you. You can never defend the truth, Wistin. It's far more powerful than any proof. There's no adequate defence for truth. And truth doesn't need any defence, either."

"But, for Susanna's sake you..."

"For your mother's sake, you mean." Fr. Grejbel promptly corrected him.

"For my mother's sake then, very well... you're too fond of making excuses for her. Why is that, Fr. Grejbel?"

The priest bowed his head and was silent. His face plainly showed that those words had wounded him deeply. "Don't you believe me?"

Wistin kept his gaze on the ground and his elbows resting on his knees. He shook his head.

"Your father himself, Wistin, can now help you come to believe all that I'm telling you. He too trod along this path."

"For me to believe, Fr. Grejbel, you must perform a miracle!"

"Well then let me tell you. If afterwards you'd believe, well then I'll try to make one happen! I'll tell you one thing: without faith, everything, but everything in life is absurd."

"I don't have faith, Fr. Grejbel."

"I'm not understanding. Speak plainly, Wistin."

"I look at the sea and try to imagine the depths, and I gaze at the earth and skies and say to myself, I ask myself: But where is He? Is He looking down here at this moment?"

"First of all you need to be certain He exists, that He is alive, and then it will dawn on you quietly that He is indeed present, accompanying us along the way. It's not a straight road, Wistin. For anybody. Everyone has questions like yours, Wistin, to a lesser or greater extent. And the answer comes from within, like a heartbeat. Otherwise it has no value."

"If that's what you believe and just what I can't believe, well then, Fr. Grejbel, that's already a miracle!"

"Our miracles, Wistin, are small ones because we, people, are small, but He is kind and merciful and considers them big miracles! His magnifying glass sees everything on a larger scale, on purpose, and so He sees everything close-up and nothing escapes Him."

"Nothing? Nothing? Not even if someone escapes from the village?" Wistin paused and then changed tack. "And afterwards, you didn't stay in the village, did you?"

Fr. Grejbel nodded affirmation.

"And you went very far away from here?"

"Yes, yes."

"Because of Susanna."

"It was God's will."

"But the story goes on. I know, I know, but in the meantime, you didn't lose that faith you talked about? Did you still believe?"

"Of course, of course I did, Wistin."

"Should I believe you now, Fr. Grejbel?"

"The important thing now, Wistin, is not to believe me but for you to start feeling the same."

"I can't, I'm sorry, but I just can't!"

"Maybe it's still too soon."

"Yes, maybe it's too soon, like Grandma Katarina likes to say."

"Everything is calling you back, Wistin. All your future lies in the upbringing you've had. Even your love for Antonja. She, too, grew up in the same soil you did, and that's where she'd like to go on."

Wistin's face lit up as soon as Fr. Grejbel mentioned Antonja.

Chapter 8

It was still very early. Wistin could not rest with all the thoughts jostling around and growing in his mind after Fr. Grejbel had talked to him. He spent the entire night trying to decide what he should do. He was reluctant to return to his mother's house but he was also unwilling to let days go by without discussing what he felt with someone. He knew he could always seek his father out somewhere in that neighbourhood. He was certain to find him in one of those bars that were open in the evenings, or somewhere along the quay, chatting with friends, all of them proud of their boat tied up and bobbing about in mid-harbour, ready for work and waiting for a new day's work to begin. But at the same time, he did not feel the need to go looking for his father to have a talk with him. In the short time since he had made his acquaintance, he had become used to him, was at ease with him. Maybe it was because he still remembered his mother introducing Stiefnu to him without saying who he really was, beside his grandfather Saverju's grave when he, Wistin, was still a little boy.

Many years had to pass before Wistin discovered that the man, standing by his mother's side on the day when she took him to see Grandpa Saverju's grave on purpose, was none other than Stiefnu. He was still a little boy flying his kite then, and on that day, just before going to the cemetery, he had left his kite lying torn on the ground. His grandmother had gone to look for his mother and him there, but she had only found the torn kite, which she recognized and picked up. Katarina searched for them and had gone to the cemetery on a hunch, finding the three of them there. Susanna took Wistin there and Stiefnu turned up to meet them as prearranged. In this way, Stiefnu saw his son and the boy saw his grandfather's grave. Grandma Katarina had stood beyond the iron gate. Wistin had called out to her loudly when he saw her but she had put her forefinger across her lips, motioning him to silence, making him aware of the need to keep quiet in a cemetery. Susanna had helped him make the Sign of the Cross, putting her hand over his and guiding it, first to his forehead, then down to his chest and then across to his left shoulder. He had shaken off her hand at that point, wanting to continue making the Sign of the Cross on his own. In his other hand he held a bunch of flowers. His mother had told him to put it down on the gravestone and then to greet his grandfather, telling him, 'I love you'. The three of them started walking back to the gate, with him in the middle. One of his hands was clasped in his mother's hand and the other was held by his father. Wistin could recall very clearly his father letting go of his hand, saying goodbye and departing. After all these years, he no longer went to fly a kite or made the Sign of the Cross all that often, Wistin reflected. He had grown up. He decided there and then to go to his grandmother, feeling sure of an unconditional welcome from that quarter, as if nothing had happened.

He knocked twice on her door but the house seemed deserted. He turned and walked to the church. He was certain his grandmother was somewhere there. He entered the church and looked all around, but he did not feel like getting down on his knees to pray. He wished he could behave like the other people there, having faith and going regularly to church, and most of all he wished he could feel like they did, filling up the place with their fervent prayers. He could hear them praying earnestly, endlessly, untiringly, with great seriousness, with a rhythm that resembled the sound of a deep breath, and the church echoed with waves of sound formed by their continuous chanted prayers. He too, a long time before, used to pray when his mother and his grandmother took him along with them, and he used to get down on his knees, make the Sign of the Cross, open his hands palm upward as the adults were in the habit of doing, and then go near one of the niches holding the statue of a saint to light a candle. He used to feel proud and a good boy. The men used to remove their cap on entering church, and the women used to put on their veil, holding the two ends together with their hands, as if afraid that the slightest movement or breeze would uncover their head. That would cause them enormous embarrassment. He used to smile indulgently at people who stopped to pray in front of every niche, saying a prayer whilst stretching out a hand to touch the glass pane and bringing it back to their lips. He used to admire the altar boys, and the priest, and the sacristan, but nowadays he knew for sure that he could no longer feel the way they felt. He waited for mass to be over.

He had already seen where she was, in her usual corner, head lowered respectfully and inclined to one side, holding her rosary beads. He reckoned that she would soon rise from the chair and walk towards St. Joseph's niche, stopping to say a prayer there. St. Joseph's statue was beautiful and it pleased him, but he had never stopped to recite a prayer in front of it, though the statue's face drew his attention. He knew on whose behalf Grandma Katarina would recite a prayer. He followed her movements with his eyes till she left the church and started making her way home. She did not remove her veil till she was halfway across the square.

"You couldn't make me happier than this, Wistin," she beamed at him as soon as she saw him before her eyes.

"I'm very happy to see you again, too. I wasn't very far away from here," he responded.

"Everywhere is far away for us, dear. Anywhere beyond the village is far. That's what being far means, anywhere that is not right here."

"The next village is far away for you, Gran?" he asked her banteringly.

Katarina pulled out the large iron key that was her latchkey from her skirt pocket and opened her front door.

204

"Your mother went to live in the next village because she got married," she told him, almost as if she were scolding him. "That's why she went there, dear."

"She got married in the other village. The people there are different, aren't they?"

"People fall into one of two categories. Good or bad. People from these parts are all good, or nearly so. How can I say otherwise if they're neighbours? When your mother got married, your grandfather and I didn't go to the wedding. We stayed at home, gazing at each other, and your grandfather wanted me to lock up early, as if imagining the day would then be over more quickly. She and her husband were there alone. His mother and father were dead and Saverju and I were here. Poor bride and bridegroom."

"Because of me. That's why, wasn't it Gran?"

Katarina pretended not to hear him. "And we refused to speak to them for a long time."

"That's what Grandpa Saverju wanted, wasn't it?"

"Yes, that's what your grandfather wanted. That's what he thought he should do and so that's what he did."

"I'd like to go to see his grave one of these days, Gran. The way you speak about him makes me think he was very different from you."

"We can go whenever you want. Do you want to go today, Wistin?"

"If you want us to go today, yes. But before that there's something I want to tell you, Gran."

"You want to tell me something?" she matched her mood to his, easing herself onto her rocking chair as if wishing to fall asleep for a long, long time. "Ahh!" she exclaimed. "What can you tell me, now in my old age, that I can't guess at? What could possibly surprise me in all that you're about to say? I've lived long enough not to be surprised by anything anymore. Go on, tell me."

The tone of her voice spoke volumes to Wistin, making him realize how annoyed she was with him and possibly that she was also offended. He knew he had let her down badly but he was also certain that she was a good, kind woman and that as usual, she would be ready to excuse and forgive him without effort. She spoilt him and he counted on it.

"Gran, do you know that Mum...?"

"The heart, my dear, stays beating as long as it's alive," she interjected to cut him short. She was waiting to hear him start talking about Susanna.

"My mum. Do you know that Mum has started seeing someone?"

Katarina stopped the rocking chair's movement with a violent kick to the ground and as soon as its motion was arrested, she rose to her feet and in a voice that held no tremors, unusually so for her, barked out, "How do you know?"

"How do I know! Why shouldn't I know? People told me, Gran."

"They shouldn't have said anything to you. They don't mean you any good."

"Even my father knows."

"What does your father know?"

"Mum is seeing Pawlu *tal-Ħaxix*. They meet every day somewhere near the Valley. She's working for him, selling flowers and plants, and people buy from her because they tell each other she was Lady's servant and was married to Mr. Arturu. The villagers look upon her respectfully, because she lives in a grand house that's very different from their own and they also buy from her because it's Pawlu who employs her and he too is a rich man."

"Yes, yes, my dear, that's so. If it was up to me, your mother would remain a widow till the end of her days. You should only marry once in your life. But if she wants to go courting with another man, what can I, from this armchair here, do about it?"

"Are you happy to see all this happening?"

Katarina did not say a word. She kicked her rocking chair into motion again and gently rocked herself to and fro. "I do my best, Wistin. I'm going to tell you something, listen carefully: I saved you once when I could. And the onus falls on me again to save you once more, in the way I can manage. This goes against my wish but there are times and then there are other times, and now, in order to save you, I must do something else."

"Do something else? Do you mean close your eyes, pretend you don't know, or you're not taking any notice? Is that what you mean, Gran?"

"My eyes don't close so easily, Wistin. I don't sleep much. No, no, I don't close my eyes. But I must see what can be done. We haven't had an easy life, that's what it boils down to."

"Well, Gran, Mum has taken up the courting game again," he answered half seriously and half-jokingly.

"Your mother is trying to save you, Wistin. Don't you know all this? Aren't you living in the Port neighbourhood? You've left these parts." She was suddenly afraid that her words would enrage him and she softened her voice and looked back at him with a smile. "Try to understand what I feel, Wistin, in my old age, after having thought that my last vow was granted and that it was going to be truly my last one. Well, it wasn't!"

"Did you make another vow, Gran?" he asked her slyly, as if mocking her.

"Yes, Wistin, I made another vow."

"Because of me."

"Needs must, my dear."

"I know to whom you made the vow, Gran."

Katarina turned to face him, waiting to hear him speak.

"You made the vow to St. Joseph."

"Are you going to church again, by any chance?" she exclaimed happily, a smile starting across her face.

"No, no, Gran. I'm not a churchgoer anymore. I saw the face of St. Joseph painted on my father's boat. I recognized it straightaway. It's the face painted on the statue of St. Joseph in our village church, the very same one."

"Really? So you know where your father keeps his boat?"

"Of course I know. And sometimes I sleep in it too."

Katarina was startled on hearing this. "And if the sea is rough? And if the boat rocks hard with you on board? And what if a storm should break whilst you're sleeping in it?" In her mind's eye, she conjured up images of the boat's rope coming undone, the boat starting to drift away out into the open sea beyond the Port with Wistin aboard. With an effort she reined in her imagination and told him sorrowfully, "You've forgotten this village, Wistin. You've forgotten us."

"I don't know what you mean."

"Don't you understand what I mean?"

"No, Gran, I don't. I'd like to know though."

"Simple. It means, do you still feel something for your mother, Wistin?"

Wistin was silent.

"Your mother went out to work to be able to pay your way, so that you can have enough to live on. Didn't you know?"

"No, I didn't."

"Don't you know?"

"What has my mother got to do with my life?" he asked her angrily. "I work in the Port, I seek employment day after day, and that's all."

"And whenever you want, you can return to your mother, Wistin. There's an entire house lying empty in your absence."

Wistin did not answer her.

"Why don't you go back to your mother's house? She lives there all alone in that enormous house, waiting for you to turn up from one day to the next. Dreaming, worrying, peeping out of the window in the hope of seeing you coming."

"And she goes courting, too."

Katarina drew a deep breath, saying, "Yes my dear, you're right about that."

"Meaning it doesn't please you to see her look at another man and coming to love him. This time you're not siding with her."

"Wistin, a person's heart..."

"Has wings, a person's heart has wings. Isn't that what you're going to say?"

"Well maybe that's so it can fly." she admitted unwillingly.

"Like the kite I had as a boy, Gran. So, you no longer have any hold over her heart, Gran?"

Katarina had not expected such words. She turned to face him swiftly and in a strong voice told him, "Wistin, I know what you're going to tell me but I want to ask you all the same. Where did you learn to say such words?"

"At sea, Gran. The sea holds much wisdom because it's very deep."

"I'm not joking with you here, Wistin. Who spoke to you about your mother?"

"Can't you guess, Gran?" he answered in a firm voice.

Katarina immediately brought to mind all that Fr. Grejbel had told her: "Be careful of the least word you say to Wistin. Make sure you don't put him at loggerheads with his father because that's not right, and it will serve you ill. The more you have to say against his father, the more distance you'll be putting between you and him. If you want him to approach you, show him your love, and nothing else. Love can work miracles and goes a long way. One day, love will be proved right."

"My father, Stiefnu the trader on a bumboat, Gran, that's who talked to me about my mother."

"Then let me tell you this, Wistin. I don't control my daughter's heart. If I could, I would close my eyes right now and imagine the three of you, your mother, your father and you, together."

"Do you really wish that, Gran? Are you sure of what you're telling me?"

Katarina did not answer him.

Wistin rose from his grandmother's side and told her he was leaving.

"Stay with me, Wistin! I have no one else left. I'm trying to husband all the strength I have left to be of use to you. Otherwise why would I want to linger here any longer?"

"You want to go near Grandpa?"

"My place is by his side, Wistin, because he was, and will always be, my husband. But down here I have no one."

"You have my mother, you have Susanna."

"I don't hold her heart anymore, Wistin. Can't you understand that?"

"That means my mother has someone else, then."

"Yes, she has someone else," his grandmother answered him wearily.

"And my father doesn't come into this at all, Gran?"

"Wistin, you need to learn this lesson too. Children's hearts don't belong to their mother and father."

"Do you want my mother to marry Pawlu *tal-Ħaxix*?"

Katarina was flustered, as if caught between two conflicting positions and she said, "I don't know. I still don't know what to think. Up to now, I've never had to face such a situation. Give me some time to think it over and I will think long and hard about it and let you know. But for now, no, no, I just don't know what to think."

Wistin went up to his grandmother and kissed her lightly on her forehead, giving her right hand a gentle squeeze, and then he went out of the room.

"Won't you ask for my blessing? What should you say, Wistin?"

"Bl-ess-me," he chanted as he opened the front door and stepped out, slamming the door shut behind him.

The slamming of the door, though entirely expected, still managed to startle Katarina. With both her feet she kicked her rocking chair into motion. Her gaze was directed at something far away and she bit her lower lip to stop herself uttering a single word.

***

Susanna still went to market every day. She had become used to selling flowers and plants and people had become used to her as well. The shyness she had felt at first gradually slipped away and slowly, slowly, she also learnt how to call out to make people come and buy her goods. She remembered some regular customers by name. She chose a few words to say and called them out, loudly, occasionally trying to sing them too, like the chants she heard all the other sellers use. The market thus resembled a choir. Whatever housewives bought from her could never amount to much. Rich customers were few and far between and most probably the rest were used to making do with meagre amounts of everything. Not everybody could afford to buy flowers because these were often an extravagance or a luxury. Some villagers liked to have a small bunch of flowers in a vase on the kitchen table where they had their meals, and in another vase kept in front of Our Lady's image which was to be found somewhere or other in every home. The plants she sold were sought after though, but she had a soft spot for the flowers she sold, whatever kind they happened to be. She considered them all to be beautiful and they all had some sort of fragrance. Their mere colours were enough to please and she used to gaze at them lost in thought and then raise her head to give her attention to passers-by, hoping they would stop and buy something. When it was time to pack up and go home, in the early hours of the afternoon, she would pick up her two reed baskets, holding them one on each hip with her hands coming to rest halfway across her stomach, and she would make her way back to Pawlu's house. Sometimes she would pin the most beautiful flower that was left to her bodice. If someone stopped her on her way in order to buy something, she would still serve the last-minute customer graciously. She greeted everyone and people used to smile back at her, even those who never bought anything.

"How did it go today?" Pawlu would ask her.

"These are the flowers that are left," she used to reply.

"Take them with you to adorn your home."

In this way, her house never lacked for colours or fragrance. It was not the first time that she gathered up the flowers that were left into a bouquet and made straight for the church where she put them in front of one statue or another. One time she shared them out between children she met in the street and they ran home gleefully handing their flower to their mother, though some children approached people and tried to sell their flower to earn something.

Pawlu was reluctant to see her go. He had been drawn to her for a very long time. She was a good and decent woman who minded her own business, a good worker and withal, very beautiful. Now that he had seen many pretty faces on women, frequenting the market or coming out of the church or strolling about in the village square, he could weigh things calmly and decide sensibly. "Stay here a bit. I can find you some other work to do today. And the more you work, the more I'll pay you," he told her one fine day, taking the plunge.

"It's time to go home now and I'd better go."

"It's time? For whom? I live alone and don't have much else to occupy me. Same as usual. And you too, no?"

Susanna ducked her head and did not reply.

"Aren't you alone too? Tell me. Now you'll go home and how will you spend the rest of the day?"

"Maybe my mother will call round. She might come and if she makes the effort I don't want it to be in vain. She would surely worry if she knocked on my door and I didn't answer it.

You know how relatives think. They smell danger at the drop of a hat."

"And if she doesn't turn up?" he asked her with a smile. "She has a fair distance if she comes on foot. And by now, if she has to walk back it will be dark till she gets home."

"Well, maybe my son will come. I'm always waiting for him to turn up, day and night. He may appear unexpectedly, one of these days."

"Is that what you think, Susanna?"

"Yes. At least, I'd like to think that." She had frequently opened her heart to him, telling him that she lived only for the day when she would see Wistin come back home and have him treat her with respect. After all this time, she said, she was ready to content herself with crumbs of comfort, just a tiny bit of his love.

Pawlu put down what he was holding. He approached her as she was sitting around the table, resting his hands on the table surface and telling her, "Susanna, listen to me."

"No, no, Pawlu. Thank you, but I'd better go. Some other time, I promise."

"Do you want us to go and look for Wistin?"

"No, no! Let him walk wherever his heart dictates. That's the advice I got. He must come back of his own free will, out of love, otherwise..."

Pawlu told her he knew the Port and its environs well, and they could get there in a short time. He had done business with several people and he knew to whom he should turn.

Susanna reiterated her thanks and the matter rested there.

"Well then, just one more thing. I have to say this and then you can go."

"What is it?" she asked, full of apprehension.

"Stiefnu wants money from you."

"He came to tell you that himself?"

Pawlu nodded.

"Doesn't Stiefnu know I've gone out to work for my son's sake?"

"Aren't you happy to be working, and with me?"

"Of course! Of course I'm glad, but I started working..."

"You started working for his sake. He knows that, too." Pawlu was about to put his hand across her mouth to stop her speaking, but he held back.

"Doesn't he know that I immediately started looking for work? Thank the Lord you welcomed me with open arms. What more does he want? He can wait a while till I save up a pretty sum and then I'll send it to him."

"I can take it myself, don't worry."

"Very well, very well."

"But Stiefnu wants a large amount, a lump sum, and after that he won't bother you again."

"The money Arturu left me has to serve me for my daily needs, as was the custom in his family. There's a chest containing money. I knew that when the money ran out, I would have to go out to work, like I did before. But Arturu didn't want me to go out to work. At the time, I was pregnant with his baby," she continued, "but then he closed his eyes forever and I lost the baby, as well." Susanna came to a stop, trying hard to stem her tears. Pawlu did not speak, waiting for her to go on.

"I need that money to live on," she said, speaking as if to herself.

"It's not that money he has in mind."

Susanna paused to gather her thoughts together and then gave a jerk as it all suddenly dawned on her. "How can he stoop so low? It comes to this, then? Well, never mind! Very well," she said grimly. "If I knew all this would serve to make Wistin's life easier, I will do whatever it takes. I will sell the house and everything in it, except those pieces dear to Arturu's heart because they were the best keepsakes of his family. I will keep whatever I can out of respect for him, because he gave me everything I have. But I don't need the rest. I know, yes I know I don't need them. If I was sure that all this will serve to make Wistin happy."

Pawlu advised her to take her time in thinking it over. It was a big step to take and she would do well to consult a lawyer.

"Can I depend on your help?" she begged him. "I don't know about these things and I'll only make some mistake or other."

"I myself am telling you I'm at your service. You can trust me, don't worry. Dealing with money is my job. And just so you can set your mind at rest completely, we can include Fr. Grejbel in this business, if you want. You can then be sure there's no deceit and our combined experience should prevent any mistakes. Fr. Grejbel doesn't live a life of luxury but he knows what it means to be responsible for money since he runs a parish."

Susanna appeared very pleased with this suggestion. "Thank you so much! I was about to mention Fr. Grejbel myself, even though I don't want to bother him more than I already have. Where do matters stand with Stiefnu?"

"He's going to come round again in a few days' time. I'm going to tell him."

"Tell him Susanna will give him the sum he wants. At least that way he'll know what kind of mother I am! I was a mother from the start, a good mother! I always stayed with my son, whenever I could, and now Wistin... I don't know, I don't know," she said, her voice breaking. "And now I would like Wistin to know that, to understand that I'm at his side."

"He'll come to realize that soon enough, don't you worry," Pawlu said encouragingly.

Susanna went straight to her mother, telling her she had decided to sell the house she had gained on her marriage in order to give Stiefnu the means to support Wistin. At least, that's what Stiefnu had decided.

Katarina was taken aback and drew in a sharp breath. She told her daughter to be careful and not rush into something

215

like that without proper advice. "Consult someone who knows about such things, daughter. We're the sort of people who are bound to the land and we have no experience in such matters. Don't take such a step on your own!"

"I've already taken advice, Mother, don't worry," she replied, thoughtful.

"By any chance, did you ask for advice from...?"

"I took advice from the right quarter, Mother, and it was good advice."

"Did you bring any flowers with you today? Yes, yes, there," Katarina changed the subject, turning her back to look at one side of the room, "I didn't even notice that bouquet! Well, they're fresh flowers at least, with really pretty colours, I can't deny. One more beautiful than the next. They only need a butterfly to come fluttering by and alight on them! But flowers wither soon enough, and they soon won't smell so sweet daughter. You'll have to throw them away then."

"Mother, stop wittering on about flowers."

"Oh very well! And then, after you sell the house, what are you going to do?"

"Well, then, if you're willing, I'd like to come here and live with you."

"Here with me? With all my heart, dear daughter! If all this will be in your best interest, and that of your son, and maybe, why not, maybe..."

"The pot stands on a tripod, doesn't it, Mother?"

"Yes, on three supports, that's it, on three. Let's wait and see."

Pawlu and Fr. Grejbel took care of the whole matter. In a short time, Susanna had a large sum of money in her hands and she could give Stiefnu some of it. All that remained was for the two men to meet him and hand over the money.

"The best thing to do is to meet over at your place," Pawlu told the priest. "See which day is most convenient for you and at what time."

Fr. Grejbel agreed and Stiefnu came to the meeting as arranged. They negotiated the terms till they reached an agreement and Stiefnu was satisfied.

"You can tell Susanna I'm completely satisfied now," Stiefnu told Pawlu and Fr. Grejbel.

"You mean, in this way Wistin too will be happy and satisfied, don't you Stiefnu? Do I understand you well?" Fr. Grejbel insisted. "All that we're doing here, the three of us, is for Wistin's benefit. Since you want to have a lump sum now, and not a small regular amount of money. If you really want to take care of your son, it would be better to have a small sum occasionally, and that way you can eke it out better."

"We all make a decision in the way we feel. That's how I feel. We all do what we think is best."

"For us."

"What's best. That's all."

"Which means," Fr. Grejbel insisted, "Wistin will content himself this way." He brought to mind what Stiefnu had told him some time before.

"If I'm happy and content, then everyone is. Can I say better than that? The agreement has been reached with me."

"With you, because you're Wistin's father," Fr. Grejbel reminded him.

"Of course, of course, and as Stiefnu the trader on a bumboat," Stiefnu replied half-jokingly. "With me not with Wistin. Actually, Wistin shouldn't know about it at all."

"This is all for Wistin's benefit, isn't it?" Pawlu asked Stiefnu.

"It's all as you say, Mr. Pawlu."

Days passed but Susanna did not hear from Stiefnu or Wistin. She continued going to market to sell her flowers and plants expecting to see one or the other, coming to buy something like an ordinary customer or at least coming to have a word with her. She told Pawlu she was ready to go with her two reed baskets and sell her goods even in the Port environs, if Pawlu wanted to send her there.

"As if! Susanna, what are you thinking of?" She told him she was still living in hope. She did not even believe her own words. Now that Stiefnu had acquired what he had wanted so much from her, she was expecting him to relent and if he had been keeping Wistin away from her, he would now let him come to her. Sometimes she entertained doubts about this, as well. All that money in Stiefnu's hands meant Wistin could be taken care of, but nothing more. It did not mean he would leave the Port and its neighbourhood to return to the village fields. What was there to draw him back, now? Susanna wished Fr. Grejbel could convince Wistin not to leave and go far, far away. She was afraid he would go and live in some distant village or worse still, leave from the open doorway of the Port aboard some ship and never return. Even Antonja's mother and father were afraid of losing their daughter.

The change from Arturu's grand house to Katarina's tiny dwelling did not have much of an impact on Susanna. It was more in the nature of a return to humble beginnings. Her only regret was that she had let Arturu down in some way. However, he had once assured her that he was leaving everything in her hands, to do as she saw fit. "Take care of everything, but according to what you feel is best. You know I've made my will," he had told her a short while before his death.

She had never realized how deeply Wistin's behaviour had wounded Arturu. It was only later that she realized Arturu was feeling he was treated as an outsider in his own house. He did not discuss it with her so as not escalate things. Ever since they had come together again, he had wanted to ensure nothing hurt Susanna at all costs, almost as if to make amends for the anger he had directed at Susanna and at himself. He also wanted to prove Fr. Grejbel right. He wanted the priest to think that all the trouble he had brought on himself for their sake had not been in vain. Even Fr. Grejbel had the right to find satisfaction in this.

"Nothing is left now," Susanna observed sadly. But then she would cheer herself up with the thought that at some time or other, Wistin would remember the happy years he had spent with her, and stories and the kite would work their magic over him once more. "He can't possibly throw all that away now. If only I could fill him up with happiness and lull him to sleep with stories again. If I could, I would start telling him... Once upon a time..."

***

Although he would be within the four walls of his room, surrounded only by a few people he could trust, far away from the squares, streets and alleyways, the Bishop made every effort to follow whatever was happening, both in the vicinity and far away. He wished he knew every priest in his diocese well, even though the distant, reclusive villages dotting the countryside were worlds apart. As the shepherd of a large flock, he was convinced that his gaze should reach the far corners of his domain, far, far away, even where his eyes would find it hard to penetrate. However, there was no way he could fail to distinguish Fr. Grejbel from anyone else or forget him, even amongst all the other priests and people. The suffering endured by the country priest was not something he could ever forget, especially since it was he himself who had summoned him and ordered him to leave the country and exile himself somewhere else, in some distant land. Throughout that time, he had observed that Fr. Grejbel could hold his peace, bow down in obedience, and continue to wait in hope. These were very important lessons. And the Bishop did not forget the huge welcome the villagers had accorded the priest on his return by ship, either. They had flocked down to the harbour, waiting for the ship to berth, and they had greeted him and celebrated his return by holding a feast, one of those feasts normally held only in their patron saint's honour. From that day onwards, the Bishop held Fr. Grejbel in high respect.

219

One fine day, a short while after celebrating mass and entering the sacristy, Fr. Grejbel found a man waiting for him. The man had just descended from a *karozzin* and entered the sacristy, asked for him by name, scrutinized him carefully to make sure he was who he said he was, and given him a letter.

Fr. Grejbel smiled at him and kept his gaze on him.

"The Bishop sent you this letter," the man told him. Nodding a farewell, the man went out and left on the *karozzin* that had brought him there.

The next day, Fr. Grejbel found himself in the Bishop's office, sitting down in an armchair which he felt was too large and luxurious for him, with his hands gripping his hat across his lap. Sometimes, out of nervousness or embarrassment, he crushed the hat between his hands and the hat received a further battering. It was an old hat.

"Nowadays I'm a tired old man, who has travelled a long, hard road," the Bishop told him. "I know the end cannot be far away for me. And I have no wish to linger on. This is a time when I need to show, even to myself, conviction in all that I appeared to stand for. Why should I show any reluctance to meet my Lord, now? Otherwise, what have I believed in for all these years? What was I convinced of? What sort of future would I have been assured of?"

In that silence, amidst the sturdy walls of that grand old building, every word assumed greater importance. There was no other sound, no other voice.

"I have to leave this world, just like everybody else, true... But I'm very much afraid that the weight I carry will be far greater than that of anyone else." The Bishop paused and gazed earnestly at the priest, seeming to seek comfort.

Fr. Grejbel, who was still trying to find a comfortable position in the armchair, and who was still clutching and mangling his hat, was at a loss for words and so he merely nodded, as if listening to and agreeing with the Bishop.

The Bishop realized it was time to change the subject. "Never mind, don't worry, that's my problem, the last one, and the biggest one I've had to face. But please, Fr. Grejbel," he went on saying with a more satisfied air, "don't forget to pray for your Bishop."

"Of course I will pray for you, Your Excellency."

"And how are you going to pray? What will you say to the Lord for my sake?"

Once again, Fr. Grejbel did not know what to say and he ducked his head. He felt very embarrassed and began to feel slightly annoyed as well. "I will pray as usual."

The Bishop smiled and changing his tone of voice asked, "How are the lessons on the alphabet going?"

"The lessons on the alphabet?" Fr. Grejbel stammered, flustered and astonished, as if in that moment he was unable to understand what the Bishop was talking about.

"It's a good job you're doing there, teaching people how to read and write."

"Yes, yes," he answered, relieved and happy with the compliment. "Maybe it will help them to think in a better way. Knowing the alphabet broadens one's mind, your Excellency. As soon as I teach them how to read a word, even a short simple one, they are overjoyed, as if they've just made a new discovery, a skill they didn't even know they possessed. Every new word they learnt ended up bringing them great joy."

"Great joy? Because they've discovered the alphabet?"

"Yes, Your Excellency. Even if you've grown up, become a man already, to learn the alphabet you seem to become young again. A child."

"The alphabet turns us all into children. Isn't that what you're telling me? Really, Fr. Grejbel? Well then, the wine tavern, or bar as they say nowadays, isn't what people make it out to be."

"The wine bar, Your Excellency, is another classroom, like another small church."

"It's another small church? Is that possible?" the Bishop paused, gazing at nothing and then continued. "But, but, Fr.

Grejbel, I didn't send for you to learn what you're doing in the village tavern. I entertain no doubts that you know what you're doing, how to conduct yourself, at what time you go and how long you stay. In any case, you need to find some considerable time for yourself every day to read your breviary. Don't you?"

"That's right, Your Excellency. Reading the breviary takes up a long time. And as I read the Latin I find myself getting somewhat tired too. I don't understand everything. The alphabet always remains something difficult."

"Even when we grow up?"

"Yes, that's what I think, Your Excellency. These men know how to read now, but the problems begin when we learn how to read. How are we to understand?"

"Understand what? What? What are you saying?" the Bishop interrupted him, visibly annoyed.

"I need more time to understand the simplest things, Your Excellency. With all my knowledge of the alphabet, I still find it hard to understand some things."

"Like what, for example?"

"Well, for example I find it hard to understand the relationship between a father and his son or between a mother and her son. These questions are too hard for me, and they are different every time."

"Fr. Grejbel! Fr. Grejbel! Bring me some comfort! I'd like to hear something else from you. I need to hear something different!"

"From me, Your Excellency?"

"You see before you a man who did his utmost to convince people to believe ... well there you are, to believe all that you know, all that we believe in and live for. There's nothing new. Here I am, an old, tired and troubled man, recalling the past spread out before me, as if it was a film like those being shown lately in cinemas, some distance from here. What should I be believing, here and now?"

"I don't really know what to tell you, Your Excellency, but I suppose you should continue to think in the way you always have. That's it, yes! You must continue to think in the same way."

"The same? Always the same? What do you think He's going to ask me when I appear before Him? Am I to blame if life seems to be changing? What was I supposed to have done when I saw a way of life I had never even imagined before?"

"I don't know what He'll ask you, Your Excellency, but maybe He'll ask you the same thing."

The Bishop was not very happy with that reply and he ploughed on, "Aren't you concerned about what will happen after we've gone, Fr. Grejbel? Will it all tumble down, all that we've built up in entire centuries? Do you think that the long tradition we've been brought up on will be broken?"

Fr. Grejbel felt dizzy assaulted by this torrent of words about things he had never thought about. "I don't know, Your Excellency, I just don't know. These thoughts have never crossed my mind."

"Will our villages be split wide open, one of these days, Fr. Grejbel? Is it possible that they will be invaded by things that have never managed to infiltrate them up to now? Will the sea rise and cover the land and drag everything back in it, do you think? Do you know what I mean?"

"I don't know, Your Excellency," the priest answered with rising trepidation in a voice thick with tension.

"Our fields, the walls we've built, will they stand up to the coming storm? Is it possible that one day they will all fall down, tumble down stone by stone?"

"I don't know, Your Excellency, I just don't know," Fr. Grejbel replied again in a wail, midway between fear and calm, as if he could not quite fathom the sense of all these questions.

"You're familiar with the Port area, aren't you? Do you think the Port will bewitch our youths and they will leave us and go to live somewhere else? Don't you worry about the fascination that the Port exerts, Fr. Grejbel?"

"I don't know, Your Excellency."

"What do you mean you don't know? Do you think I'm not aware how familiar you've become with the Port and its environs? You know the area very well indeed, and you know what a trader on a bumboat is and what a ship chandler does and everything! You wanted to remain in an obscure little village in a remote corner of the world but in the meantime you've also come to know the other end, the sea, the Port. So you know both sides. Who else can I ask if not you? I want an answer from you. I need to have an answer because if He asks me..."

"If He asks you... Ah, now I get it! I know why you need an answer now, Your Excellency. In case He asks you," Fr. Grejbel exclaimed, glad to have found something to say.

"Tell me, tell me, what will happen when our village youths start emigrating? They will see a ship and fall under its spell! Will they remain the same children we brought up with iron discipline that was for their own good?"

"I don't know, Your Excellency," Fr. Grejbel replied sadly, almost moaning. He wanted to have an answer but it eluded him. Not a single idea occurred to him.

"You don't know! You don't know! How can you not know? You yourself have already been through all this. And what will happen when the alphabet is taught more widely and people will learn how to read and write, and when more books will become available, and more newspapers? What will happen, huh? And when instead of the bicycle..."

"Wistin's bicycle," interjected the priest cutting the Bishop's words off. "Wistin likes to ride his bicycle."

"The bicycle, yes, yes, Wistin's bicycle," the Bishop broke in impatiently. "But understand me well. When instead of the bicycle we'll be seeing cars, what then? And what about the cinema? And pictures?"

"I don't know, Your Excellency," the priest fell back on the refrain.

"Do you think everything we've built up will fall down and break, one day?" the Bishop fell silent, drawing in a deep breath.

Fr. Grejbel rose in the same instant, was silent for a few moments and then said, in a high, clear voice full of decision, "No, no, Your Excellency. All this won't fall down and break. It can't break! The Cross will remain on the hill, in fair weather or foul, but especially during a storm!"

"So, you think our life hasn't been all in vain?"

"No, no, Your Excellency, our life hasn't been all in vain. Nothing will be wasted."

"Not even a single tear, a single grief?"

"No, nothing will go to waste, Your Excellency," Fr. Grejbel went on with a determination never seen before in him.

"Are you certain of that?" the Bishop asked in amazement, seeing the priest speaking in such a manner now.

"Yes, I'm certain of it, Your Excellency."

"And when were you most certain about it?"

"When I felt I was alone, Your Excellency, completely alone," Fr. Grejbel replied brokenly, his voice betraying the grief he had experienced. He felt so choked with feeling that he could hardly speak.

"When it was you up on Golgotha you mean, don't you?"

"Yes, Your Excellency, that was the time when I felt most alone, and yet when at the same time I felt most certain I hadn't been abandoned. I know that in fact I was not alone."

"Alone, but in reality not alone. Do I understand you correctly? Do you have any proof of this, Fr. Grejbel?"

"No, I have no proof. No, Your Excellency."

"You don't?" the Bishop replied in disappointment.

"I don't need any proof. I am absolutely sure about it!" The Bishop was greatly struck by these words, and remained staring back at the priest, and then he rose slowly, approached Fr. Grejbel and embraced him. "So you're certain we're not alone."

"Yes, Your Excellency, I'm certain."

The Bishop allowed a few moments to pass and then continued in an altered tone of voice, "Do you know why I wished to have this meeting with you today?"

"No, Your Excellency, I don't know. As you can see, I know nothing, almost nothing. I only know what I feel. I have a heart, but a mind... no. I'm nothing more than a simple village priest. All heart, able to feel much, that's true."

The Bishop smiled. "You have everything then. The mind is there for us to use and then discard along the way. The more we come close to the heart of things, the more we need a heart that's able to keep the mind in its hands, in its pockets, like something that's been used already. I have long suspected this. But I've reached that conclusion today. With your help, once more, Fr. Grejbel."

"With my help, Your Excellency?"

The Bishop did not reply and appeared to want to change the subject. "Well then, let me tell you what you wanted to know. Antonja and Wistin are going to get married, aren't they?"

"Yes, I think they will marry, that's true, Your Excellency."

"Well, when they're about to get married I'd like you to inform me, please. When and where."

"Of course, of course, I'll let you know when they're getting married."

"I would like to come to the village and marry them myself."

Fr. Grejbel raised his head slowly, thunderstruck. "Come yourself, to the village, to marry them? Come to the far end of the world, you? How can that be?"

"Yes, Fr. Grejbel, that's what I'd like to do."

"But that's something that's never happened before!"

"Then this will be the first time."

Fr. Grejbel realized it was time to leave the Bishop's office. He slowly got up from the armchair, holding his hat in both hands.

"Today I learnt how I must answer when my time comes, when He calls me to Him. With your help. If He asks me where I learnt all this, set your mind at rest, Fr. Grejbel. I will mention your name," the Bishop told him with a smile, feeling very happy.

Fr. Grejbel went down on his knees to kiss the Bishop's hand but the Bishop did not allow it.

Chapter 9

People were already starting to leave their place and making the Sign of the Cross for the last time before paying a quick visit to their favourite saint's statue in its niche and leaving the church. Fr. Grejbel had just finished celebrating mass and had gone into the sacristy. He was divesting himself of the vestments and silently mouthing some prayers he knew by heart, as all priests do after celebrating mass. The sacristan called out "Well done" in a loud voice and bobbed his head in respect, as he was wont to do in those particular moments, standing smartly by in readiness to help the priest.

Suddenly, Wistin appeared at the end of the sacristy, out of breath, his hair tousled, gazing straight at the priest with a fixed stare. He came forward slowly and then in a rush said, "I want to confess."

Fr. Grejbel nodded to the sacristan and the altar boy to leave. No one else was in the room. He put on the purple stole around his neck, went to the *prie-dieu* kneeler and invited the youth to approach and kneel down. The priest then sat down on a chair, bent his head and made the Sign of the Cross and waited.

Meanwhile, Wistin had remained standing up. "No, no, Fr. Grejbel, I don't really want you to hear a confession. But I would like to have a word with you, alone," he said apologetically, feeling uncomfortable about having lied for a few moments.

"It doesn't matter," Fr. Grejbel reassured him, rising and removing the stole and then going up to Wistin.

"I want to tell you something. Please, help me. I kept thinking about what you told me last time. Then I went to the market hoping to see her, just that, nothing more, to catch a glimpse of her even at a distance at the spot where people told me she is usually to be found, selling flowers and plants. She stays there all day long, in the same spot, for hours on end, people told me. But she wasn't there. I didn't have enough courage to approach Pawlu *tal-Ħaxix* and ask after her. I know he's set his sights on her. Maybe he doesn't want to talk to me, and maybe I wouldn't be doing the right thing in talking to him, either. I don't know him at all. I've never been near him. I don't have any excuse to ask after my mother."

"Your mother hasn't been well, lately, Wistin."

"Has it been long since you saw her last?"

"No, not long. But, more importantly, she's not going to keep selling flowers and plants. She doesn't want to go on doing it."

"She's found some other work, then?"

Fr. Grejbel did not reply and bowed his head. "Is that all, Wistin?"

"No, no, there's more! I went looking for her at home. I thought I might pluck up courage and knock on her door. I supposed she would still open the door to me, even though I had abandoned her. I knocked and waited, looking around. I waited for a long time. There was perfect silence. At first, nobody opened the door but then a woman came out, a servant going by her clothes, and she said, "Who are you looking for, my lad?" I thought she was my mother's maid and I was taken aback. My mother never ever had a maid in the house. She never wanted to have one. I stood there, stammering, and that servant waited impatiently for me to reply, appearing on tenterhooks to draw back in and slam the door in my face. 'Susanna' I stuttered, 'I'd like to see the lady of the house, Susanna,' I replied, having fixed in my mind that my mother had taken on a servant. 'There's no Susanna here, dear. My lady's name isn't Susanna,' she declared. I was completely confused. 'But I'm sure the lady Susanna lives here,' I insisted. 'You're mistaken. But wait here a moment. Maybe she's someone who lives in the vicinity but unknown to me. Maybe my lady will know. I'll go and ask her and I'll come back and tell you,' she said wanting to be helpful, and she closed the door. I waited there. She soon came back with a reply, telling me, 'The lady Susanna doesn't live here anymore. This is no longer her house.' At that very moment I heard a hand bell ring upstairs and immediately recognized it as a signal for the maid to get rid of me and close the door so that I would go away."

"And you left," Fr. Grejbel added, almost with a smile.

"I left, yes of course."

"But you're still looking for your mother, aren't you?"

Wistin did not answer him at first, appearing reluctant to admit it. "I just wanted to see her, and I still would like to see her. I'm a bit worried about her. I think I worry more than I used to. Maybe I'm getting older."

"That's right, you're getting older and wiser."

"That's it, yes, yes, perhaps that's it."

"And what else do you want to know, Wistin?"

"I'd like to know where she is. She's not well you said? If she doesn't live in that house any longer, where has she gone then?"

"Has it been a long time since you visited your grandmother, Wistin?"

"I don't want to worry her any more than I have already. I know I didn't behave very well to her. But perhaps she finds an excuse for my behaviour."

"Your mother is staying with your grandmother, Wistin. You can set your mind at rest," Fr. Grejbel assured him.

"Thank you! Thank you!" Wistin replied, his face alight with happiness, approaching the priest and taking his hand to give it a squeeze. It was a habit he had picked up in the harbour area, when he had observed it in men with a solid background and a world of experience behind them. "But

230

what did that maid mean? Is it true my mother doesn't live there anymore? What's happened? That's the house where I grew up. That's my home."

"Don't you know what's happened, Wistin?"

"No I don't know. Truly."

"Your mother sold everything. That house is no longer hers."

"That's no longer her house?" Wistin was thunderstruck and he raised his hands and covered his eyes.

Fr. Grejbel bowed his head, almost against his will, and remained like that without saying a word. He could not find the words in him to say anything.

"She sold everything? And you're going to tell me she did it for my sake? She's always done everything for my sake?"

The priest remained silent but nodded as if to affirm what Wistin was thinking. He felt that the youth should have realized a long time before how many sacrifices his mother had made for him. The priest did not want to force the issue; rather he wanted Wistin to arrive at that conclusion all by himself. Perhaps it was still too soon. And because of that, Fr. Grejbel had asked himself many times what more he could do to convince the lad.

Wistin paused to gather his thoughts. Then, in the manner of one accustomed to take a quick decision, he turned to the priest and asked him, "Please, Fr. Grejbel, come with me to my father. I beg you to come with me. Don't leave me on my own in this."

The two of them went to the village square together, and there they found a coachman with his *karozzin* and asked him to take them to the Port. They sat facing each other inside in order to read each other's expression and mood as they talked. Wherever they looked, the countryside appeared to them like a beautiful spectacle sheathed in a peace and tranquillity that comes through a life of humble toil. It was an unravelling panorama of tiny houses, old farmsteads, and narrow and winding country lanes, small chapels whose domes and

231

steeples towered above and dominated all other buildings. The fields offered a large rolling vista but of people there were few. Occasionally, some animal would give voice or some man or woman would call out and these sounds would break the silence for a while. Only some bell in a belfry or the barking of a dog or the call of a shepherd or farmer sounded, otherwise nothing at all.

"So my mother sold everything," Wistin repeated to himself but aloud, full of disbelief. "She sold the house and so many other things. It seems like another fairy-tale, a colourful story like those I used to hear when I was young. But why? I want to know what happened."

Fr. Grejbel did not reveal anything. "It's not really up to me to tell you, Wistin. I wouldn't like to say more than I should and cause irreparable harm. Every word counts and it can heal or it can wound." He paused and tried to change the subject. "What sort of work are you doing now? Do you have a job?"

"No, not at the moment. I go all over the Port looking for work. I know every corner of the place, blindfold. I run the occasional errand, offer my services for anything that turns up but otherwise nothing. I dream up jobs! Imagine it through! Perhaps there's a chance of being taken on as a ferryman. But I don't have an answer yet." As soon as they came to the neighbourhood of the Port, the priest asked the coachman to let them down and they descended from the *karozzin*. They walked along the quayside looking for Stiefnu. They called out his name, loudly, and as soon as their call echoed around, two beggar boys appeared, eager to run an errand to earn some money.

"All you need to do is run along and shout the name Stiefnu as loudly as you can, 'Stiefnu! Stiefnu!' That's all, children!" the priest instructed, throwing a few coins into their outstretched palm.

They were ecstatic and jumping in glee dashed off immediately raising their voices and shouting, "Stiefnu! Stiefnu!"

The man who approached them a short while later was like an old decrepit statue, neglected and forgotten by all, swaying endlessly from side to side. Both of them realized it was Stiefnu but neither wanted to be the first to admit it. They let the man draw closer, both of them standing stock still, waiting, wanting to make certain that the man was Stiefnu. The man continued lurching from side to side on unsteady legs and then he gave a final jerk as if drawing on all the strength he had left, moving slowly to lean against the wall and falling with a thump on the ground, sprawling on the ground like an empty sack. The sound of his fall was very loud in the stillness of that hour in that spot.

Wistin had no more doubts. "That's my father! That's my father!"

In an instant, Fr. Grejbel went to the man at a run and tried hard to raise him to his feet, but the man's strength had given out and he slumped down again in a sitting position with his back resting against the wall.

"Dad, Dad," Wistin called out. That heavy sound, like a shot, of his father's fall startled and dismayed him. He had not expected to see his father in that condition. Up to that day, his father had always led Wistin to believe him a powerful man, hard to put down. He had promised him he was about to become a wealthy man shortly and that he was undaunted by anything and that his heart was at no one's mercy.

Fr. Grejbel held Stiefnu in his arms and helped him sit up. "Do you recognize me, Stiefnu? Come on, look at me closely and remember. Can't you place me?"

Stiefnu looked back at the priest vacantly, wordless, but then slowly, slowly he focused on the priest and in a surprisingly decisive voice replied, "Of course I recognize you. You are that priest with a heart of gold. That's what people say of you and it's true."

Wistin and the priest gave him a breathing space and then helped him to his feet, and keeping him upright between them, they took him to a nearby bar and gave him coffee to drink.

They helped him sip it till they realized he did not want to drink anymore of it.

"Dad! Dad, what's happened?" Wistin wanted to know.

"I'm happy, son, today I'm happy! At last, I'm happy! I've eaten a big supper and drank well too. I awarded myself a feast! And do you know why? Because I've never had so much money in my pockets before. I've had to eat swill for so long but not today, no, today I didn't go and lick up every last crumb of swill. And I told my friends I was going to go to the best restaurant round here and order a special meal. 'What's happened? Are you mad?' they told me almost envious. 'I'm mad because I'm so happy?' I retorted. They didn't believe me when I said I'd become rich. 'Did you win the lottery?' they wanted to know. 'No, I didn't win any lottery prize money', I said, and I wasn't lying you know. 'So, have you suddenly inherited a large sum of money?' they asked me again. 'No, neither!' I replied. After all, it was none of their business. They didn't want to believe me. Anyway, at last I've eaten a huge meal like any ship chandler!"

"Aren't you a trader on a bumboat anymore, Dad?" Wistin was curious to know.

Stiefnu began to moan and he ducked his head and buried his face in his hands as if he wanted to hide it, but then, with an effort of will, he continued to say, "Yes, yes, I'm still a trader on a bumboat. But I wanted to imagine I'd become a ship chandler. I wanted to make believe that one minute I was still a trader on a bumboat, a small time trader on board a boat, rowing it toward some ship and berthing alongside it to sell all my goods to the people on board, and the next minute I'd succeeded in becoming a ship chandler. I grew up all at once, the way I've always wanted to! At last I had become a ship chandler, able to provision an entire ship! A very influential merchant! Always waiting for my ship to enter port! And then I would go on board without any trouble whatsoever and talk with the captain and bring him all the provisions he asks for. Food and anything else! A ship chandler! I could provision the ship from my stores. And if I lacked any goods, I would buy them from other stores. And when any goods weren't available locally, I would board a ship myself and leave port to go and buy the goods from abroad, from out there, like any other ship chandler. A ship chandler can go and see the world."

Fr. Grejbel squeezed Stiefnu's hands and congratulated him. "Well done! Well done indeed, Stiefnu!"

Stiefnu's voice broke all at once. "No, no, Fr. Grejbel! I haven't become a ship chandler," he admitted. "It's not true, none of it. I'm only wishing and dreaming it up. I had told Susanna that's what I'd become one day. And I'd even told Arturu that, God rest his soul. But I was only a trader on a bumboat and that's what I still am. I sell a few things from on board my boat. I'm a failure. I've seen many people come and go in all the years I've been here but I've stayed in the same position. I go out on my boat and try to sell my goods."

"No you're not a failure, Stiefnu. You've done your work just like everybody else. A trader on a bumboat is an important person too."

"I've failed, Fr. Grejbel. Do you want to see my boat? It's still full of stuff. Go there, see, out in mid-harbour. Look, look, there it is, waiting. I haven't managed to sell anything today!"

"Well then, let me buy all those things, Dad!" Wistin exclaimed trying to jolly him along.

"Ah, but today I can pay you, son. Today I'm flush with money."

Fr. Grejbel bent his head and remained silent.

"You've got money, Dad?"

"Yes, son. Ask me for anything today and I'll give it to you! Quickly now, quickly, before I change my mind," he told him, making a joke out of it. "But there, it's true enough. Today you can ask me for anything and I'll give it to you, as if I've really become a ship chandler! Only make-believe of course, I haven't really become one. But don't tell your mother that."

Wistin gave Fr. Grejbel a look, as if coming to an understanding with him, and then turning to his father he asked, "Dad, I want to ask for something, then..."

"Tell me, tell me, however much it costs. Today I can give it to you."

"Will you give it to me, for sure?"

"For sure!"

Wistin hesitated, trying to find the courage and the right words, and then burst out with, "Dad, please marry my mother. That's all I want from you now! I want to see you together, a married couple."

The three of them gazed at each other in silence, overwhelmed.

"What are you saying, Wistin? Where on earth did you get such an idea, son?"

"It's nothing more than I wish for. I've been thinking about the same thing for a long time. At last, I thought, we can be together, the three of us."

Stiefnu drew on all his strength and standing straight, his feet firmly planted on the ground and his gaze fixed on the Port, he replied, "I can't, Wistin. I can't! If I could, I would tell you yes, especially since it was my fault that you suffered, though that wasn't my intention. But I can't. I'd like to be able to say yes, but no, I can't, I know I can't."

"You can't bring yourself to love my mother?" Wistin persisted.

"No, I can't, no," Stiefnu reiterated, on the point of repeating it over and over again. "I can't give you what I don't possess. Ask me for something else, please. Don't let me have to say no to you. I would so much like to say yes, after all these years!"

"You won't say yes if I ask you to do it out of respect for me, Dad? Love my mother for my sake, Dad."

Stiefnu kept shaking his head, a clear signal of refusal.

"So that I can be happy and content, Dad."

"No, not even for that, son. Not even to bring you happiness. I can't put my heart where it doesn't want to stay. I've been rowing my boat for many years, now. Just imagine it, with the wind blowing. The boat is my woman."

"Don't tell me you too want to start telling me stories, Dad! I don't want to hear any more fairy tales," Wistin interjected rather angrily.

"Your mother and I tried to come to an understanding a long time ago, but there's nothing that can bring us together. Have patience and resign yourself to this, too."

"But my mother, Dad, did all she could for me. I know that now. I'm starting to realize that."

"She's your mother, the mother of my son. But she isn't my wife. That's all there is to it, Wistin. Maybe it's too soon for you to understand it but slowly, slowly you'll have to. Everybody takes their time to understand something, at their own pace. You've started too soon, son!"

"I'm going to talk to her and I'm going to tell her that I'm asking you to do this. This something that I want. Maybe she loves you, Dad."

"You can tell her all you want Wistin, but you can be sure that I won't be changing my mind. Don't waste any more time, son. You've got your whole life ahead of you now. Our love, between me and your mother, has got nothing to do with your own future. There's nothing left between us. Don't expect anything more."

"Nothing? Absolutely nothing? Can't I even tell her to hope?" Wistin pleaded. "I can tell her my father needs some more time to think it over, to decide, and he's waiting to earn a good sum and will shortly become a ship chandler with his own stores. I can at least hold out some hope."

"No, son, not even that."

"I'll tell her, look Dad, I'll tell her... 'Look, my father may change his mind.' That's what I'll tell her, even though it's not true."

"No, son, that would be a lie."

"But, Dad, that way Mum can be happy for a while, at least."

"No, son, not even for that reason."

"So what shall I tell her, Dad?" Wistin wanted to know.

"Nothing, son. It's a closed book now."

"There isn't even any hope?"

"No, not even any hope of that, son. Wistin, you just don't know anything about it. Even hope has faded. Your mother doesn't want what you're wishing for, either. You're a son and she's a mother. There's a great distance between the two!"

Wistin grimaced and he turned to Fr. Grejbel almost angrily telling him, "Let's go back, please. I'm very sorry to have brought you here for nothing. Please forgive me this time as well." Stiefnu remained there standing ramrod straight.

The priest and Wistin walked away from the quay till they arrived at the spot where the *karozzini* stood in a row, waiting for a fare. They went up to one of the coachmen and requested a trip back to their village.

"Wistin! Wistin! Listen to me!" Stiefnu's cry rang out.

Fr. Grejbel asked the coachman to wait a bit before driving off.

In a few moments, Stiefnu's powerful voice eddied around the entire neighbourhood as if the deep sea swell was carrying him from one side to another to make sure Wistin could find no excuse for misunderstanding his every word. "Wistin! Wistin! My boat here is all for you! For you, my son, this boat's for you!" Stiefnu began shouting almost in a chant. "Look at it, look at it full of things. I earned them all with many hard days' work. I didn't inherit them. I never found anything ready for me in my whole life. From this very moment that's your boat, it all belongs to you. You can come and take it right now. Come, come! I too did all I could for you. Take this boat here, work as a trader on a bumboat instead of me, and start rowing towards the big ships from this very moment. This is all I can give you. You can be a small time trader on the sea. But for the rest, don't ask me for anything more!"

Wistin heard it all but did not say a word.

When Stiefnu stopped shouting, Fr. Grejbel asked the coachman to set out and they left. The *karozzin* kept up a steady pace and they soon left the environs of the Port and took up the road that would lead them straight to their village. As they were moving along, they looked at each other, pondering about what had just occurred.

"Well then, Fr. Grejbel, it's clear my father doesn't love my mother," Wistin spoke despondently, his gaze fixed on the moving countryside beyond the *karozzin*. It was a large tranquil space, a stretch of peace and orderliness.

"He's still your father, Wistin, and will be forever. As he always was from the very beginning and will be right up to the end, your father. In the meantime, nothing's changed."

"And so, I'm duty bound to love him. Always, at whatever cost. That's what you want to say, isn't it?"

"Yes, that's right, Wistin." Fr. Grejbel did not want to discuss the subject but he had expected Wistin to bring it up.

"And what if my mother doesn't love my father, Fr. Grejbel?"

"She'll still be your mother, Wistin, right till the end." He paused and drawing in a sharp breath, he asked Wistin, "Why are you asking me?" Fr. Grejbel felt the weighty presence of many unasked questions which involved other people and once more felt afraid to answer.

"Because I too realized my mother doesn't love him. I didn't want to tell my father that. I wanted him to think Mum loves him. I kept hoping they would come together again finally, maybe for my sake if anything. And I wanted it to be me to bring it about, even if it was with a white lie. But this is very hard for me, it's a great grief."

"Well then, you must nurse that grief well, Wistin, and make sure it won't be wasted."

"A grief that can't be wasted?"

"Yes, a grief that's not in vain. It's the best thing you have at the moment. And now, if you want, we'll go straight to your mother at your grandmother's house, Wistin."

"To Gran's house! So my mother is once again staying in her mother's house. There's a huge difference between Mr. Arturu's grand house and Grandma Katarina's tiny dwelling." As soon as they arrived at one end of the street where Katarina's house was situated, they observed several women in front of Katarina's house sitting on chairs grouped around Susanna who was reading a passage from a story in the latest penny dreadful. Each edition of these story papers consisted of a few pages. A boy, engaged to distribute them in return for a pittance, would come round every few days knocking on doors to sell the eight-page rag that held another instalment of a novel that was being serialized. A novel was something serious, a story that was written little by little by someone who was shaping a narrative that gave people pleasure when they read it. The author would use his imagination and dream up a tale and the people who read or heard the story would enter another world. In-between instalments the author, writing from home, would have enough time to develop the various intricacies of the plot and sub-plots. Love, envy, ambition, vendetta, sentimental feelings, all the instalments held more or less to this pattern. Katarina used to pay the boy with a few coins when he came round and he would promise to come by in a few days' time with another freshly printed edition. Every edition held a fresh instalment of the story, slowly progressing to the end with many a startling twist and heart-rending turns in the tale. The people who waited eagerly for each instalment and promptly bought it were motivated by curiosity. Though Katarina herself could not read, Susanna carefully collected each instalment in numerical order and kept them in the cupboard drawer for when her mother felt like hearing some of the story. The closeness of their small village made the novel seem more beautiful, like a distant and different world, and it nurtured a need to dream and rely on one's memory. From time to time, people who did not physically journey to other places occasionally felt the urge to undertake a mental journey, though they would be sitting comfortably on a stool or chair. They would close their eyes, cross their arms and listen hard in perfect silence. Nothing satisfied this need like a penny dreadful.

"Read us a bit more from the novel in the story paper, Susanna!" Katarina sometimes urged Susanna. "That story you were reading to us, how did it go on?"

"Very well! Let me read aloud that story for you. I'd like to know how it went on, too. Go and tell the neighbours to come round and I'll go and get the latest instalment and see where we left off," Susanna would answer.

The neighbours would be called and they would happily come out of their homes clutching a chair and gather round Susanna outside Katarina's front door. Susanna read the story out slowly, pausing to repeat a sentence or paragraph when her listeners stopped her because they had not heard or understood properly. When she picked up the pace they would ask her to slow down and when a particularly heart-breaking piece was narrated, they would all break into tears and sobs and the reading would stop for a while till the handkerchiefs would have mopped up the tears in their eyes. Some women felt embarrassed about crying in public but the sobs and whimpers around them were too powerful and their shyness would be overwhelmed and they would cry their eyes out as much as the rest. Only women sat and listened to these stories.

Susanna was looking at the pages in her hands. The other women, with their arms crossed and with their gaze most likely fixed on the ground, were silently listening. No one dared make the least sound and drown out a word. The story was very interesting. Katarina was immensely proud that these story sessions were held outside her house and that the one who was doing the reading for the benefit of all those women was none other than her own daughter. Nearly all the other women present could not read.

Fr. Grejbel and Wistin were seen approaching Katarina's house and everyone was startled.

"Lady of Mercy!" Susanna exclaimed in shock, as soon as she stopped reading and raised her eyes from the pages in her hands, her gaze fixed on the two figures. She could not believe her eyes. The pages slipped from her grasp as she palmed her face and gazed at the two of them in disbelief. Then she got up from her chair and treading past the knot of women sitting around her she went up to Wistin and clasped him to her in a strong embrace.

Wistin could not drum up enough courage to say a word to her. With a huge visible effort he managed to tell her, "Mum! Mum, here I am. This time I won't abandon you again."

"Where were you, son? Where did I lose you again? Haven't I had to spend too much time without you already?"

"Do you still love me?"

"Yes, of course I do, more than ever before." Susanna did not have the strength to say more and she clasped him to her more strongly. She looked at Fr. Grejbel who had hung back, standing still, and with a slight nod she offered up her thanks to him once more. Her tear-filled eyes met his gaze and he lowered his head, much moved.

Meanwhile, the other women had got to their feet and were standing there gripping the chair each of them had purposely brought out from their own house, ready to return home with it. It was getting late but more than that, the scene that was taking place before their eyes proved to be too upsetting and in any case, they all realized this was a private family matter. Slowly, slowly, they drifted back to their own house until only the four figures remained outside Katarina's house.

"We can go inside now," Katarina urged the others, taking up the chair but having it promptly taken out of her hands by Fr. Grejbel and carried inside to the first room one entered within her house.

"My father wants to have nothing to do with you, Mum. He doesn't want to hear any more about it," Wistin addressed her as soon as he could speak. "He told me so, over and over."

"It feels like a hundred years since I saw you, son," Susanna said, wanting to speak to him but deliberately avoiding a reply.

Katarina went to the kitchen and brought out four coffee cups. She was intent on hearing every word Wistin spoke. She was happy but at the same time rather worried. She would have liked to question him about his father but something held her back every time she was about to speak and remembering that discretion was the better part of valour, she held her tongue. In a short while she re-entered the room with four steaming cups of coffee and she took her place around the table next to the others.

Wistin told his mother that he had gone to look for her at the other house but had not found her.

"I don't live there anymore, Wistin. I had to sell everything, well, nearly everything. After all this time I had to return back here, to Katarina's tiny house. Isn't that so, Mother?"

"The house may be small but the heart is big," Katarina replied, voicing a slight disappointment.

"I am back where we all used to live a long time ago, before you were born, Wistin."

"So you no longer live there? I mean, don't we? That house isn't ours any longer?"

"That's right. It's not our house any longer. But I have no regrets if it had to come to that. Actually, not only do I have no regrets but I'm happy about it," his mother reassured him. "Unity is the best thing, my dear. The main thing is that you're here now."

"I don't understand, Mum."

Susanna and Katarina exchanged glances, wordlessly. Fr. Grejbel looked into the distance with a preoccupied air in order to remain silent as well. He had no wish to speak of the matter before the women broached the subject themselves.

"Yes, I'm here now, that's true. But, but... what's that got to do with the house, Mum?"

"With that sum of money, son, you'll be able to live decently. You'll have someone to support you for a very long time."

"Support me for a very long time? Who?"

"What do you mean, who?" Susanna wanted to know, taken aback.

"My father? Is he the one you mean?" he asked her impatiently.

"With the money I gave him for you. A very large sum of money. I had to give it to him."

"A very large sum? For me?"

Susanna realized that Wistin knew nothing at all about it. She told him how his father had demanded a lump sum of money which she hoped he was going to use to support Wistin so that he would not leave the country.

"I never knew anything about this."

"Your father never mentioned anything?"

"Of course not. So that means you're living in Gran's house because..."

Susanna bowed her head in acquiescence.

"So my father really wanted that money for himself," he concluded in a serious tone.

"But for you too, no? So you wouldn't emigrate."

"I have no thought of emigrating, Mum. I don't have a steady job but I've managed so far. My heart is bound to this place, now more than ever before."

"Don't you want to come back to the village?"

"I'm not going away, Mum," he reassured her. "Now that I've found both of you again, I don't want to live far away from you. Even though you're not together, at least I know where both of you are."

"Thank you, son. You've made me very happy."

That night, Katarina, Susanna and Wistin slept peacefully feeling happy and content.

Days passed and an endless procession of thoughts continued to march past in the youth's mind. The same troublesome thoughts continued coming and going, like a wave in the harbour, like a breeze across a field. Wistin would have liked to ignore them but he did not succeed. There was something he was not sure of. He thought that by now he understood his mother and father reasonably well, though they were very different from each other although both were children born and bred in the fields. Their upbringing had been different and Stiefnu had long since grown a pair of wings and learnt to fly, while Susanna had remained rooted to the ground walking barefoot on the soil and selling flowers and herbs. Wistin kept turning over these thoughts in his mind for days on end. He was glad that they were so different from each other but now he realized that this difference meant a separation. Well, at least his father had not hidden behind a smokescreen of words and his mother did not nurture any vain hopes. He could now see them clearly and respect them for the kind of persons they were.

He imagined his father strolling about in the Port neighbourhood, his pockets bulging with paper money and sovereigns in danger of falling out and spilling onto the road at any unsteady step he took or at the moment of stepping onto his boat. He imagined the paper money floating on the surface of the sea. He could just see in his mind's eye his father carelessly squandering money, foolishly puffed up with himself thinking he looked important, a rich man. Wistin could well imagine his father spending the whole sum all at once on a whim, buying something expensive just for the pleasure of it. His father could also take up gambling, games of chance, betting and playing cards. What did his father's last words to him mean? Wistin heard his father once again shouting to him that the boat was all his now. It was stacked full of goods as if on that day Stiefnu had not wanted to sell anything on purpose, in order to leave the boat to his son as it was, full of things to sell. His father had said quite plainly that he had not inherited them but had worked hard alone to earn everything over many years. It was a taunt and Wistin understood that immediately. And his father had also invited him to start working as a trader on a bumboat instead of him. Finally, he had warned him not to expect anything else from him. For days on end, the same thoughts swirled around in Wistin's head, coming and going, word by word.

"If you come back to live in the village, we'll find you a job for sure, take my word for it," Susanna declared. "You can continue with your visits to the Port to see your father and talk to him, whenever you want. I'm not going to hold you back. But live here. Stay here. Sleep here. The village is quite big enough, even to hold you! Please!" Susanna eagerly entreated him, certain she could prevail on Pawlu to find him some employment. Pawlu would not let her down. He had never denied her anything. Maybe Pawlu would offer Wistin the job she had held, selling flowers and herbs in the market.

"My father promised to give me his own job, Mum."

"Work alongside him, you mean, as a trader on a bumboat?"

"No Mum, that's not what he said. He told me to take his boat because that was all he possessed and he could give me nothing more. He gave it to me, telling me it was mine from that very moment. I could start going to work with it, be self-employed. I don't really know what he meant by it."

Suddenly, a suffocating silence fell in the room as if something new, something unexpected and unwelcome had dawned on everyone at the very same moment.

"He could give you nothing more? What does that mean?" Katarina burst out.

"Mum, Mum," Wistin exclaimed at the same precise moment in a very excited voice, as if he had just then realized something. "I'm going but I'll be back soon. I promise. But I'm going to try and find him." He rose from the table and left the room at a run.

"Where are you going, Wistin? Don't leave me again! Don't go! Don't go! Leave the sea alone! The sea is not for you," his mother pleaded.

Susanna and Katarina both stood up and walked to the front door, speechless, looking at his back as he disappeared down the street.

Wistin searched for his father in every nook and cranny of the Port neighbourhood. Stiefnu could not be found on land. When Wistin gave up looking for him on land he turned his attention to the sea. Wistin went down the quay, pulled at the rope of the nearest boat and scrambled on board. Then he untied the rope and took up the oars, beginning to row out to sea, one powerful pull on the oars after another, in a regular unending rhythm, searching for his father's boat. It had to be there, somewhere. Laboriously he wove in-between boats, paying extreme attention not to bump into any of them, till he arrived at his father's boat. He jumped into it and stood there for a few moments, standing and swaying with the rocking motion and then he fell to his knees in the uncluttered space facing aft, where he knew that the image of St. Joseph was painted. He gazed at the image for a long time, recalling that it was the exact same face painted on the statue of St. Joseph in their village. Wistin faced the fact that it had been a long time since he had said any prayers and he could not now decide whether he should try to say that litany of words he had learnt as a child. There had been a time when he had known all those prayers by heart, every last word of them, and he had been able to recite them correctly every day without fail, in a kind of chant that children saw as music. He used to say a prayer as soon as he woke up, before eating a meal and before going to bed. There had been a time when he felt proud of being able to recite all those prayers on his own, happily and with conviction, with his clasped hands held in front of his face, right under his nose. He tried to recall some of those prayers now. But he had all but forgotten them completely.

However, the simple words he uttered at that moment came straight from his heart and Wistin's prayer reflected the way he felt. "St. Joseph, find my father. Find him for me this time, once again. Where is he? Where is he? My mother used to tell me about you, that you could see everywhere from up there, keep an eye over everyone, even beyond the Port. Is this

247

true? This is the story she used to tell me about you. If you want, I can tell it to you right now. I remember it very well. You know where the ships go when they leave from that wide-open door, and you also know where they arrive. People pray to you for a safe journey, so that no strong waves would swell up and cause the ship to founder. Find my father for me once again and I promise I'll start going to church again and will start saying my prayers again, and everything else I used to do as a boy. I make this vow. Find him again for me!" The sea was calm, a deep blue.

Wistin made the Sign of the Cross in a hurry, paused in indecision for a few moments and then stood up and jumped back into the other boat and rowed himself back to shore. He was quite certain that his father was no longer in those parts.

***

Stiefnu had long since gathered up his personal belongings in a sack and closed it with a big knot, convinced and ready to leave. His luck was contained within that sack and he was certain a different life awaited him somewhere else, a better life. He stood for some time on the quay, ready and waiting, and when the opportunity came, he went aboard the ship that was ready to go and he left for a distant country. He had heard many people talk about a big country full of wealth and opportunities, very far away from the Port there, where all sorts of employment and good things were to be had. This country needed a lot of people to go to work there because there were so many jobs available but not enough people to take them on or able to do the work involved. He could continue working as a trader on a bumboat there, or maybe even become a ship chandler, but he might also take up a different kind of occupation. He would be able to consider everything, even a complete change in his life. Many people from different countries were emigrating to this big wealthy country. They would usually find it hard to get used to the different life at first and might even feel homesick and want to return because they would frequently stop and think about their homeland and countrymen and would conclude they had made a mistake to emigrate. Their heart would pine for home and order them to return but their mind would demand they stay. Later, as they steadily made money, they would get used to their new life.

Stiefnu learnt all about this when one day, after a day's work where he had barely earned anything, he had gone to a bar for a drink and found a man who had just returned from a distant country regaling everyone with his luck in as loud a voice as he could manage in order to reach everyone present in that bar. He spoke in a different accent, unlike any man Stiefnu had ever heard, and his appearance alone proclaimed his arrival from abroad.

All the men were gaping at him, hearing him out with admiration in their eyes. He was not an ordinary looking man. Even his clothes showed him to be a man coming from a far distant land: his shirt, his tie, his shoes, the colours of all the clothes he was wearing, and most of all, his hat, a huge tall affair that made his head appear too small.

"So, you won't be going back, then?" the people in the bar asked him, almost with one voice.

"No, of course not! I'll be staying now. I don't need to go back there. I've made enough money to last me a lifetime. I went with a dream in my mind and in time it's been fulfilled. And now that it's come true, what else do I need but to take my leisure, watch the world go by and enjoy it? There's nothing better than that in all the world. You can stay calm, gaze around, enjoy what you see and wait leisurely in seeing time going by!"

"You don't work at all, then?" the others in the bar asked.

"No, of course I don't work at all. I don't need to," he replied.

"You mean, you wake up in the morning, yawn and stretch, and know you don't have to go to work?" they insisted on asking for every detail.

"That's it! Precisely!"

"Is that true? But how can that be?" the rest of the men wondered aloud.

"True? Of course it's true!" he replied with a smile spread wide across his face. He stretched his right hand out to the landlord, who was behind the bar counter, and in a voice full of self-satisfaction he ordered a round. "A bottle of beer for everyone. My treat!" And he brought out money from his pocket and put it down on the bar counter. "Here's the money for it. There's more than enough. You can keep the change. Keep the change!"

Stiefnu had been much struck by all this, although at first he had not believed it. But now that the opportunity, to make the long journey to that distant land, had come knocking at his door he entertained no more doubts that fortune was finally smiling at him. The only thing that remained to be done was to wait for the ship that would take him to that land of opportunity and overcome any difficulties to prevent him from embarking on it. After that it should all be plain sailing and he would use his head and grab any opportunity that offered itself to him. He had decided on this venture and felt certain of success.

***

A short while later, Fr. Grejbel received a letter. He realized it was not really meant for him. He opened it and began to read: "I am Stiefnu, Wistin's father, and I am writing this from abroad. I arrived here by ship, safe and sound thanks be to God. I would like you to pass on this letter to Wistin. He knows how to read. A friend of mine wrote this letter for me because I still don't know how to write yet, though I'm learning. Over here I had to learn how to read and write, and I hope to start writing on my own soon..."

Fr. Grejbel did not read anymore of the letter because he realized that the rest of it was meant for Wistin. He carried the letter to Susanna and asked for Wistin. Wistin then asked the priest to read it to him.

Susanna and Katarina remained in the next room, full of curiosity, torn between wanting to hear and not wanting to hear its contents. They wanted to know what was in it but were afraid that it might contain something undesirable in their eyes. Wistin called out to them and invited them to hear what was written and Fr. Grejbel began to read it aloud.

Right at the end of the letter Stiefnu asked for Wistin's forgiveness and understanding for his, Stiefnu's, actions. "Tell your mother that as soon as I've earned enough money, I will start returning the sum she gave me, little by little. I needed a lump sum of money to get to this place. And I will send you money too, depending on how much I earn. I am working to support you too, and I'd like to show you I can be a rich man in a modest way. You'll see. I'm doing well at work. And as for you, don't forget to look after that boat well."

Susanna was certain Stiefnu would never come back "He's the very same person as the youth in the Valley I met so long ago," she reflected. "In all these years he's remained the same as ever. Not even that new land out there has changed him."

"An angel butterfly, always fluttering here and there," Katarina muttered shaking her head but taking care not to be overheard.

Wistin wrote back to his father and told him he was expecting some money from him so that he and Antonja could make plans to get married. He told him he could expect no financial help from his mother now. His mother could not even offer them a roof over their heads in the large house that used to belong to her not so long before. His grandmother's house was far too small to accommodate them all. After some time, Stiefnu wrote to Fr. Grejbel again enclosing some money for Wistin. He instructed him: "Give Wistin this sum so he can get married. Tell him I won't be coming back. He shouldn't hold out any hope of seeing me return. This country has made me very welcome and I consider it my home for

251

evermore. I'm also thinking of getting married and starting a family here. I feel very happy and content."

Susanna heard Fr. Grejbel out and pursed her lips in disapproval. "Never mind. Wistin will be able to get married all the same."

Katarina looked askance at her but waited to hear more.

"Wistin won't find it hard to find work, Mother. Pawlu is offering to take him on. Wistin will start selling flowers and herbs."

"Sell flowers? Just like you used to do?"

"Yes, Mother. The same flowers from the same fields. And the same herbs. And I too have a job. Everyone is remaining here, Mother. Are you happy and content?"

Katarina was speechless. She nodded her head and gazed down at the floor.

***

Katarina kept up the rocking motion, regularly and unceasingly tapping her feet to keep up the rhythm of the rocking chair. She continued gazing vacantly out of the window, looking in the distance where the edge of the fields and the spread of sky appeared to meet.

"Shall I help you to bed, Mother, or do you want to stay on a bit?" Susanna asked her as she passed a cup of tea to her.

"I don't know, daughter, really, I can't make up my mind. Well maybe I'll stay here a bit longer."

"You're not sure of yourself, Mother," Susanna spoke banteringly to her. "Well then, you stay on a bit here and in the meantime I'll go and drink my own tea. I can't stand it if it cools."

"Go and bring your tea here and keep me company then. I don't feel like being alone, daughter."

"What are you thinking about then, Mother?"

"I'm thinking about all the things you're wishing for."

"I've spent all my dreams. It's as if I went to the market and frittered them all away. I have nothing else left to wish for, Mother, except to see Wistin safely married and well set-up in his own household."

"Take this cup and go and put it back in its place."

"Aren't you going to drink more of it, Mother?"

Katarina passed her cup to Susanna and leaned back against the back of the rocking chair with her head resting at an angle. After a few moments she appeared to have gone to sleep, and the rocking chair gradually came to a complete stop.

Susanna put her hand on the chair back and started rocking her mother gently in order to wake her up without startling her. She did not wish to see her mother go to sleep so soon. "What are you thinking about, Mother?"

Katarina came awake hastily and replied, "I'm thinking that finally I'll soon be seeing the very end of this long drawn out story. Wistin isn't going to leave aboard a ship. Tumas and Ester seem to be happy with our Wistin and they know their Antonja won't be leaving this neighbourhood. And Antonja and Wistin love each other, I'm certain of it, and they'll be getting married."

"Wistin wants to have what I didn't have, Mother. At least that's what I think. And Fr. Grejbel agrees with me. I asked him if I was thinking along the right lines," Susanna replied. "What do you think, Mother?"

"That's what I think, too. Wistin wants to have his own nest and he wants to build it properly."

"You seem to have set your heart on that, Mother."

"And then, all that remains is for you and Pawlu to get married. I'm going to have many wonderful stories to tell, daughter. I hope I'll be able to remember them all when the time comes. My memory isn't what it was."

"Tell stories? Many wonderful things? To whom, Mother? What are you saying?"

"To whom? To whom? What do you mean, to whom? To your father, who else, daughter? Who else do I have? Imagine how many questions he's going to ask me as soon as he sees me! I want to know what I'm going to say. I want to prepare my answers from now!"

"What are you saying?" Susanna exclaimed, taken aback. "My father has been dead for many years now, Mother."

"But you only get married once, my dear. Saverju was, and will always remain, my husband. And as soon as I meet up with him again, I will tell him all that's happened since he died. He left everything in my hands and I'm duty-bound to account for everything I did and show him I discharged my duty well."

"So, when you're up in Heaven you're going to talk about down here. You're going to ruin all your happiness then."

"I will talk about all that's happening down here. And most of all I'll be talking about... do you know about whom?"

"Mother, there's no one like you in all the world!" Susanna exclaimed, looking fondly at her mother, guessing what she was about to tell her.

"Do you know about whom? About you, daughter. Even up in Heaven, I will be thinking of you, I promise. And up there I'll be able to talk face-to-face with St. Joseph and make sure you won't lack anything. Even up there I'll want to ask him a favour – for you! Now I won't need to make any more vows. I don't want to spend my time in Heaven worried about you. I want to feel reassured about you, otherwise how can I be happy in Heaven?"

"Does that mean you can't only get married once in your life, Mother?" Susanna asked her, wanting to know how her mother felt about the love she felt for Pawlu.

Katarina drew in a long sharp breath and raised her head slightly off the back of the rocking chair. "I don't know, daughter, I don't know. There are moments when I feel one way and then I start feeling the opposite. I swing from one position to another. My whole life has been like a swing, daughter. All I know is that I want to see you happy and content. Your father didn't swerve from his position before he died. And he demanded I follow his example. But I, here and now, and after all this time, I just don't know what to think. Maybe it's God's will that you and Pawlu come together and belong to each other. But I really don't know. I only have one soul to safeguard. That's what my husband used to say, and I echo that sentiment now, me too. Think carefully about the step you're taking."

"So you haven't decided yet, Mother..."

Katarina did not reply, appearing not to have heard her. Susanna continued gently rocking her mother till she appeared to have fallen asleep indeed. She did not wish to disturb her by moving her to her bed. She was afraid that if she woke up her mother now, Katarina would not be able to fall asleep so easily again. Susanna went and brought a blanket and she spread it over her mother, moved the rocking chair up against the wall to prevent it moving, kissed her mother lightly on her brow and blew out the lamp. She tiptoed out of the room soundlessly and went to her own bedroom. She herself was not sleepy at all.